# IRISH
# PARADE
# MURDER

Books by Leslie Meier

MISTLETOE MURDER
TIPPY TOE MURDER
TRICK OR TREAT MURDER
BACK TO SCHOOL MURDER
VALENTINE MURDER
CHRISTMAS COOKIE MURDER
TURKEY DAY MURDER
WEDDING DAY MURDER
BIRTHDAY PARTY MURDER
FATHER'S DAY MURDER
STAR SPANGLED MURDER
NEW YEAR'S EVE MURDER
BAKE SALE MURDER
CANDY CANE MURDER
ST. PATRICK'S DAY MURDER
MOTHER'S DAY MURDER
WICKED WITCH MURDER
GINGERBREAD COOKIE MURDER
ENGLISH TEA MURDER
CHOCOLATE COVERED MURDER
EASTER BUNNY MURDER
CHRISTMAS CAROL MURDER
FRENCH PASTRY MURDER
CANDY CORN MURDER
BRITISH MANOR MURDER
EGGNOG MURDER
TURKEY TROT MURDER
SILVER ANNIVERSARY MURDER
YULE LOG MURDER
HAUNTED HOUSE MURDER
INVITATION ONLY MURDER
CHRISTMAS SWEETS
CHRISTMAS CARD MURDER
IRISH PARADE MURDER

Published by Kensington Publishing Corp.

A Lucy Stone Mystery

# IRISH PARADE MURDER

## LESLIE MEIER

**KENSINGTON**
PUBLISHING CORP.

www.kensingtonbooks.com

KENSINGTON BOOKS are published by

Kensington Publishing Corp.
119 West 40th Street
New York, NY 10018

All Kensington titles, imprints, and distributed lines are available at special quantity discounts for bulk purchases for sales promotion, premiums, fundraising, educational, or institutional use.

Special book excerpts or customized printings can also be created to fit specific needs. For details, write or phone the office of the Kensington Special Sales Manager: Attn. Special Sales Department. Kensington Publishing Corp., 119 West 40th Street, New York, NY 10018. Phone: 1-800-221-2647.

Library of Congress Card Catalogue Number: 2020944028

The K logo is a trademark of Kensington Publishing Corp.

ISBN-13: 978-1-4967-1039-0
ISBN-10: 1-4967-1039-8
First Kensington Hardcover Edition: February 2021

ISBN-13: 978-1-4967-1041-3 (ebook)
ISBN-10: 1-4967-1041-X (ebook)

10 9 8 7 6 5 4 3 2 1

Printed in the United States of America

*For Beryl and Kevin Daley*

# IRISH
# PARADE
# MURDER

# Chapter One

"I just want to say that this was absolutely the loveliest, most beautiful funeral I've ever attended," said the woman, grasping Lucy Stone's hand and leaning in a bit too close for Lucy's comfort. Some people were like that, and Lucy resisted the urge to draw away, and smiled instead at the woman, who was middle-aged and dressed appropriately for such a somber occasion in a simple navy-blue dress and pearls. Her hair was a warm brown, probably colored, and she had applied her makeup with a light hand: a touch of foundation, mascara, and soft pink lipstick. Lucy didn't know the woman, but she didn't know most of the people she was greeting in the reception line at her father-in-law's funeral, and she assumed she was a friend or neighbor.

"You know, it made me feel as if I actually knew Mr. Stone," continued the woman, exploding that theory. "And what a wonderful family you have."

A bit weird, thought Lucy, wondering if the woman made a hobby of attending total strangers' funeral services. They were listed in the newspaper, after all, and anyone who had a passing interest could come. It was because of those listings that the funeral director had advised them to make sure someone stayed at the house, since burglars were known to take advantage of those notices, too.

"What a nice thing to say, and thank you for coming," said Lucy, passing the woman along to her husband, Bill, who was next in the reception line, and greeting Maria Dolan, who was Edna's best friend and one of the few people at the reception that she actually knew.

"Edna seems to be holding up," observed Maria, glancing at Lucy's newly widowed mother-in-law, "but I'll be keeping an eye on her and making sure she doesn't get lonely. I know you Maine folks can't be popping down to Florida every time she feels a bit blue."

"Thank you so much. I really appreciate that," said Lucy, who was finding her present situation somewhat surreal. It was only two weeks ago, when Lucy was still clearing away the Christmas decorations, that Edna had called, saying Bill Senior had suffered a heart attack but was going to be just fine. She had insisted on downplaying the situation, but Bill, an only child, had immediately booked a seat on the next flight to Tampa.

When he called Lucy from the hospital, he reported that Edna was either in denial or hadn't understood the seriousness of the situation, as his father was in the ICU in critical condition and wasn't expected to survive. He asked Lucy to inform the kids and prepare them for their grandfather's death. He also urged her to book a flight as soon as possible, as they would have to plan a funeral and support his mother. But even as her husband lay dying, Edna refused to believe there was any cause for concern and insisted that her son was making too much of a fuss. And when her husband finally did slip away in the final days of January, she opted for a quick cremation, to be followed by a simple memorial service. "No need for the kids to come all this way. My Bill wouldn't want a big fuss. He always said he hated funerals and didn't even want to attend his own," she said. "Elizabeth's in Paris, Toby's in Alaska, and Sara is just starting her new job in Boston, and their granddad would want them to look to the future. Young people don't want to waste time at some dreary memorial service, and why should they?"

But much to Edna's surprise, the kids immediately made plans to come to Florida. Elizabeth insisted she had to say a final *adieu* to her *grand-père*, Toby and his wife, Molly, brought Patrick to remember his Poppop, and Sara, who was waiting until June to start her new job at the Museum of Science in Boston, offered to stay with her grandma for a week or two to help out. Zoe, the youngest, who was still in college, wasn't sure she'd be able to make it, but in the end was able to postpone some exams and joined the grieving family that had gathered in Edna's spacious ranch house.

Lucy wasn't sure what to expect, but it turned out that people in Florida weren't much different from folks in Tinker's Cove, Maine. There was a steady stream of visitors offering sympathy, and many brought casseroles and desserts for the mourning family. And when they all finally gathered in the modern church, all angles and abstract stained glass, which was so different from the centuries-old church in Maine, with its clear glass windows and tall white steeple, the memorial service wasn't dreary at all, but was instead a true celebration of Bill Sr.'s life.

The service began with one of his favorite hymns, "For the Beauty of the Earth," and was followed by a favorite Irish prayer that he often repeated: "May you be in heaven before the devil knows you're dead." The kids all spoke of favorite memories they cherished of their grandfather. Elizabeth remembered the rainbow-colored Life Savers he always carried and shared with her, Patrick remembered catching his first fish with Poppop's help, Sara recalled the loud rock and roll he favored, which grew even louder as his hearing began to fail, and Zoe remembered countless games of checkers that Poppop somehow never won. Toby recalled that, as a child, he loved helping Poppop wash his car, but admitted that the time he tried to do it himself, as a surprise, didn't go well because the car was a convertible and the top was down, but Poppop had just laughed and said it was about time the inside got washed, too.

Lucy knew all these stories, of course, except for Toby's misadventure, which was a surprise to her. It was the minister's eulogy, however, that revealed her father-in-law's deep spirituality and faith, which she hadn't appreciated. "Bill Stone was a man who practiced his faith through action," said Rev. Florence Robb, "and he spent countless hours delivering Meals on Wheels, giving rides to the homebound, and working at the local food pantry. He helped at worship services, sometimes as an usher, sometimes reading the lessons and prayers. If something was needed, he provided it, often before it was missed. He replaced light bulbs, tightened screws, polished the brass, and those were only the things he did inside the church. Outside, he mowed the grass, weeded the flower beds, pruned the bushes, and repaired the church sign when it was torn down in a storm. In his quiet way, he made a huge difference in many people's lives, and he will be missed." She paused, and her voice breaking, added, "Greatly missed."

All this was running through Lucy's mind as she smiled and accepted the condolences offered by the people who had attended the funeral—dear friends, neighbors, and people whose lives had been touched by Bill Stone Sr. And also, as the reception line finally petered out, at least one total stranger who admitted she hadn't known Bill Stone Sr. at all.

Finally released from her duties on the reception line, Lucy glanced around the room, making sure everyone was all right. Bill had taken charge of his mother and had led her to the buffet table, where he was filling a plate for her. The kids were gathered in a corner, taking advantage of this rare opportunity to hang together and catch up with each other. There was plenty of food and drink, and there was a steady buzz of conversation punctuated with laughter, as was usual after the solemnities had been dispensed with and people took the time to reminisce, renew acquaintances, and enjoy each other's company. As she scanned the crowd, Lucy looked for the woman in the blue dress and pearls, but didn't see her. She did see Bill, however, trying to catch her eye, and she quickly joined him and Edna.

"Quite a nice turnout," she said, taking Edna's arm and leading her to one of the chairs that were lined up against the wall. "It's good to know that Pop was appreciated by so many people."

"I suppose so," said Edna, pushing her potato salad around with a plastic fork. She sighed. "I don't know what I'm going to do with myself, now that he's gone."

"He was a force to be reckoned with, that's for sure," said Lucy, squeezing Edna's hand. "But you're not alone. We're here for a few more days, Sara plans to stay for a week or more, and I hope you'll come visit us in Maine very soon. There's always a place for you at our house, you know."

"I know," said Edna, but she didn't sound as if she really believed it.

\*    \*    \*

A week later, the Florida sun was only a memory as Lucy was back at her job in wintry Maine, working as a part-time reporter and feature writer for the *Pennysaver*, the weekly newspaper in the quaint coastal town of Tinker's Cove, but she was having a hard time concentrating on the intricacies of the rather complicated changes being proposed to the town's zoning laws. "What exactly is an overlay district?" she asked Phyllis, the paper's receptionist, who was seated at her desk across the room, tucked behind the counter where members of the public filled out orders for classified ads, renewed subscriptions, dropped off letters to the editor, and occasionally complained.

"Beats me," said Phyllis, with a shrug of her shoulders. She was occupied with entering the week's new batch of classified ads and was peering through the heart-shaped reading glasses that were perched on her nose and that matched her colorful sweatshirt, which was bedecked with hearts and flowers, in contrast to the dreary reality of lingering dirty snow outside. "I don't know where to put this thank-you to Sheriff Murphy," she groaned. "Is it an announcement?"

Lucy perked up, her curiosity piqued. "What thank-you?"

"All about his help for some fund drive."

"Who submitted it?"

"Uh, it's right here." Phyllis studied the slip. "Someone named Margaret Mary Houlihan, corresponding secretary of the Hibernian Knights Society. Do you know her?"

"No, can't say I do. The Hibernian Knights present the big St. Patrick's Day parade over in Gilead, but the thank-you is a new one on me."

"Where do you think I should put it?"

"That I don't know. Better ask Ted." Ted Stillings was the publisher, editor, and chief reporter for the paper, which he'd inherited from his grandfather, a noted regional journalist. Times had changed since his day, however, and Lucy knew that Ted was hard-pressed to keep the little weekly paper afloat. Like newspapers throughout the country, the *Pennysaver* was faced with a diminishing list of advertisers and subscribers, and constantly increasing production costs.

"Well, I would if he was here, but he hardly ever is these days," complained Phyllis. After a pause she added, "Is it me, or do things seem a bit weird around here?"

"Weirder than usual?" asked Lucy, who hadn't really been paying much attention since she'd returned from Florida. She'd been focused on staying in touch with Edna and keeping Bill's spirits up.

"Yeah. While you were gone Ted's had a lot of meetings with, well, folks who aren't from around here. Fancy types, in city-slicker clothes."

"Really?" Lucy's interest was piqued. "Like who?"

"Well, there was a middle-aged man, with quite a big belly, dressed in a suit and tie. He was nice enough, made a lot of jokes, and laughed a lot, but didn't give his name or business. Then Ted arrived and whisked him off—took him out to lunch, I think."

"And when Ted got back from lunch, did he offer any explanation?"

"Nope. I asked if he was buying life insurance. It kind of just popped out. I guess the guy seemed kind of like a salesman, but Ted just chuckled and gave me a big pile of listings for the Events column." Phyllis paused to polish her glasses. "I definitely got the feeling he didn't want to continue the discussion."

"He is always complaining about the rising cost of newsprint . . ." said Lucy.

"And the declining number of subscribers," added Phyllis. "And that's another thing. He had me research all sorts of facts and figures, like ad revenue, classified ad revenue, production costs . . ." She let out a big sigh. "Not exactly my cup of tea, if you know what I mean."

"How did the figures look?" asked Lucy, beginning to feel rather uneasy. Was it possible that Ted wasn't just worrying out loud but that the *Pennysaver* was really in dire financial straits? Was he thinking of selling the paper, or even shutting it down permanently?

"Not good," admitted Phyllis, "but I'm no accountant. I can't even balance my checkbook."

"Neither can I," admitted Lucy. "I just cross my fingers, and if the bank says I have more money than I think I have, then it's a good month."

"Wilf manages our money," confessed Phyllis, sounding a bit smug as she referred to her husband. They had married late in life, and she was clearly enjoying married life. "And then there was that woman, done up to the nines, with high-heeled boots and that bleached-blond hair that looks natural so you know it must cost a fortune."

Lucy noticed that Phyllis's tone had changed; she sounded worried when she spoke about the woman. "I'm confused," admitted Lucy. "Does Wilf know this woman?"

"No way." Phyllis dismissed that idea with a flap of her hand. "She came here to the office and, again, no introduction. Ted just dragged her off. He was gone for a couple of hours, and when he got back, not a word. He just sat down and started pounding out his weekly editorial."

"You have no idea who she was?" Lucy considered possible identities for a woman with a city hairdo and high heels. "Maybe she was some sort of sales rep? A high-flying real estate agent?"

"Your guess is as good as mine," said Phyllis, "but she looked like trouble to me."

Lucy was inclined to agree. She tended to be suspicious of women in high heels, who clearly did not have to negotiate the icy sidewalks and muddy driveways that were an annual feature in Maine as winter began to loosen its grip and temperatures began to rise above freezing in the day, only to refreeze at night. Everyone she knew, male and female, wore duck boots beginning with the first February thaw and right on through June.

"Any other suspicious characters?" asked Lucy, thinking this was beginning to sound like a Sherlock Holmes story. Of course, Sherlock would immediately identify the jovial man as having come from Portland, where he'd recently stopped for gas and a stale tuna sandwich. The woman, he would assert, undoubtedly came from Chestnut Hill, where she raised Dobermans and ran a sado-masochistic dungeon patronized by wealthy men with guilty consciences.

"A tall, skinny man in a plaid shirt and jeans with a big Adam's apple," offered Phyllis, interrupting Lucy's thoughts. "He had a deep voice. He greeted me politely, 'Good morning, ma'am,' he said. That's how I know about his voice."

Ah, thought Lucy, a radio announcer for the country-western channel. "No introduction?"

"Nothing. He asked for Ted, called him 'Mr. Stillings.' Ted happened to be in the morgue, but he popped out like a jack-in-a-box when he heard the man's voice. Then they were gone, and again, no explanation when he returned."

"I dunno," said Lucy, shaking her head in puzzlement.

"Either he's working on a feature story of some sort about little-known celebrities, or it's got something to do with the business. Maybe he's once again on the brink of bankruptcy and is trying to refinance, or . . ." Here she stopped, unwilling to continue and voice the notion that Ted might be selling the *Pennysaver*.

The bell on the door jangled, and they both turned to see who their next visitor might be. This time the stranger was tall, dark, and undeniably handsome. He was also young, and dressed in brand-new country duds: ironed jeans with a crease down the leg, a plaid shirt topped with a barn jacket, and fresh-from-the-box duck shoes that hadn't yet ventured into muddy territory.

"What can I do for you?" asked Phyllis, in her polite receptionist voice.

"I have an appointment with Ted Stillings. Will you let him know I'm here?"

Phyllis and Lucy both perked up, presented with an opportunity to ascertain the fellow's name. "Gladly," said Phyllis, with a big smile. "Who shall I say is here?"

"Rrr," he began, then caught himself. "Just say his eleven o'clock is here."

Phyllis's ample bosom seemed to deflate a trifle. "Actually, you'd better take a seat. Ted's not here, but I expect him shortly, Mr. Rrr . . ."

"Thanks," he said, smiling and revealing a dazzling white perfect bite. He sat down on one of the chairs next to the door, opposite the reception counter; even bent at the knee, his long legs pretty much filled the intervening space. He picked up the latest copy of the *Pennysaver* from the table between the chairs and began reading it.

Lucy took this opportunity to study him, taking in his thick, Kennedy-esque hair, his sweeping black brows, hawkish nose, square jaw, broad shoulders, and large

hands. Dudley Do-Right, she considered, recalling the car-
toon character. Clearly, she was no Sherlock Holmes.

"Did you travel far?" she asked.

"Not too far," he said, with a shrug.

"So you're familiar with Maine?" she continued.

"Sure," he said. "Lobsters, blueberries, and moose."

"Would you like some coffee while you wait?" asked
Phyllis.

"No, thanks." He nodded. "I'm good."

"We also have tea," offered Lucy. "If you're a tea
drinker."

"Thanks, but I'm all set," he answered, turning the page
of the paper and burying his nose in it. Lucy doubted he
was really all that interested in the Tinker's Cove High
School's basketball team's recent defeat at the hands of the
Dover Devils, and figured he was trying to avoid conversation. But why? Why were all these recent visitors so se-
cretive, and what was Ted trying to hide?

She glanced at the antique Regulator clock that hung on
the wall above the stranger's head, just as the big hand
clicked into place at twelve, indicating it was exactly
eleven o'clock. Like clockwork, the bell jangled as the
door opened and Ted arrived, bristling with energy and
rubbing his hands together. "Ah, you're already here," he
said, extending his hand.

The stranger stood up and took Ted's hand, giving it a
manly shake. "Good to meet you," he said.

"Same here," said Ted. "Did you have a good drive?"

"Not bad," said the stranger. "Bit of traffic in Portland,
but otherwise clear sailing."

Lucy and Phyllis picked up on that last, and their eyes
met. Was this a clue to his identity? Was he a fisherman? A
yachtsman?

"That's great," said Ted. "Well, I don't know about

you, but I'm usually ready for a coffee around now. We don't have Starbucks, but we've got our own Jake's. How about it?"

"Sounds great," said the stranger.

Ted opened the door, holding it for the visitor, who stepped outside. Ted followed, and the two walked past the plate-glass window with the old-fashioned wooden blinds, their progress followed by the two women inside the office. Then they were out of view, leaving nothing behind except questions.

"Who is he?" asked Phyllis.

"Why is here?" asked Lucy.

"What's Ted up to?" asked Phyllis.

"I wish we had some answers," said Lucy.

# Chapter Two

By the time Wednesday, deadline day, rolled around, Lucy and Phyllis were increasingly concerned about the future of the *Pennysaver*, and their jobs. Ted's strange behavior had continued, with increasingly frequent unexplained absences, and the parade of unidentified visitors had not abated. Worst of all was the day Ted's wife, Pam, dropped by and tucked a bottle of champagne in the office fridge. Lucy and Pam were good friends, but when Lucy asked about the bottle, Pam had just replied with an enigmatic little grin. After she left, the bell on the door was still jangling when Lucy finally spoke the unspeakable.

"It's over. They've sold the paper."

"I think you're right," said Phyllis, her plump cheeks drained of color. "But who'd buy it? Weeklies like the *Pennysaver* are going the way of the dodo."

"Yeah, but think of the real estate. This building is right in the middle of Main Street and is probably worth a pretty penny. We'll be gone, replaced by tacky T-shirts and postcards for the tourists." Lucy glanced around at the newsroom, which didn't seem to have changed much since 1910, apart from the addition of PCs on each scarred wooden desk. "Or maybe a retro coffee shop? Scuffed and worn is kind of chic now."

"And Ted and Pam will probably buy themselves a condo someplace warm," said Phyllis, picturing them lounging by a turquoise pool. "Not that I blame them," she added, with a shrug.

"Yeah," agreed Lucy. "Ted fought the good fight, but we all know it's a losing battle. The media is the enemy of the people, the news is fake, and newspapers are just clutter that doesn't bring joy when you can get all your news on your cell phone."

"Shhh," hissed Phyllis, spying Ted through the window. "Ted's coming back."

The door flew open, the bell jangled, and Ted strode in, . positively vibrating with energy and good cheer. "Heidy-high, heidy-ho," he exclaimed. "How are you ladies this fine day?"

Lucy and Phyllis exchanged a nervous glance. "Pretty good," offered Phyllis.

"Busy," said Lucy, hitting the keyboard. "I'm working on the big story about the proposed zoning changes."

"Terr-rr-rific," growled Ted, sounding like Tony the Tiger. "Nobody can do zoning like you, Lucy. You actually make it interesting."

"I do my best," said Lucy, with a sick feeling growing in her stomach.

Ted practically danced through the office and perched on the edge of his chair, powering up the PC that sat on his totally impractical but beloved antique rolltop desk. Then he popped up and fixed himself a cup of coffee, took a few sips while peering out the window through the old-fashioned wooden blinds, then abandoned the half-drunk cup, setting it down by the coffeepot. He bounced on the balls of his feet, then cleared his throat.

Here it comes, thought Lucy. At least I'll be able to collect unemployment, and maybe I'll get severance. No, not likely; the most I'll get is unused vacation time.

"Don't go anywhere," ordered Ted, raising his pointer finger. "I've got to go out, but when I come back, I'll have an important announcement." Then he was gone, the bell gave a few sad little jangles, and Lucy moaned aloud, resting her forehead on her desk.

"The visiting nurses are hiring home health aides," said Phyllis. "Maybe I could do that." She didn't sound very excited at the prospect.

"Unemployment will probably get me through the winter," said Lucy, trying to sound hopeful. "Come summer, the IGA will probably be hiring, or I could work at the fudge shop."

"Yeah," said Phyllis, trying to sound encouraging. "There's lots of opportunities."

"No, there aren't," said Lucy, facing reality. "If there were, we wouldn't be working here—now, would we? The pay's lousy, the benefits nonexistent, and our boss is borderline abusive."

Phyllis laughed. "You love it, you know you do."

"I do," admitted Lucy. "The first time I saw my byline in print, I thought I'd died and gone to heaven."

"Yeah," said Phyllis, with a big sigh. "It was sure fun while it lasted, but all good things come to an end." Her attention was caught by a shadowy figure outside the door, and the two women watched as the door opened and the mysterious tall, dark, and handsome stranger stepped inside.

"Welcome back," said Phyllis. "What can I do for you?"

"Uh, nothing," he said, giving them a brief, but dazzling smile. "I've got a meeting with Ted."

"Too bad you missed him," said Lucy. "He just went out."

The stranger consulted his phone. "No problem. He'll be back."

Cripes, thought Lucy. Talk about being out of the loop. This guy gets text updates from Ted, while Phyllis and I are left completely in the dark. It was enough to make you want to quit, except it was too late for that.

"Take a seat," said Phyllis, with a wave of her hand. "Can I get you coffee? Tea? Water?"

"No, thanks, I'll just catch up on the news," he said, grinning and plucking a copy of last week's issue off the pile on the reception desk.

"It's old news," said Lucy. "Today's deadline day. The paper comes out tomorrow."

The stranger seated himself, stretching out his long, blue-jeaned legs, and started reading the second section, which featured Ted's over-optimistic analysis of the high school girls' basketball team's chances of making it to the state championship. Phyllis returned her attention to the pile of last-minute ads she was entering into the classified section, and Lucy resumed her struggle to make the proposed zoning regulations comprehensible to the average reader. The office was silent, apart from the quiet clicks of the two keyboards, the rustle of the paper when the stranger turned the page, and the ticking of the big old Regulator clock on the wall.

Lucy finished the zoning story and filed it for editing, thinking it was probably the last story she would ever write for the *Pennysaver*. Too bad she couldn't go out with a bang, a real scoop, instead of this tedious collection of details that hardly anyone would bother to read. She was thinking back on some of the big stories she'd written uncovering corruption, arson, and even murder. Well, that was all in the past, she thought, when Ted returned along with Sam Wilson, the publisher of the *Gilead Gabber*. The *Gabber* was similar to the *Pennysaver*, except it had the advantage of covering a neighboring town that happened to be the county seat, where the courts and county government were located. She figured Ted must have sold the *Pennysaver* to Sam, who was known as a shrewd businessman, and wondered if Sam would be keeping her and Phyllis on or letting them go. Probably letting us go, she decided, considering that Sam already had a complete staff in place.

As she watched, Ted went straight to the little fridge and grabbed the bottle of champagne. The stranger stood up, and the three men gathered in a loose little knot. "I have an announcement," said Ted, looking very pleased with himself. "So listen up, ladies, and Lucy, can you grab some paper cups?"

Somewhat resentfully, Lucy got to her feet and rummaged in the cupboard beneath the coffee station, producing the cups. Wasn't it bad enough she was going to be fired? Did Ted actually expect her to celebrate?

"I know there's been a lot of unexplained activity around here lately, but it's all been for a good cause," began Ted, peeling the foil off the bottle. "I am delighted to announce that I am now the proud owner of the *Gilead Gabber*, and I've hired a new reporter. Let me introduce Rob Callahan, who comes to us straight from the *Cleveland Plain Dealer*."

The tall, dark stranger gave them all a big smile, and Ted popped the cork. "Champagne all round, to our exciting new venture!"

Lucy and Phyllis were dumbstruck, Ted was giggling with glee, Sam Wilson was nodding with satisfaction, and Rob was passing around the paper cups of champagne.

"To a new venture!" exclaimed Ted.

"To a new venture," they all repeated, before sipping the bubbly.

"We thought you were selling the *Pennysaver*," confessed Lucy. "This is quite a surprise."

"We were braced for the worst," said Phyllis.

"I won't lie. I was considering it, but then I heard about this new project to improve and support local news outlets. It's called the TRUTH Project. Do you want to tell them about it, Rob?"

"Sure." He nodded. "We know that democracy depends upon an informed electorate, and this project is an effort to respond to the increasing number of news deserts that are appearing in the country as local papers find it impossible to remain in business. There are lots of towns that don't have or are in danger of losing their reliable source of local news, which is typically a weekly paper like the *Gabber* or the *Pennysaver*. The project is funded by a charitable foundation and will offer financial support and journalistic expertise to improve local news, because we know that what happens on the local level has national and international impact. School boards can vote to distort or even eliminate subjects like evolution, state legislatures can gerrymander voting districts to skew elections, health departments can limit resources for AIDS education and addiction. These issues are most often decided on the local level, and voters need to be informed when they go into the voting booth."

"So, thanks to a grant from the TRUTH Project, I've been able to purchase the *Gabber,* and increase staff," said Ted. "We're going to be covering the entire county, and that includes the courts and the county sheriff, the community college—it's a whole new ball game."

"Wow," said Lucy, sitting down in her chair and taking another sip of champagne. "I don't know what to say."

"What about you, Sam?" asked Phyllis. "What's next for you?"

"Retirement," he said. "I'm not getting any younger, you know, and I've wanted to retire for quite a while now, but I didn't feel it was right to quit. It means a lot to me that the *Gabber*'s in good hands." He put down his glass and shook hands with Ted. "So I'm out of here. I know you're eager to get started, and I wish you all the good luck in the world."

"Are we going to be moving to Gilead?" asked Phyllis, narrowing her eyes in suspicion. She lived only a few blocks from the office and usually walked to work.

"Are you keeping the entire *Gabber* staff?" asked Lucy, aware of that paper's head reporter, Fran Croydon, who'd won numerous awards for her warm and fuzzy feature stories.

"I'm not making any changes immediately. I'll be splitting my time between the two offices," said Ted. "The two papers will operate independently for the time being, under their own banners, but the content will be shared. So the *Gabber* will have your stories, Lucy, and the *Penny-saver* will now have the county news, too. And we're also going to have an online edition."

"That's going to be expensive," said Phyllis.

"And a lot more work," said Lucy.

"Well, I've got money from the TRUTH Project, and we've got Rob to help," said Ted, draining his paper cup and setting it down. "I'm planning on merging the two eventually, but for now I'm feeling my way. So let's get to work on next week's news section. The big news, of course, is the purchase of the *Gabber*, and I'll write that up myself. The other big story is the upcoming election of the grand marshal for the St. Patrick's Day parade over in Gilead—we need to profile the candidates."

"Won't Fran cover that?" asked Lucy, aware of Fran's numerous contacts and figuring she'd have to cede some of her usual assignments.

"No. She's on leave. She had to have cardiac bypass surgery," said Ted.

"All that sugary sweetness probably got to her," said Lucy, regretting the words the moment they flew out of her mouth.

"Bad attitude, Lucy. She's only on leave; she's planning on coming back when the doctor gives her the okay." He took a moment to think. "That's a good story for Rob to cut his teeth on; he can get a feel for the area and the power players."

"I always write that story for the *Pennysaver*," said Lucy, protesting.

"Actually," said Rob, "I have a story in mind about this puppet maker, Rosie Capshaw. I ran into her by accident at the gas station, and we got talking. I thought it would be a nice human-interest sort of piece and a good way for me to introduce myself to the readers. You know, kind of reassure them that I'm not some sort of muckraker."

"Sounds interesting," said Ted, "and the perfect story for Lucy. She's great with features."

"I can do that and the grand-marshal story," offered Lucy, who had just read a magazine article advising working women to lean in and seize opportunities.

"No, Rob can do the grand marshal. Remember, you've got all the local meetings, too, Lucy."

"Oh, right." Lucy stared into her cup, where the remaining champagne had gone quite flat. Just like her future, she thought, fearing that Rob would get the real news stories while she was stuck with puff pieces and boring town committee meetings.

"That's all for now," said Ted, checking his phone. "I've got to get over to Gilead to get things rolling over there."

"But it's almost deadline, and you haven't edited my stories yet," protested Lucy.

Ted caught himself in mid-stride and turned to Rob. "You can handle a little copyediting, can't you?"

Lucy's jaw dropped, waiting for Rob's answer.

"Sure thing," said Rob, seating himself at Ted's desk and cupping his hand on the mouse.

"So Rob will wrap up the paper. We'll finish up the budget tomorrow morning. Be here at noon. Right?"

"Right, boss," replied Rob, eagerly, and he added a little salute.

Lucy and Phyllis just nodded, exhibiting little enthusiasm for Ted's changes. Lucy was definitely disgruntled, irked at the way Ted took her for granted, and resentful of the way he'd assigned Rob to edit her stories. She'd show him, and she'd show that bunch over at the *Gabber*!

Hearing her phone, she was surprised to see Bill was the caller. He was a busy restoration carpenter, and he rarely called during the workday unless something was wrong, so she was a bit concerned when she answered. "What's up?"

"How about lunch?" he asked, surprising her. They rarely had lunch together, and usually only if they happened to be at home.

"Okay, but there's not much in the house. I could make egg salad . . ."

"I was thinking of pizza. Meet me at Pizzapalooza?"

"Eat out?" Lucy was shocked.

"Yeah. Why not?"

"Okay," agreed Lucy, glancing at the clock and seeing it was already noon. "I was just leaving the office."

"Great. I've got something I want to talk to you about. Meet you in ten," he said, ending the call.

What next, wondered Lucy, gathering up her things and intending to leave the office for the short walk down Main Street. She was on her way to the door when Rob called her by name.

"Lucy, where are you going? I haven't finished editing your story, and I've got some questions for you."

Lucy stopped and gave him the look that had reliably stopped all four of her kids in their tracks. "It's noon, and I'm done for the day," she said. "Phyllis can help you if there's anything you don't understand, or"—she added a shrug—"you could call Ted." Satisfied that she had put this overreaching young smartie in his place, she turned and marched out the door, giving it an extra little shake so the bell's jangle was extra loud. Pleased with herself, she continued on her way to the pizza place.

Pizzapalooza was a new arrival on Main Street, offering gourmet pizzas with creative toppings like avocado and vegan cheese. It had replaced the old-fashioned Tony's—known for its greasy Formica tables, vinyl seats repaired with duct tape, and flickering fluorescents—with cheery, bright décor and classy pendant lights that dangled over each freshly reupholstered booth, but Lucy rather missed the older, grubbier place. Everyone agreed that the pizza wasn't nearly as good, and she and Bill ordered a classic cheese with pepperoni, unwilling to experiment.

"I miss Tony's crust," said Lucy. "It was leathery, like New York pizza," said Lucy, as they made their way to one of the many empty tables.

"It was a lot cheaper, too," said Bill, replacing his wallet in his rear pocket before sliding onto the seat opposite her.

They looked up as the server brought them their Cokes and promised the pizza would be ready soon. After taking a sip, Lucy asked her husband what was on his mind.

"The funeral director sent me this," he said, producing a long, white envelope from the roomy pocket of his barn jacket.

"A bill?" asked Lucy. "I thought your mother paid for the funeral."

"Not a bill," he said. "Read it, and tell me what you think."

Opening the envelope, Lucy found several sheets of paper, folded in thirds. The top was a letter from a woman named Catherine Klein, introducing herself as Bill's half sister.

"This is crazy," said Lucy. "You're an only child, and your parents didn't have any previous marriages. Edna loves telling how she met your dad when she was seventeen, and they had to wait until she turned eighteen before her folks would let her marry. They were devoted to each other."

"That's what I thought," said Bill. "Keep reading."

The next two pages were copies of a DNA report from Genious.com, which featured a pie chart indicating that Catherine Klein was 40 percent English, 40 percent German, and 20 percent Swedish. The second page provided a family tree, which identified Bill Stone Sr. as her father, a nameless woman as her mother, and Bill himself as a half brother. Lucy stared at the diagrams for a long time, considering various explanations.

"Did your Dad ever mention sowing any wild oats?" she finally asked.

"Not to me," said Bill. "And this woman is younger than I am, which means Dad must have cheated on my mother, which I find hard to believe."

"Me, too," said Lucy, folding up the papers and replacing them in the envelope, as if that could erase this disturbing news or contain it somehow. Cover it up and hide it. Then a troubling thought occurred to her. "Does your mother know?"

"I don't think so. The funeral director wrote that this woman asked for Mom's address, but he refused to provide it and offered instead to forward the letter. He said it was given to him in a sealed envelope, and he decided it would be better to send it to me rather than Mom. He said this sort of thing happens quite often; someone appears from the past and wants to reestablish relations with long-lost relatives, but he tends to be cautious about troubling—that was his word, *troubling*—recently bereaved people, especially older widows. I got the impression a lot of these folk are after money."

"I suppose some people simply want to belong to a family. That must be why she did the DNA search." She paused, as the server arrived with their fragrant, steaming-hot pizza and set it on their table. "Do you have any idea who she is? Was she at the funeral?"

"She sent a photo," said Bill, producing a two-by-three-inch head shot and sliding it across the table to Lucy.

"Oh my goodness," exclaimed Lucy, recognizing the face. "I remember her from the funeral. She made a big fuss about how nice the service was. She said we were a wonderful family."

"So wonderful she wants to join it," said Bill, helping himself to a slice. "Do you think she's for real?" he asked, then bit off the end.

"Maybe," said Lucy, taking a piece for herself. "But I think we need to be skeptical. People aren't always who they say they are."

Bill sighed. "But DNA doesn't lie, does it?"

"I guess we'll find out," said Lucy, plucking a piece of pepperoni off her slice, popping it in her mouth, and deciding that Tony's pizza was definitely better.

# Chapter Three

Lucy chewed thoughtfully, trying to imagine Bill's folks as young parents. She'd seen photos, of course, but photos didn't always tell the truth. People said "cheese" and smiled automatically when faced with a camera, revealing little of what they were truly feeling. Good looks covered a lot, too, she thought, remembering a news photo of an adorable, dimpled mass shooter with a killer smile. Edna and Bill were pictured in plenty of old photos, photos that were now curling with age, and they'd seemed happily married and terribly proud of their new baby, Bill. "There's quite a few years before kids become aware and remember things," she said, picking up her slice. "Those early years are pretty much a blank, right?" she asked, before taking a bite.

"That's what I was thinking," admitted Bill. "Maybe Mom had postpartum depression . . . maybe Dad freaked out about being responsible for a baby . . . I guess there could have been a period when they were separated."

"But they never mentioned it," said Lucy.

"No." Bill shook his head. "And I remember asking Dad for advice a few times, when things weren't so great between us."

"What do you mean?" challenged Lucy. "When was this?"

He shrugged. "Oh, when you went back to school and took that course; it was years ago."

"Oh," said Lucy, looking down and studying her pizza with great interest. That was an episode she wasn't proud of, when she was attracted to a young professor but hadn't realized that Bill had noticed. "What did your dad say?"

Bill chuckled. "He said not to worry, that you were a good girl."

"And so I am," said Lucy, eager to regain the high ground. "But I guess the question is, was your dad a good boy?"

"I've certainly never had any reason to think otherwise," said Bill. "But he was pretty private; you didn't always know what he was thinking."

Lucy asked the question she'd been wanting to ask since the funeral. "Is that why you didn't speak about him at the memorial service? I thought for sure you'd tell about the Christmas he sent the surprise check, the money that got us through that awful first winter in Maine."

Bill chuckled. "I figured that if I told that story, he'd materialize someow and rise right up out of the urn and brain me. That was between us and him; it wasn't for anybody else to know about."

Lucy sipped at her diet Coke. "So you're kind of saying he might've had an affair."

"I don't really know, Lucy, but it's possible." He sighed. "And if he did, I doubt that he ever would have told my mother."

"She might have figured it out," suggested Lucy. "Men aren't very good at hiding evidence, and you learn a lot from doing the laundry."

Bill smiled naughtily. "I guess I'll have to be more careful in the future about those lipstick stains." He took a bite of pizza and chewed thoughtfully. "But I'm sure not going to ask my mother if she had any suspicions about Dad. Not now, not while she's grieving."

"So what are you going to do about this Catherine Klein?" asked Lucy.

"Beats me," said Bill, wiping his mouth with a paper napkin.

Dinner that night was unusually silent, as both Bill and Lucy were occupied with their own thoughts. Bill was worrying about his mother and how she would take this news, and Lucy's mind kept flitting between the problem of Catherine Klein and the new situation at work. The girls, however, were in high spirits, describing the float they were already planning to build as members of the Interact Committee at Winchester College for the upcoming St. Patrick's Day parade.

"We're going to have students dressed in their national costumes," said Zoe, taking a drumstick and passing the platter of chicken.

"And there'll be flags from all different nations," added Sara, choosing a thigh.

"And music, too," said Zoe, looking curiously at her mother, who was staring at the bowl of mashed potatoes as if it held the secret of the universe or might at least give some inkling of what the future held for her at the *Penny-saver*.

Aware of Zoe's glance, she quickly said, "Uh, nice," and passed the potatoes to Bill, who passed them on to Sara without taking any.

The girls looked at each other. "Is something the matter?" asked Sara.

"Yeah, what's going on?" demanded Zoe. "I don't think either of you have heard a word we've said."

"I have," insisted Bill, helping himself to salad. "But I don't understand why you're having all this international stuff for an Irish parade."

"Because we're the Interact Club; it's the club for exchange students," explained Sara.

"Are any of them from Ireland?" asked Bill, in a rather confrontational tone. "And how come nobody passed me the potatoes?"

"We did," snapped Zoe, "but you didn't take any, which, frankly, was kind of weird."

Lucy could sense that Zoe didn't appreciate her father's line of questions and decided to change the subject. "Actually, you're right. I have been distracted. Ted hired a new guy at the paper, and I'm worried he's going to get all the big news stories."

"I thought Ted was hanging on by a thread and the paper could fold any minute," said Sara.

"He was, and it could have," admitted Lucy. "But he got a grant from this TRUTH Project outfit to buy the *Gilead Gabber* and hire this hotshot who's supposed to help us improve local news coverage." She picked up her fork. "And now the new guy, Rob, is going to cover the grand-marshal selection, which is a big story. I've got the usual committee meetings, and believe it or not, Ted actually assigned Rob to edit my stories this morning. It looks like this guy might actually be our new editor."

"That's not fair," protested Sara. "You've been there forever."

"And I've developed lots of contacts, and I've got the background knowledge," said Lucy.

"Well, whatever you do, don't share anything," advised

Zoe. "I can just see this guy asking for help, and you're too nice to tell him to figure it out for himself."

"Especially since he's supposed to be the big expert!" declared Sara.

"Women do this all the time," said Zoe. "They take pity on the helpless male, who ends up undercutting their work in the end, and getting all the credit."

"I object," said Bill, helping himself to another piece of chicken. "You're making it sound as if men are inferior to women. And why shouldn't your Mom help the new guy out if it helps the paper?"

"Because women have to work twice as hard to earn three-quarters of what men make, that's why," said Sara.

"It's not a level playing field, Dad," declared Zoe, "and women lose every time they help some dumb guy climb right over them to get the promotion, or the raise, or the award."

"Women have got to do what men do, which is play the game to win."

"But there's no 'I' in team," offered Bill, rather feebly.

"Building a career is not a team sport," said Sara. "It's an individual accomplishment, and Mom has worked hard to make her byline mean something."

"Yeah, Dad," said Zoe. "It's about time Mom got the credit she deserves. She's worked hard all these years, and she's an amazing journalist, and she doesn't need anybody telling her how to do her job."

Sitting there, listening to her daughters defend her, Lucy was stunned. "Golly, guys, I didn't know you'd noticed."

Everybody laughed, but later, as she cleared the table and loaded the dishwasher, Lucy thought about what the girls had said and vowed to take her work more seriously. Sure, she was only a part-time reporter and feature writer, but she was very good at her job and didn't need to take a back seat to anyone, especially not some young whipper-snapper like Rob Callahan!

On Thursday morning. Lucy joined her friends for breakfast at Jake's Donut Shack. The weekly gathering had developed as a substitute for the casual meetings the four friends had enjoyed at school and sports events when their kids were younger. As their nests emptied and the kids flew off to college and careers, they realized they needed to get together regularly to share advice and offer each other support with life's challenges. Lucy always enjoyed these breakfasts; she had missed them while she was away in Florida and greeted her three friends with a big smile. Rachel Goodman, who was a psych major in college and never got over it, was quick to offer Lucy sympathy when she joined the group.

"Lucy, I'm so sorry about Bill's father. How are you all coping?" she asked, peering over her coffee mug with big, brown eyes. Rachel's husband, Bob, was a busy lawyer in town, and Rachel was a caregiver for Miss Julia Ward Tilley, who was Tinker's Cove's oldest resident.

"Thanks," said Lucy, sliding into a seat. "It was kind of sudden, but I was really encouraged by the kids' reaction. They gathered round. Elizabeth even came from Paris, and they all spoke so nicely at the service. They had wonderful memories of Grandpa—even a few stories that were news to me."

"That's great," said Rachel, "and such a positive way for them to deal with their grief. How is your mother-in-law doing?"

"Edna's not one to get overly emotional," said Lucy. "I know she misses Bill Senior, and we want her to come for a visit real soon, but I'm not at all convinced she'll do it."

"You should encourage her to open up and express her

feelings," advised Rachel, as Norine, the waitress approached, order pad in hand.

"Easier said than done," said Lucy, giving Norine a big smile.

"So is it the regular orders for everyone?" asked Norine, licking her pencil. "Sunshine muffin for Rachel, organic yogurt parfait for Pam, hash and eggs for Lucy and"—she narrowed her eyes and glared at Sue Finch— "black coffee for you."

Sue, perfectly turned out, as always, in skinny jeans and a cashmere sweater, flicked a lock of shiny black hair away from her face with a beautifully manicured hand and smiled a polite little smile. "Thanks, Norine."

"A donut wouldn't kill you, you know," said Norine.

"I just don't have any appetite in the morning," said Sue, with a little sigh. Truth be told, nobody had seen Sue eat any solid food in years, and Lucy suspected she survived on a liquid diet of white wine and black coffee.

"I'll be back with the coffeepot," promised Norine, who quickly returned to supply Lucy with a mug and to top off the others' with fresh coffee. When they were all supplied with caffeine, Pam called for attention, tapping her water glass with a spoon.

"I have a big announcement," she said, with a toss of the ponytail she always wore. "Lucy knows already, but Ted and I have bought the *Gilead Gabber*. Now the *Pennysaver* won't be limited to Tinker's Cove news; the expanded paper will cover the whole county. It's very exciting."

"Congratulations!" trilled Sue, raising her mug. "We must toast to your success!"

"Here, here," added Rachel.

"To success," said Lucy, who was still uneasy about the paper's expansion.

"This will mean a lot of changes, I suppose," said Rachel, who had picked up on Lucy's muted response.

"Changes for the better," said Pam, who had been a high school cheerleader and was still given to bursts of enthusiasm. "Ted found out about this foundation that is dedicated to improving local news. Do you know that there are news deserts in this country, where people have no way of knowing what their local governments are up to because they've lost their local papers? And Tinker's Cove came close, quite a few times. We even got a second mortgage on the house at one point, just to keep the *Pennysaver* going. Now, thanks to this grant from the TRUTH Project—that's what it's called—Ted has been able to acquire the *Gabber* and he's also hired a big-city reporter who's going to, uh, professionalize the paper."

"How do you feel about this, Lucy?" asked Rachel.

"Absolutely great," said Lucy, unwilling to rain on Pam's parade. "I mean, I don't really know what I'm doing. I didn't go to journalism school, so I've been operating on instinct. I'm sure this guy, Rob, can give me some valuable advice."

"Or maybe you could give him some," said Sue, tapping her mug with a Ballet Pink nail.

"This isn't a put-down of you, Lucy," said Pam, reaching across the table and taking her hand. "You do great work, and I made sure that this new guy isn't making a lot more money than you. He's full-time, of course, but I told Ted we are certainly not going to have wage inequality at our paper."

"Well, thanks," said Lucy, who wasn't sure she believed Pam. For all she knew, and actually suspected, Rob was probably getting a handsome stipend from the TRUTH

Project in addition to whatever pittance Ted was paying him. "That's good to know."

"What's right is right," insisted Pam. "And I know Ted is very eager to begin covering the county, which we all know has been pretty much a closed book. Sam Wilson's one of those go-along-to-get-along types; he just printed whatever the sheriff or the county commissioners wanted him to print in the *Gabber*. He never questioned anything, never looked under any rocks, probably for fear that if he did they would cut him off and stop sending press releases."

"That sheriff, Murphy, is a powerful guy," said Rachel, with a little nod. "A small-time megalomaniac, with some real control issues. He runs the county jail, he hires the corrections officers and the deputy sheriffs, who are like his own private little gang, and he even runs the St. Patrick's Day parade. He's the sort of person who can be very dangerous if he feels threatened. I'd be very careful before I upset his apple cart. What do you think, Lucy?"

"I'm not tackling the powers that be. I'm leaving that to the new guy and sticking to what I do best, which is human interest, stuff like that." She paused, taking a sip of coffee. "Today, for example, I'm interviewing this girl who makes puppets. A puppeteer."

"Rosie Capshaw!" exclaimed Sue. "She's fabulous. She's a poor relation, a cousin, who's set up a workshop on the Van Vorst estate where she makes these amazing creations. She approached me about doing something at Little Prodigies, maybe a puppet show or even a workshop, but I haven't had a chance to discuss it with Chris." Sue was part owner of Little Prodigies Child Care Center, where she formerly taught but nowadays limited herself to an administrative role. "That should be a terrific story, Lucy."

"Sorry about the delay," apologized Norine, arriving with their orders. "Our usual cook, Sandra, is out sick, and the guy who's filling in isn't quite up to speed."

"Typical male," said Sue, with a shrug. "If you want it done right, get a girl. Right, ladies?"

The women all laughed as they dug into their breakfasts, but Lucy wasn't all that amused. While they were frustrated by their husbands', or sons', occasional lapses and incompetence, she was faced with more than the usual male failure to turn off the lights or difficulty finding things that were right in front of their eyes. For the first time in her career, she had to deal with a male rival, and she wasn't sure how she was going to deal with the challenges he presented. She could, as she'd said, stick to the female sphere and focus on human-interest stories, but she suspected she would want to do more. If Ted's new, expanded paper was actually going to challenge the powerful and expose corruption in the county, she knew she wanted to be part of it, but she didn't have a clue how to make that happen. In the past, she'd simply followed stories where they led, and sometimes she'd broken some major scoops that went national, but now she would have to compete with Rob whenever some tantalizing lead appeared. The thing she feared the most was discovering a potentially big story, only to have it snatched away from her and assigned to Rob. What would she do then? Would she fight, would she threaten to quit, or would she knuckle under and let him exercise his male prerogative?

She was still mulling over that problem as she drove along Shore Road on her way to the Van Vorst estate. The road ran atop a series of cliffs overlooking the Atlantic Ocean, which was gray and choppy on this February day. Flocks of seabirds bobbed on the water, black ducks and eiders, and she wondered at their ability to endure in the often-hostile environment without any shelter. They had special oils, downy feathers, and body fat to keep them warm, and she hoped that she, too, had special qualities that would enable her to succeed in this new work environment.

Driving along the stone wall that bounded the Van Vorst estate, she turned through the open gate and followed the drive past the stately mansion and on to the area where the stables and barns were located. The estate had once been largely self-supporting, with its own farm producing milk, eggs, vegetables, and even pork and poultry meat, but nowadays it was used as a country retreat by supermodel Juliette Duff, who had inherited the estate. A small residential staff maintained the mansion and property, with help from daily workers.

Lucy wasn't sure which brick building contained the puppet workshop, but as soon as she stepped out of her car, she was greeted by her subject, Rosie Capshaw.

"Over here," yelled Rosie, who had a mass of curly black hair tied back by a red bandanna and was wearing a paint-stained farmer's bib overall atop a thick thermal sweatshirt. "You must be Lucy," she exclaimed, grabbing Lucy's hand and shaking it. "I love your work! I'm so honored that you're interested in writing about me."

"Golly," replied Lucy, with an embarrassed smile. "People aren't usually that excited about talking to me." She pulled her phone out of her oversized Fish Ladder Restoration Fund tote bag and held it up. "How about letting me snap your photo before I get to the tough questions and you throw me out?"

"Not likely." Rosie obliged with a smiling pose. "I'm a whore for publicity, and you know what they say, there's no such thing as bad publicity."

"Well, lead on, and tell me about your puppets. I guess you do shows for kids, stuff like that," began Lucy, thinking of the kiddie shows featuring fairy tales and superheroes she'd attended at the library with her youngsters.

"Sort of," said Rosie, sliding the barn door open and revealing the interior, which was populated with huge, oversized constructions that bore no similarity to the hand puppets and marionettes Lucy had expected. A number of the creations were lined up along a wall, and several work benches contained parts of others that were still being built. The barn smelled of paint, sawdust, and glue, reminding Lucy of her grandfather's basement wood workshop.

"This is not what I expected," admitted Lucy, looking around in awe.

"I know. You say you build puppets and people think of Mr. Rogers and Daniel Tiger." Rosie shrugged. "It all started when I saw the show *War Horse* on Broadway. The horse was a life-size puppet operated by several actors, and I was enthralled. They were able to convey so much emotion, it was so lifelike, that I was blown away. I knew it was something I wanted to do, and believe me, I was a girl without a clue. But when I saw that horse, everything fell into place for me. I got myself hired as a stagehand . . ."

"For *War Horse*? On Broadway?" Lucy was amazed.

"Yeah." Rosie shrugged. "I couldn't believe it myself. I just walked in one day and asked for a job, and next thing I knew, I was painting and gluing and patching up that puppet horse, keeping it in shape for the show."

"And that led to all this?" suggested Lucy, waving a hand at the huge creations populating the barn.

"Yeah, that was the beginning. Want a tour?" Rosie led the way, pointing as she went. "Okay," she began, standing in front of a figure covered with fake leaves, "this is a Green Man; he was part of a farm festival in Vermont. And here I've got Mother Jones," she said, moving to the next figure, which was a woman dressed in a long skirt and shawl. "She was involved in the early days of the labor movement, and I made her for a Me Too event. These guys, these ghosts and ghouls, they were for a Halloween haunted house."

"So you provide these figures for who? Organizations? Private parties? Stage?"

"All of the above," said Rosie. "Want to see what I'm working on now?"

"Sure," said Lucy, leaving the huge ghoulish figures and following her to a nearby workbench.

"This is going to be St. Patrick," said Rosie, lifting up a large, bearded head she was constructing out of a big fishing buoy. "I like to recycle, use found objects where I can. He's going to be great when he's finished. I figure I can use him, along with Mother Jones, and I can rework one of the ghouls into a banshee . . ."

"Is this for a special event? A party?" asked Lucy.

"Oh, no. It's for the St. Patrick's Day parade."

"In Boston?" asked Lucy.

"No. The one right here, in Gilead."

"They've asked you to participate?" inquired Lucy, who knew the parade featured bands, step-dancers, floats from community organizations, and lots of marching firemen and policemen. She was rather doubtful that the notoriously conservative Hibernian Knights, who organized the parade, would welcome Rosie's oversized puppets.

"Oh, no, but I figured this would be a great opportunity to showcase my work. I don't expect them to pay me or anything."

"You'd better sit down," said Lucy, indicating a couple of stools by the workbench. When they were both seated, she broke the news. "The parade is run by this club, the Hibernian Knights; they're all of Irish descent, and they have a strict vetting process. Anyone who wants to march has to apply for permission, and last year they refused to let the Gay Vets march in the parade. They're very conservative, and they don't welcome newcomers."

"I didn't realize I had to apply," said Rosie, missing Lucy's point. "How do I get in touch with these Hibernian Knights?"

"They have a website," said Lucy, "but it's probably not worth the bother. I don't see them going for your giant puppets."

"Don't be so negative," said Rosie. "They're going to love my St. Patrick and his snakes."

Sure, thought Lucy, and pigs can fly. "Let me get some photos of the gang," said Lucy, with a nod toward Rosie's creations. "They are amazing."

"Yeah." Rosie smiled fondly at the Green Man. "Isn't he gorgeous? And he's green. He could be in the St. Pat's parade, too. I don't know why I didn't think of it. And Mother Jones was Irish. This is going to be the best parade ever! You'll see."

# Chapter Four

Lucy was driving back to the office to make Ted's budget meeting when her cell phone rang; since she was on
Shore Road, where a moment's inattention could send you
over the cliff into the ocean, she pulled into the driveway
of a vacant summer home. Most of the big houses overlooking the water were empty this time of year, while
their owners were making big bucks in New York or
Boston. The call was coming from Town Hall, she realized; she recognized the number with a sinking feeling,
figuring she'd gotten something wrong in that stupid
zoning story.

Her suspicion was correct. The caller was Nancy
Braithwaite, the town planner. "I was surprised when I
read the article, Lucy," she began, "since you so rarely get
anything wrong. But I thought I made it clear that the
proposed changes would allow for more mixed-use development in town, and would also encourage in-law
apartments, which have previously not been allowed."

"That's what I wrote," responded Lucy, puzzled.

"Well, it's not what the story says. Do you want me to
read it to you?"

"No, I'm on way to the office anyway, and I'll take a look. I think I know what happened," she said, convinced that Rob had made erroneous changes when he edited her story. "I'll make sure we print a correction."

"The vote is coming up in a few weeks, and it's important that people have the right information," said Nancy, sounding worried. "The planning committee and I have been working on this for over a year. I'd hate to see all our hard work go for naught."

"I'm really sorry this happened. We've got a new guy, and he's not quite up to speed."

"I didn't think it was your mistake, Lucy." Nancy paused. "To tell the truth, the writing wasn't very good; it wasn't your style." She lowered her voice. "There were misplaced apostrophes."

"Thanks for calling, Nancy, and I'll make sure that correction is right on page one."

Ending the call, Lucy sat in the car and focused on the horizon, where gray water met gray sky. Her emotions were out of control; she was furious with Rob, and she wanted to scream at him and let him know exactly what she thought of his editing. Not just his editing, his presumed superiority. So Super-Journalist Rob was going to help them, was going to show them how to improve the paper. Good work, so far, Rob. Misplaced apostrophes!

Let it out, now, she told herself, letting loose with a scream that sent a flock of blackbirds perched on the electric line scattering into the sky. Let it all out, because she was going to have to be ever so professional, and rational, and reasonable when she got to the office. Confrontation would get her nowhere, but she had to find a way to make sure that Ted, and her readers, knew that she was a reliable and trustworthy reporter, with a solid grasp of correct grammar. Shifting into drive, she pulled onto Shore Road and continued to the office, pondering her dilemma.

It wasn't quite noon when she arrived, and neither Ted nor Rob were in the office. Phyllis was at her desk, where her computer screen was decorated with red heart stickers, and greeted Lucy with a big smile. "Guess what?" she demanded, by way of greeting.

"Guess what yourself," replied Lucy, somewhat confused.

"You'll never guess." Phyllis was smiling, bursting with some unexpected news.

"You're pregnant?" guessed Lucy, thinking this was one for the *Guinness Book of Records*.

"No. I'm part Native American." She nodded. "I really am. Five percent."

"I'm guessing you did one of those cheek-swab DNA kits," said Lucy.

"I did, and so did Wilf. No surprises there, really, except that he's not one hundred percent Swedish, like he thought; there is some Czech mixed in. And I guess I shouldn't be so surprised about being partly Native American since my ancestors have been here for centuries, and there probably weren't too many possible mates available for those early settlers."

"It could've been rape, you know," said Lucy, plucking one of the new *Pennysaver* issues from the stack on the reception counter. "A lot of bad stuff happened back then between the natives and the settlers. It wasn't always love."

"Lucy! Shame on you! My ancestors were undoubtedly good, upstanding folk; they'd never do anything like that!"

"Just saying, if you read your history books . . ."

"I think it was like John Smith and Pocahontas, begging her chieftain father to spare his life; that's history for you."

"Probably a tall tale," laughed Lucy. "As it happens, Bill just heard from some woman who did a DNA test and claims she's his half sister. It's kind of thrown him for a loop, coming so soon after his father's death."

"Half sister? Out of nowhere?"

"Yeah." Lucy had hung her jacket on the coatrack and had seated herself at her desk, where she powered up her computer and waited for it to complete the laborious business of waking up, complete with groans and grinds. "If it's true, it means his father must've had an affair, or maybe a previous marriage. Bill's not at all sure his mother is ready for this."

"I think you'd better be very careful. I've read there are a lot of DNA cons going on. People claiming to be related, especially after a death, in hopes of cashing in on some sort of inheritance. Like if a will says "to my issue," instead of naming each heir, they could make a claim on the estate."

"Come to think of it, I don't know anything about a will, if there even is one," said Lucy, glancing at the *Pennysaver*, which featured her zoning story on the front page.

"Then you could be in big trouble because the state's inheritance laws will take over," continued Phyllis. "I don't what they are in Florida, but a lot of times, they divide the estate among the spouse and the kids, even though most couples leave everything to the surviving spouse. That's what Wilf and I did, but of course we don't have kids."

"Not that you know about," said Lucy, turning her attention to the story, which she read quickly, growing angrier with each mangled sentence. She'd just finished reading when the bell on the door announced Ted's arrival, accompanied by Rob.

Lucy thought the two men seemed to be sharing some sort of joke, chuckling and nodding along with each other, just short of slapping each other on the back or punching each other's arms as they removed their jackets and hung them up. She realized she was going to have to deal delicately with the matter of the correction, so she decided to avoid confrontation and take the matter into her own hands by writing it herself. "Due to an editing error," she began, quickly completing the text and sending it to Ted.

Ted was busy fixing himself a cup of coffee and inquiring if anybody else wanted one before they went into the morgue for the budget meeting. Rob wanted one, cream and two sugars, and Ted fixed it for him; then they all gathered around the table in the room that served as both conference room and library.

"Wow," enthused Rob, gazing at the huge bound volumes of previous issues dating back to the early 1800s. "I bet there's some history here."

"Sure is," said Ted, beaming at his protégé. "Shay's Rebellion, the Civil War, Lincoln's assassination, world wars, it's all here." He sat down, took a sip of coffee, and rubbed his hands together. "Okay, let's get to work. Lucy, how's your feature looking?"

"Great. I interviewed Rosie Capshaw this morning and got a lot of material. I can write it up this afternoon. There aren't very many meetings this week, just the selectmen, so if you've got anything else for me, I can certainly handle it."

"If I may," said Rob, raising a finger and getting a nod from Ted, "it's a common failing—no, that's not the right word—common practice on a lot of local papers to rush the writing process. If you have a light week, why not take the time to polish your story and make it really shine?"

Lucy felt her cheeks redden. She'd always been a fast worker, and Ted rarely made any changes in her work, which had won numerous awards from the regional press association. And here Rob was advising her to polish her work, when his editing had ruined a perfectly correct story that happened to be quite well-written, too.

"Good point, Rob," said Ted. "And there's always the possibility of breaking news, so it will be good to have a light budget this week. You're doing the parade grand-marshal selection; how's that going?"

"Well, actually, maybe that is a story for Lucy," said Rob, giving her a condescending little smile. "I think my experience could be put to better use, especially when there's hard news begging to be covered. I've done a little digging around, and this little parade doesn't seem terribly significant."

"It's not a little parade," said Phyllis, whose dander was up. "It goes on for hours, with bands and floats. The governor always comes, and all the local politicians show up, and there's police and fire departments from all over the state."

"Yeah, people come from all over to watch, even from as far as California," added Lucy. "Choosing the marshal is a big deal; it's an enormous honor."

"And there's a woman in the running this year. They've never had a woman as grand marshal, and if she gets chosen, it will be huge," declared Phyllis.

"That's right. It will probably be James Ryan, he's a big-shot banker," said Ted. "But Brendan Coyle's got an outside chance—he does that Walk to End Hunger every year—and Eileen Clancy is undoubtedly popular; she runs that dance school where all the kids learn to step-dance."

"And their mothers, and their grandmothers," asserted Phyllis, who was clearly rooting for Eileen.

"That's the thing," said Lucy, speaking her thoughts as they developed. "People have favorites; they root for the person they want. Phyllis likes Eileen Clancy, but I'd really like to see Brendan Coyle chosen, and I think we're pretty typical. Most everyone in the community gets involved." She paused for a breath. "And the parade brings a lot of money into the county. The bars and restaurants do a huge business; so do the inns and motels, not to mention the gift shops."

"Well, you clearly know more about this than I do, so why don't you do the story?" said Rob, who wasn't about to give up the argument. "I've been studying the town reports for the past few years, and I was shocked to see that the same handful of people have been sitting on the board of selectmen for decades. It's an abuse of power that needs to be investigated."

Lucy couldn't help it—she laughed. "That's because nobody wants the job, which is actually a big pain in the neck. If it wasn't for Roger Wilcox and the others, we wouldn't have any selectmen at all."

"And they do a good job," said Phyllis, with a sharp nod that made her wattles wobble and set her dangling heart earrings to shaking.

"I think we can leave that story for later," said Ted, "when elections roll around. For now, let's leave the budget as it is. I think Rob will find the Hibernian Knights are

worth investigating. Sheriff Murphy is chairman of the Hibernian board, and he and the other board members also
happen to be county commissioners. They pretty much
run the county."

"But I'm only supposed to cover this grand-marshal selection?" Rob was incredulous. "Why didn't you tell me
the sheriff's crooked?"

"Baby steps, Rob," cautioned Ted. "We don't know
that he's crooked; as far as I know, nobody's ever investigated to find out. We need to start slowly, gain his confidence. Remember, we're the new guys in town, and we're
going to have to win his trust. We'll give him a nice, folksy
story about the grand-marshal candidates."

"I see your point, but I think that approach is risky. Before you know it, we'll be swallowing his blarney."

Ted looked amused. "I think we're up to the challenge,"
he said. "So we're sticking with the budget." He looked
around the table. "Anything else?"

Lucy was tempted to mention Rob's hack job on her
story but decided to let it go for the moment and wait until
Ted saw the correction. She shook her head, Ted rose, and
they all trooped back into the newsroom.

"I'm heading over to Gilead," announced Ted, "so Rob
can use my desk until we get him settled with his own."

Lucy figured it was now or never, if she wanted to clear
up the mess Rob had made of her story. "Oh, before you
go, Ted, I want you to look at a correction I wrote," said
Lucy, standing awkwardly in the middle of the room.

"What correction?"

"Um, well, Rob made some changes when he edited my
story that turned out to be incorrect. The town planner
called, and she was pretty upset, so I told her I'd make
sure we ran a correction."

Rob wasn't about to let this accusation pass. "That's ridiculous!" he exclaimed heatedly. "I made very few changes, just a few typos and misspellings."

"That's not true," said Lucy, looking him straight in the eye. "You messed the whole thing up; it doesn't even read like my writing."

Ted looked puzzled. "Lucy's copy is usually clean. I rarely need to fix anything."

"Like I said, just a few little tweaks," insisted Rob, appealing to Ted.

"Well, there's one way to find out," said Ted. "Send me the original story, Lucy, so I can compare it to the edited one."

Lucy realized she'd made a big mistake. She'd sent the story to Ted's file without keeping a copy for herself. She had no way to prove that her copy had been changed. No way at all. "I don't have it. I didn't save a copy," she said.

Rob, who had just seated himself at Ted's desk, swung around in the swivel chair and met her eyes. His gloating expression said it all: *I win, you lose.*

"Well, I'll make sure we run a correction, Lucy. Meanwhile, carry on, kids," said Ted, shrugging and reaching for his jacket. "Play nicely."

Then he was gone, and Rob was peering at the computer screen. "By the way, Lucy," he began, in an offhand manner, as he began typing, "if you need any help with the puppeteer story, I'm here for you."

Speechless with fury, Lucy grabbed her bag and coat and marched out of the office and into the chilly March air. She was standing next to her car, fumbling with her keys and struggling with her jacket when her cell phone rang, and she started digging frantically in her tote, searching for the darn thing. Finally finding it after it stopped ringing, she seated herself in the car and checked her voice mail. She started the engine, wiggled into her jacket, fastened her seat belt, and played the message. It was Rosie Capshaw, informing her that her parade application had been denied. Sheriff Murphy had turned it down flat; she hadn't even been given an opportunity to present her work to the Hibernian board, or even to him. The original paperwork had merely been returned to her, with a red "Denied" stamp and his scrawled initials.

Lucy sat in the car, fingering the phone, and waiting for the heat to kick in. It was sunny and breezy; the wind was tossing tattered brown leaves about on the street and sidewalk, where patches of dirty, icy snow still lingered, making walking treacherous. Valentine's Day was just around the corner, and some of the stores had hearts in their windows or were flying holiday banners, but spring seemed very far away. She was furious with herself for letting Rob best her, but she vowed it wasn't going to happen again. From now on, she was going to save every story she wrote before she sent it on for editing. Editing! Was Rob going to be editing her work from now on? Or mangling it, which was more the case. She had to find a way to let Ted know what was really going on. Even better, she had to come up with a real scoop, a huge story that would show her brilliance as a reporter. A story that would win the Pulitzer Prize, for goodness' sake. But where was that story?

She bit her lip, pondering the possibilities. Genealogy scams? That was trendy, but maybe a bit too personal, considering the sudden appearance of Catherine Klein. She knew Bill wouldn't want to go public with his awkward family situation. She realized she was still holding her phone and started to replace it in her bag when it hit her: she was holding the story in her hand. It was the sheriff's refusal to let Rosie Capshaw's puppets appear in the parade. Suddenly energized, she shifted into gear and headed straight for the county offices in Gilead.

# Chapter Five

The county complex in Gilead was situated atop a hill that overlooked the town's main street and included the stately Superior Courthouse, built of granite in 1850, the modern brick District Court building, and, looming over both courthouses, the fenced and gated county jail. The sheriff's office was located nearby on a side street, in a colonial-style, red-brick building. When Lucy pulled into the parking area, she noticed that several prisoners were hard at work, scraping the shingles off the roof under the watchful eye of a guard. A few others were working on the ground below, and they smiled at her as she passed, but didn't pause in their work picking up the shingles that rained down and collected on the tarps that protected the windows and foundation plantings. She smiled back, then greeted the guard. "Spring's got to come sooner or later," she said.

"Looks like it's gonna be later this year," he replied, never taking his eyes off the prisoners.

Continuing on into the building, she gave the receptionist her name and asked if she could meet with the sheriff.

"Do you have an appointment?" asked the receptionist,

checking the book. "I don't see you here." From above, they could hear the roofers moving around, and the steady scraping of the shingle shovels.

"No, I'm afraid not, but if he has a spare minute, I promise I'll be brief. I just have a quick question."

The receptionist picked up the phone and relayed Lucy's message. Lucy figured she'd be sent on her way, but much to her surprise, the door behind the receptionist's desk opened, and the sheriff himself bounded out and greeted her. "Lucy Stone," he said, taking her hand in both of his huge ones, "I've been an admirer of your work for a long time. And now that Sam has sold the *Gabber*, I understand you'll be covering our little town, too. This is a great development, having a paper that covers the entire county, and I'm looking forward to meeting your boss, Ted Stillings. He's a fine journalist and committed to public service, as am I."

Wow, thought Lucy, reclaiming her hand, this was quite a charm offensive and the last thing she'd expected. Sheriff John P. Murphy was a very large, very attractive man. His great height was topped with a thick thatch of graying hair, his blue eyes twinkled, his cheeks were ruddy, and he smiled easily and often, displaying a fine set of teeth. His uniform, probably tailored, flattered his manly physique, and he easily carried the heavy utility belt containing his weapon and a shiny set of handcuffs. He radiated such a sense of confidence and strength that he really didn't need the gleaming badge that was pinned to his shirt; he was a natural leader.

"You flatter me," said Lucy, unable to resist a bit of flirtation. "But beware, I'm here to ask the tough questions."

"Ah, so you're after the dirt, Lucy Stone. I expect no less from the *Pennysaver*'s star reporter." He gave her a wink. "Come into my office, and we'll see how well I can stand up to your penetrating and insightful questions."

Shaking her head with amusement, Lucy entered the office through the door the sheriff held for her. "Take a seat," he said, indicating the leather couch that stood against one wall.

Instead, Lucy chose the visitor's chair that stood by his desk.

"You're not kidding; you are all business," said the sheriff, seating himself at his huge mahogany desk. The wall behind him was covered with awards and photos of himself with various rich and powerful people, almost all men. "Go ahead, then, ask away."

Lucy produced her notebook and flipped it open. "I'm writing a story about Rosie Capshaw and her puppets, which are most impressive. She told me that she hoped to march with the puppets in the St. Patrick's Day parade, but her application was denied. Can you tell me why it was turned down?"

"That I can," began the sheriff, with a big sigh and speaking with the faintest Irish brogue. "The decision wasn't up to me, you see. I had no choice in the matter. It's most unfortunate, but the darling girl didn't apply in time." He sighed again. "The committee has its rules, you see, and we must abide by them; that's what rules are for. It wouldn't be fair, now would it, to let the puppets in the parade when other groups that were also late weren't allowed." He leaned back and tented his hands. "And definitely not fair to the many groups that followed the rules and worked hard to get their applications in before the deadline."

"So that's all it was? A question of timing? It wasn't because of the controversial nature of her puppets?"

"Controversial?" He was all surprise and innocence. "In what way are these magnificent puppets controversial?"

"Well, Mother Jones, for example, was a labor organizer and a bit of a rabble-rouser. She's considered a heroine by the left."

"Mother Jones was indeed active in organizing labor, as were many other Irish folk. They were no strangers to oppression in Ireland, and they didn't come all the way to America to be trod under foot by the wealthy Yankee mill owners, now did they?"

"I suppose not," admitted Lucy. "So if Rosie Capshaw gets her paperwork in order next year, will the committee allow her puppets to march in the parade?"

The sheriff shrugged his enormous, epauletted shoulders. "Who knows what the committee will decide? I don't tell them what to do, but if it were up to me, I'd be happy to see St. Patrick and Mother Jones marching in the parade."

"Well, that's all I need. Thank you very much for your time," said Lucy, closing her notebook and rising from her chair.

"You're not leaving already?" he asked, seemingly downhearted at the prospect of her departure.

"I'm afraid so. I have other work to do." She smiled and shrugged. "Deadlines, you know."

"I understand." He stood up. "Remember, my door is always open to you, so don't hesitate if you have further questions."

"Oh, I'm sure I will," said Lucy, unable to resist smiling.

"Have a fine day," he said, opening his office door and holding it for her. She had reached the outer door when he spoke to the receptionist. "Now, Nora, if Lucy Stone calls or wants to see me, be sure to put her right through."

Lucy was certain he'd spoken intending her to hear, so she turned around and gave him a smile of thanks.

"I certainly will, sir," replied Nora, as Lucy opened the door and stepped outside.

She wasn't at all sure what to make of the sheriff, but she had to admit he was not at all what she'd expected. The man was charming and polite, he'd graciously made time to speak with her, and she believed his answers were sincere. Organizations had their rules and were entitled to stick to them. It was a shame that Rosie had applied too late, but there was always next year. Those were her thoughts as she drove back to the office, where she was happy to find Phyllis, but no Rob.

"So where's the boy wonder?" she asked, as the bell on the door announced her arrival.

"Raking muck, uncovering crime, exposing dirty se-crets," said Phyllis. "Oh, and covering his own tracks, the little liar. It's bad enough he messed up your story, but then he had to go and make it worse by denying it."

"I see he's won your heart," said Lucy.

"Little brat," snorted Phyllis. "He was actually advising me to make the classified's livelier reading. I told him peo-ple pay by the word and just want to get that snow blower sold in as few words as possible." She yawned and glanced at the clock. "So what were you up to this afternoon?"

Lucy plunked herself down in her desk chair and swiveled around to face Phyllis. "I did a follow-up with the sheriff, asking why he'd denied the puppeteer's request to march in the parade."

"And why did he?"

"She applied too late, after the deadline."

"There's no deadline," said Phyllis, adjusting the zebra-striped cheaters that were sliding down her nose.

"Are you sure?"

"Pretty sure. Somebody from the Hibernians called Wilf yesterday and asked if his banjo band would march. Wilf said the guy seemed pretty desperate; apparently they don't have enough bands."

"I can't believe it," said Lucy, realizing she'd been fooled, taken in by the sheriff's charm offensive.

"No, God's honest truth. I heard the call."

"I can't believe I fell for it. I swallowed that sheriff's story hook, line, and sinker. I'm an idiot."

"I don't imagine you're the first," said Phyllis, shrugging her well-upholstered shoulders. "That's how he stays in power. He beguiles his critics into submission."

"Not anymore," vowed Lucy. "Not me."

She immediately reached for the phone on her desk and called the sheriff's office. As promised, Nora put her call through immediately, and she steeled herself to resist the man's blarney.

"Ah, so soon," he cooed. "What can I do for you, Lucy?"

"Just a little thing. Could you please send me a copy of the parade guidelines? I need it for my story."

"Oh, sadly, that's the one thing I cannot do for you, my dear. You see, the guidelines belong to the Hibernian Knights, and the board must vote to release them. If it were up to me alone, you'd have them in a matter of minutes. This email is a wonderful thing, now, isn't it?"

Lucy refused to be distracted and stuck to the issue. "I'll be happy to present a request for the guidelines to the board. When do they meet?"

The sheriff clucked his tongue. "Now isn't that too sad. They just met yesterday to finalize the parade, and they won't meet again until April."

That was interesting, thought Lucy, picking up on the sheriff's admission that the board had met yesterday. "I understand the board reached out to some groups yesterday in a last-minute effort to recruit more marchers. Why couldn't they include Rosie Capshaw's puppets?"

"Ah, Lucy, it's not as simple as it seems. Those groups had submitted applications in the past, and the board was merely following up to see if they had forgotten to file new paperwork but were intending to march, that's all."

"But you must admit the Hibernian Knights have been known to exclude some groups in the past, including Vietnam vets, gays, and nonwhites."

"Ah, we mustn't rake up old grievances. There's no point, now, is there? The Hibernian Knights believe the parade should represent the entire Irish community, and the board recently voted to approve a policy that states exactly that. I believe we sent a press release containing the new policy last month."

"I remember," admitted Lucy. "So the only reason Rosie Capshaw's puppets won't be seen in the parade is because she didn't file her application in a timely manner?"

"Absolutely. You have my word on it."

"Okay. And thanks for your time," said Lucy, wrapping up.

"I've got all the time in the world for you, Lucy," he replied, ending the call.

Lucy immediately got to work and started pounding away on the keyboard, adding this latest development to the feature story she'd written previously. She included the sheriff's statement that Rosie Capshaw had applied after the deadline, as well as the Hibernian Knight's newly instated policy of inclusion, but also recapped past incidents in which groups deemed undesirable by the board had not been allowed to march.

She sent the revised story to Ted's file for editing, but only after saving it in her own folder, just in case. Realizing it was nearly five, she shut down her computer and gathered up her things, intending to stop at the IGA on her way home to pick up a few things for dinner. She was cruising the aisles, searching for the walnut oil a new recipe for salad dressing required, and failing to find it with the regular oils or in the gourmet aisle. She was headed for the health-food section when her phone buzzed and she saw a text from Ted, informing her that he had posted the Rosie Capshaw story on the brand-new online edition of *The Courier*, which was the name he'd chosen for the combined *Pennysaver* and *Gilead Gabber*. The print editions would retain their own mastheads, for the time being, although the content would be shared.

She knew that Ted had long been frustrated by the limitations inherent in publishing a weekly paper and had wanted to give readers an online option with more up-to-date news. She agreed that it was frustrating when a big story broke on Friday, the day after the *Pennysaver* came out, which meant they would be giving readers old news in the next issue. And she couldn't help feeling a little bit proud that her story had been chosen for the very first posting in the online edition. Unfortunately, she found the walnut oil and discovered that a very small bottle cost $12.99, and even though she was working harder, she wasn't seeing any increase in her paycheck. She'd have to make that salad dressing with plain old canola oil.

Much to her relief, the salad got rave reviews at the Saturday night potluck at the Community Church, and so did her story about Rosie Capshaw. Everybody there seemed to have read the "Breaking News from *The Courier*" post, which popped up on screens throughout the county. Initially sent only to subscribers who had provided contact info, the story went viral as readers forwarded it to their friends and neighbors.

"So the Hibernians are up to their old tricks," observed Reverend Marge, helping herself to a second serving of mac and cheese, which Lucy couldn't help thinking she didn't really need as her backward collar was growing a bit tight. "You just have to wonder what they're so afraid of."

"Losing control, I suppose," said Rachel, who had chosen her own quinoa casserole. "They seem to have to say no every once in a while, just because they can."

"Like two-year-olds," added Sue, drawing on her experience as a preschool teacher, now retired. Her plate contained nothing but salad, and Lucy doubted she'd actually eat it.

"Well, good for you, Lucy, for a neat bit of investigative reporting," said Bob Goodman, Rachel's husband. "And what an honor that your story was the first on Ted's new online *Courier*." Bob's plate was overloaded; he probably hadn't had time for lunch and was making up for it.

"Gee, thanks," she said, blushing. "I am kind of pumped about it."

"Well, you should be," he insisted, heading for a table. "It's something to crow about."

Or not, thought Lucy, thinking it would be wise to maintain a low profile at work. She suspected Rob would interpret any success by her as a personal slight, and she figured he would do whatever he could to tear her down in order to preserve his sense of superiority.

He was already on the attack when she arrived at the office on Monday, complaining to Ted that she had poached on his assignment, which was to interview the grand-marshal candidates. "I didn't want the stupid parade story in the first place, but you insisted," he said, facing off with Ted in front of the coffeepot. "All Lucy was supposed to do was write a cute little feature, which I gave her, about Rosie Capshaw. And now she's turned it into a big story, which should be mine. She stole it . . . it's unethical . . . it's unsporting."

"I was only . . ." began Lucy, attempting to defend herself when she was interrupted by Ted.

"It's a heck of a good story," said Ted, calmly spooning sugar into his coffee mug. "That's what a good reporter does, follows the story where it leads."

Lucy hung her jacket on the rack and went to her desk, where she powered up her computer and waited for Rob's retort.

"Well," he sniffed, "as far as I'm concerned, she can follow it from now on. She can write all she wants about the parade and the stupid grand-marshal thing. She can have it all."

Lucy didn't like the sound of this, which meant adding three interviews to an already full schedule, and she was quick to protest. "Don't forget I've got the selectmen this week, and the elementary school's Valentines for Vets is this afternoon."

Ted nodded, added some powdered coffee creamer, and resumed stirring. "I'm actually surprised you didn't follow up on Lucy's story by questioning the grand-marshal candidates about the decision to block the puppets. That would have added a new dimension to your story, which I'm still waiting to see."

"Are you insulting my work?" demanded Rob, bristling with anger and bouncing on the balls of his feet.

"What about the interviews?" asked Ted, taking a sip of coffee. "Have you started?"

"I'll get to them." Rob was defensive. "I've been doing background research . . ."

Ted was incredulous. "What's the problem? I thought you were a gung-ho sort of guy, eager to show us how to improve our local news coverage."

"I am. That's why I'm here. But this sort of little popularity contest isn't newsworthy."

"I think you're mistaken, considering the response we've gotten from the online posting. I can fill the 'Letters to the Editor' page with that topic alone. Everybody seems to have an opinion." Ted went over to his desk and set his coffee down. "I think you're right, though . . ."

"What?" protested Lucy.

"Lucy should take over covering all aspects of the parade, including the grand-marshal candidates."

Before she could say a word, Rob jumped in. "And I'll start working on the lack of candidates for local positions. I see it as a series of stories, a real investigative report."

"Uh, no. You'll cover the selectmen's meeting." Ted sat down at his desk, his back to Rob. "Nothing says local like a selectmen's meeting, and don't forget the Valentines for Vets at the elementary school. Take plenty of pics. Readers love cute photos of kids."

"It's a big deal; the kids take it quite seriously," said Lucy, trying not to smirk.

Rob didn't reply but grabbed his jacket and briefcase and marched out the door, letting it slam. The little bell jangled behind him. "I don't think that boy understands local news," Phyllis said, pushing her glasses back up her nose. "I hope he doesn't stumble into something he shouldn't and find himself in a whole mess of trouble."

# Chapter Six

Lucy didn't reply. She figured the sooner Rob decided to go back to the big city, the happier she'd be. Right now, she had to get started on her interviews of the candidates and decided to call Eileen Clancy first, aware that the dance teacher would no doubt be busy with classes when school got out later in the day. She was correct, it turned out, as Eileen was quick to agree to an interview, saying, "I'm just here in the office catching up on my paperwork."

When Lucy arrived at the dancing school, Eileen gave her a big welcome. She was a trim woman in her late fifties, with a blazing head of red hair, and carried herself with a dancer's poise. Dressed for work, she was wearing tights and a leotard, with a wrap skirt, along with a comfy-looking pair of well-worn fuzzy slippers. "Would you like a cup of tea?" she asked, leading the way through the lobby into a tiny office. "I usually have one about now."

Following her, Lucy noticed the dozens of photos on the foyer walls, all picturing posed groups of step-dancers, ranging in age from toddlers to high schoolers, in their heavily embroidered, stiff costumes. "Thanks, that would be lovely," said Lucy.

There were more photos in the office, along with a large desk covered with an untidy mass of papers, a couple of potted shamrock plants, and numerous figurines of leprechauns. "All gifts from my students," said Eileen, setting down a couple of mugs bedecked with shamrocks. "Do you take milk or sugar?"

"No, thanks," said Lucy, flipping open her reporter's notebook. "I'm a simple girl with simple tastes."

"I find a little sugar picks me up," admitted Eileen, stirring her mug. "I suppose you're here to ask about my nomination for grand marshal of the parade, right?"

"Right you are," agreed Lucy, taking a cautious sip of the hot tea. "So why do you think you should be grand marshal? Do you think you have a chance?"

"I think I have a very good chance of being chosen," said Eileen. "For one thing, they've never had a woman, and I think the Hibernian Knights are becoming a bit more open-minded and realizing they have to change with the times. I also think they want the parade to accurately reflect Irish-American culture, and step-dancing is a big part of that tradition."

"As I understand it," began Lucy, "step-dancing is much more popular here than it is in Ireland. Is that true?"

"Perhaps," replied Eileen, with a shrug. "I have taken my students to Ireland to participate in contests there, and they've done very well against some very stiff competition. I think the dancing is a treasured part of Irish culture on both sides of the Atlantic. You know why the dancers must hold their torsos so rigidly, don't you?"

"Actually, no," said Lucy.

"So it wouldn't seem as if they were dancing, which was

not approved by the church, you see. It's actually derived from Spanish flamenco dancing, but without the sinuous upper action."

"Made it G-rated," said Lucy.

"Exactly," agreed Eileen, with a big smile.

Lucy was thoughtful for a moment, considering her next question. "So how exactly would you define Irish-American culture? What makes it unique in our multicultural society?"

"I'm glad you asked, because I've been thinking about that and doing a bit of research to prepare my presentation to the Hibernian Knights' board of directors. This is what I told them: there are three qualifiers. First off, Irish-Americans must have Irish ancestry; that's a given."

"So you don't believe those 'Everyone's Irish on St. Patrick's Day' buttons?"

"Well," admitted Eileen, "an awful lot of Irish emigrated to America, and they didn't use birth control, so there certainly are a lot of us, and I recently saw a statistic that about half of those DNA genealogy tests reveal some Irish ancestry."

"So half of us are Irish?"

"Have Irish genes, I guess, but it takes more than a few genes, or a grandma from Limerick. A true Irish-American is a practicing member of the Roman Catholic Church and is militantly pro-life. We're very strong on that; we believe that life is a precious gift from God, and only He can give it or take it away."

Lucy took a rather long drink of her tea and swallowed slowly. "But nowadays a lot of American Catholics practice birth control. Does that make them not Irish-American?"

"Cafeteria Catholics," snorted Eileen. "I don't believe you can pick and choose what tenets of the faith you want to practice. It's all or nothing for me, but I'm not one to judge what others do in the privacy of their homes."

Lucy was curious, wondering about Eileen's life experience. "Are you married, and do you have children yourself?"

"Alas, no. I was not given that gift. Poor Mr. Clancy died shortly after our wedding; he was a roofer and had a terrible fall that broke his neck." She shook her head sadly. "No one compared to him, so I never remarried." She paused. "Of course, I have all these lovely little dance students. I really think of the little darlings as my own."

"So, no matter whether or not you are grand marshal, you will have a big presence in the parade. How many of your students will be marching?"

"Oh, every one, and I've got a hundred and forty-odd kids." She chuckled. "A big family."

"Very big," said Lucy, with a laugh. "Good thing you don't have to feed them, or buy them shoes."

"Indeed." Eileen smiled. "So will you be watching the parade?"

"Wouldn't miss it," said Lucy. "I wonder if you saw my story about Rosie Capshaw and her puppets. She wanted to have them in the parade, but the Hibernians denied her application. Do you have a comment?"

Eileen looked a bit confused. "I'm afraid I haven't heard about it. Is this Rosie Irish?"

"I didn't think to ask," admitted Lucy. "She does have puppets of Irish characters, though. Fabulous, giant figures of St. Patrick and Mother Jones, banshees, leprechauns. They're pretty impressive, but the board said she didn't apply in time, and so they can't be in the parade."

"Well, the Hibernians have their rules," said Eileen,

cautiously, "but I really don't want to go on the record without knowing more about it."

"That's entirely understandable," said Lucy, crossing out part of her notes. "Sometimes it's best not to say anything."

Eileen looked at her appraisingly. "And are you perchance Irish yourself. You've a bit of the green in your eyes, I see."

"Not that I know," admitted Lucy, closing her notebook and standing up. "But those DNA tests do come up with some surprising results."

"No, no way." Eileen clucked disapprovingly. "If you're Irish, you'd know it. If you don't know for sure, you're surely not Irish."

Lucy was slightly taken aback, but smiled graciously. "Thanks for the tea and the chat," she said. "And good luck with the Hibernians. If you ask me, it's high time they chose a woman for grand marshal."

"We'll see," said Eileen, with a dismissive shrug, escorting Lucy to the door. "You know I was the Rose of Tralee, back in 1990, so I know a bit about representing the Irish community."

Lucy paused. "Rose of Tralee? Is that a beauty pageant?"

"No, not a competition at all. It's a gathering of young women from all over the world, all of Irish descent, in the little Irish town of Tralee. It's a kind of homecoming. We share our stories and perform a party piece, a song or a poem, some little bit of entertainment, and one rose is chosen to represent the far-flung Irish community. Do you know that only five percent of Irish people actually live in Ireland? The rest are scattered over the globe."

"I had no idea," said Lucy.

"Though I think they went a bit too far with that rose whose father was Zambian," sniffed Eileen, lowering her voice as she continued. "That's in Africa, you know."

Lucy was thoughtful, thinking. "Would you have a photo of yourself as the Rose of Tralee?" she asked.

Eileen pointed to a large framed photo, hanging by itself between two windows, that Lucy somehow hadn't noticed. It showed a young Eileen in a green chiffon evening gown, smiling broadly as a tiara was placed on her head. "Winning isn't the point," she said, taking the photo down and handing it to Lucy. "The prize is being part of the festival." She paused. "It's a bit sad, really, that we all had to leave Ireland. But no matter where we are, we're all still Irish."

"Well, thanks for your time. I'll make sure you get the photo back."

"No problem. It might turn the tide in my favor." She opened the door for Lucy. "Have a nice day, now."

Back in the car, Lucy called James Ryan, one of the other grand-marshal candidates, catching him in his office at the bank. He was free at the moment and invited her to come right over, explaining that he was due at a Rotary Club lunch at twelve.

Lucy made it to the bank in ten minutes and was immediately shown into Ryan's office, which was tucked away through a door behind the teller's counter and down a short, carpeted hall. The office occupied a corner of the building, with windows on two sides, and was well-appointed with tasteful draperies, wallpaper, and plush carpet. Ryan himself was seated at a huge mahogany desk, but he stood up when Lucy was announced.

"You made good time," he said, extending his hand. He

was a tall, good-looking man in his late fifties, dressed in a conservative suit, starched white shirt, and striped tie that matched his bright blue eyes. His dark hair was graying at the temples, and his cheeks were ruddy. A bag of golf clubs was propped in the corner.

"Not much traffic," said Lucy, taking his hand and finding it strong and warm. "I beat the lunch rush."

"So what can I do for you? Mortgage? Home equity line?" He winked, gesturing for Lucy to sit and taking his own seat. "Or is about my being a candidate for grand marshal of the St. Patrick's Day parade?"

"You spoiled my surprise," said Lucy, taking the visitor's chair and getting right down to business. "I am here to ask why you would be the best choice for grand marshal, and what you think your chances are."

"Pretty good, I'd say. A lot of people owe me," he said, grinning. "Well, owe the bank. But I listened to their stories and made the loans, sometimes taking a bit of a risk, but having faith that my customers would make good." He paused, tenting his hands. "And they have. I'm proud of what this bank has done for the community, and the Irish-American community in particular. We Irish have been quite successful, if I do say so myself."

"In what way?" asked Lucy. "Do you mean the Kennedys?"

"Well, not everyone can be president, but you could say that the Irish have been one of the most successful, perhaps the most successful, of all the immigrant groups that have come to the shores of our melting-pot nation."

Lucy nodded, writing it down in her notebook. "But you did have two advantages, no? Being white and speaking English."

"True," he admitted. "But there was terrible discrimination against the Irish when they first came here, and no wonder. The folk who fled the famine were desperately poor and lacked everything, including social graces. But they worked hard, and the women, especially, were determined to improve their lot. My grandmother is a good example. She arrived in America just before the Depression and got hired as a skivvy, a kitchen worker for a wealthy family, but she was a quick study and ended up a parlor maid. She lived to a grand old age, and believe me, when we visited, we had to be on our best behavior and dressed in our finest bib and tucker. She gave each of her grandkids five dollars on their birthdays, and woe betide the hapless child who forgot to write a proper thank-you note."

"That does sound like Rose Kennedy," said Lucy.

"Granny loved all the Kennedys. She had plates of JFK and Jackie on her mantel, and she had a special fondness for Ethel. All those babies, you know."

"Did she have a big family?"

"No, she married late. Just had time to produce my mother, who she made sure went to college and became a teacher."

"And you became a bank president," added Lucy.

"My siblings are also successful. My sister is a CPA, and my brother is a lawyer. And my family's story is pretty typical."

"So for you the parade is a celebration of the success Irish-Americans have enjoyed in this country?"

"And the contributions they've made; don't forget that," said Ryan. "We've prospered, but we've also served in the armed forces and as first responders, as teachers and nurses. It was JFK, you know, who said, 'Ask not what your country can do for you; ask what you can do for your country.' We've done a great deal, sacrificed a lot, and we weren't always appreciated."

"Thankfully, times are changing," said Lucy, with a smile. "Nowadays it seems that everybody's Irish on St. Patrick's Day, whether they really are or not."

"Well, you don't have to be Irish to enjoy a Guinness," he said, with a grin and a wink. "The more the merrier, that's what I say."

"Ah, you've stepped into my trap," said Lucy, with a sly grin. "What do you think of the Hibernian Knights' decision not to let Rosie Capshaw march in the parade with her very fabulous puppets, including St. Patrick and Mother Jones?"

He shrugged his broad shoulders. "I understand Miss Capshaw makes marvelous creations, and I'm sure there will be many opportunities for her to display them. As for the Hibernians, they're a private club, and they're entitled to make their own rules. I don't always agree . . ."

"So you don't agree," said Lucy, pouncing.

"I didn't say that." Ryan looked her straight in the eye. "I said I don't *always* agree with the Hibernian Knights' decisions, especially their tendency in the past to exclude those they didn't approve of . . ."

"Why don't you say it? Their racist behavior? As a banker, you're forbidden by law to discriminate against people; you have to use the same standard for everyone."

"True. But the Hibernian Knights are a private organization, and they get to decide who marches in their parade. And if you ask me, they've done a mighty fine job through the years putting on a grand show for folks to enjoy. It's a shame that everything these days is political; people are always looking to criticize. Now, really, what's the matter with watching some marching bands and dancing girls? What's the matter with honoring our armed forces and our first responders?"

"Nothing at all," said Lucy, judging from his spirited defense of the Hibernian Knights that James Ryan was definitely going to be chosen grand marshal. She closed her notebook and stood up. "And thank you so much for your time. It's been a pleasure."

Ryan was immediately on his feet, extending his hand across the desk. "A pleasure for me, too, and I hope this is only the first of many conversations."

Lucy took his hand, finding it strong and warm. Reassuring somehow. Ryan was a decent man, a good man, she thought, as she left the bank. The thing that bothered her was why he was so reluctant to stand up for the things he believed in. Why was he making excuses for the Hibernian Knights?

Lucy didn't get back to the office until the next morning, when she was surprised to discover that Rob was sitting at Phyllis's desk behind the reception counter. "Where's Phyllis?" she asked, trying to remember the last time Phyllis had missed a day of work. And what was Rob doing, taking her place?

"She's taking her husband to the eye doctor this morning. He needs a ride home because of those drops; at least that's what I was told." Rob didn't sound convinced; he sounded like a man with a grievance.

"It's true about the eye drops," said Lucy, setting her bag down on her desk and shrugging out of her barn coat. She looked at him curiously. "Weren't you using Ted's desk?"

"Yeah, but there's something the matter with his PC, so

I moved over here." He furrowed his brow. "Did you think I was demoted or something?"

"No," said Lucy, who had wondered if Ted was yanking Rob's chain, although she doubted he would be so petty. "Actually, it wouldn't be a demotion. Phyllis gets the news first; she knows everything that's going on."

Rob stiffened in his seat. "Well, I'm only sitting here because Ted's computer is on the fritz." He screwed up his mouth. "Actually, the hardware in the place is practically antique. He ought to use some of the grant money to upgrade."

"Fat chance," said Lucy, seating herself. "He'll keep them going until they disintegrate." She pressed the power button and was relieved when her PC responded with its usual series of groans and pings. She checked her emails, then flipped open her notebook, eager to get started on the grand-marshal story. She knew it wasn't exactly the scoop of the century, but she wanted to write a solid story that would prove once and for all that she was a top-notch reporter. She knew she wasn't perfect—there was probably room for her to improve, and there were most likely things that Rob could teach her—but she did want to make it clear that she deserved to be treated with respect. She was trying out a couple of different leads when Rob spoke up.

"Uh, Lucy, what's the deal with Wilcox and Marzetti?" he asked, naming two long-time selectmen.

"What do you mean?"

"They don't seem to like each other much."

"Really?" Lucy was puzzled. "I never noticed that."

"At the meeting last night, Wilcox got all huffy when Marzetti said something about him being out of touch."

"That doesn't sound like Tony," said Lucy.

"And then that woman . . ."

"Franny Small?"

"I guess that's her name. You gotta wonder what she brings to the board . . ."

"Franny brings a wealth of experience. She's retired now, but she created and managed a million-dollar company, all on her own."

"Are you serious?"

"Yeah. She started making jewelry out of nuts and bolts when she worked at a local hardware store. It was good timing—punk was all the rage—and her stuff took off. She never looked back."

"She doesn't seem to have much to say . . ."

"She's like E. F. Hutton."

"Who?"

Kids today, thought Lucy, with a sigh. "It was a commercial a while ago. 'When E. F. Hutton talks, people listen.' "

"Well, anyway, they didn't seem to do much of anything at the meeting . . ."

This was a shock to Lucy. "Didn't they approve the budget?"

"Oh, that. It was just a quick vote."

"It's a big story. It's the town budget for next year. You've got to get a copy. You've got to write it up so voters will be prepared when they go into town meeting."

"The whole budget?"

"Yeah. Right down to the penny."

He groaned and pushed his chair back. "I can't believe it."

"You better believe it, and you better get on it. Fast. I heard the School Committee was asking for a big increase, and if the selectmen approved it, well, that's going to be controversial. To say the least."

"I'm not really a numbers guy," he began, reaching for his jacket. "I'm more into issues and personalities . . ."

"Go! Now! Straight to Town Hall. Get the budget!"

"Aye, aye, captain." Rob saluted and marched to the door, but Lucy saw through the window that as soon as he was outside, his back drooped and his walk slowed. It seemed that local news wasn't really all he'd hoped it would be.

# Chapter Seven

When Lucy finished writing up her notes from the two interviews, she saw it was time for her appointment with the third grand-marshal candidate, Brendan Coyle. She was looking forward to her meeting with Coyle, whom she'd interviewed several times in the past regarding his work as director of the local food pantry, and she had always come away with the encouraging belief that all must be right in the world if it could contain such a good-hearted soul as Brendan Coyle.

Aware that she was running a bit late, she was tempted to speed, but thought better of it when she noticed one of the deputy sheriff's vehicles behind her. It wasn't necessarily following her, she told herself; most likely, they were simply both headed in the same direction. Nevertheless, she felt somewhat relieved when she reached the Gilead church that housed the food pantry and turned into the parking area, and the deputy continued on down the road.

Exiting her car, she walked along the cement path to the church basement, passing the last of the afternoon's clients, who were toting heavy bags of groceries home. Lucy knew that the pantry's client list kept growing longer, despite the booming national economy that had somehow never arrived in small towns like Gilead and Tinker's Cove. Jobs were few in the coastal community, and pay was low and often irregular, as people juggled several jobs in an effort to make ends meet in what was largely a seasonal tourist economy. Observing a young mom who was toting a baby on her back and pushing a stroller loaded with a toddler and several bags of groceries, she was reminded how the lack of reliable and affordable child care complicated matters for working parents, who had to rely on aging grandparents or kind-hearted neighbors to keep an eye on the kids while they were on the job.

Stepping inside, it took a moment for her eyes to adjust to the dim interior light, but there was no mistaking Brendan Coyle. He was a big man, well over six feet, with broad shoulders, a big belly, and a booming voice. "Over here, Lucy," he boomed, waving her toward the former Sunday school classroom that now served as a storage space for the pantry. A row of long tables held the day's offerings, mostly picked over now, and Coyle was packing up the remainders to store for another day.

"Peanut butter, tomato soup, elbow macaroni, and day-old bread," he muttered, shaking his head. "I wish we could give these folks some fresh fruits and vegetables. We do get donations in the summer from people's gardens, mostly zucchini and tomatoes, but this time of year, it's nothing but sprouting potatoes and mushy onions." He held up a floppy bunch of carrots. "Fit for nothing but soup."

"I saw some of your clients leaving," said Lucy, "and nobody was complaining."

"Well, maybe they should," declared Brendan. "Maybe it's time for some resistance, some demonstrations . . ."

"Whoa," laughed Lucy. "That sounds like rabble-rousing, and that will never do for the St. Patrick's parade grand marshal."

Brendan laughed as he pulled out a chair for Lucy and one for himself. "Take a load off, Lucy. You're looking tired, and it's only a bit past noon."

"My days are a lot busier, now that Ted's bought the *Gabber*. Plus we've got that new guy . . ."

"The one who's supposed to show you how it's done," said Brendan, with a wink.

"Yeah," sighed Lucy. "He needs a lot of help and takes up a lot of my time. I'm not sure it's a net gain, if you know what I mean."

"I suspect I do," said Brendan. He looked around the classroom, where a few boxes of groceries remained on the tables. "I love the volunteers, I need the volunteers, but sometimes it seems they're more trouble than they're worth." He grinned. "Some are absolute gems, always on time, ready to pitch in, but others, oh my word. 'Well, I can't make it this week because I've got to see my podiatrist, and my cousin is coming . . . I hope it's not a problem for you.' "

"So I suppose," began Lucy, flipping open her notebook, "that if you are chosen grand marshal, it would be an opportunity for you to promote your social programs. The food pantry, the annual Walk to End Hunger and Prevent Homelessness, the recovery groups . . ."

"Indeed," agreed Brendan. "And I have to say that the Hibernian Knights, as well as the Irish-American community at large, have always been very generous, very involved in helping those who need a hand up. They haven't forgotten how tough things were for their grandparents; we Irish have long memories."

"So for you it's that tradition that's most important. It's not necessarily being a practicing Catholic, or being against abortion?"

"Do you know they just voted two to one in the Irish Republic to legalize abortion? In Ireland, where they used to lock up the poor unwed mothers in convents and make them virtual slaves, laboring endlessly in laundries and such."

"I do know, and I've also heard that there is no St. Patrick's Day parade in Ireland. It's apparently an American thing."

"True," agreed Brendan, with raised eyebrows and a sharp nod. "I guess nothing makes the heart grow fonder than absence. I often wonder how much these fervent Irish-Americans would really make of the new Ireland, with no border to speak of between the North and South, and old grievances put aside." He shrugged. "For the moment, anyway."

"I guess prosperity makes it that much easier to forget the troubles," ventured Lucy.

"Knowing the Irish, it will all bubble up again." He sighed. "Those long memories, and the authors and journalists who insist on revisiting the past."

"Don't blame me. I'm not one for digging up old skeletons," protested Lucy. "So tell me when the next walk is scheduled, and how folks can sign up, and I'll put in a plea for food-pantry donations, maybe ask for a volunteer gardener or two . . ."

"Great idea, Lucy. There's space here behind the church for a garden. It would be great if we could grow our own. I bet some of the clients would be happy to dig in, no pun intended."

"And it would be a teaching opportunity for your clients, so they could plant their own gardens."

"I think there's a bit of the community organizer in you, Lucy."

Lucy laughed and closed her notebook. "No way, I'll leave that to you," she said, standing up. "You do a much better job. And good luck with the grand marshal . . ."

"Oh, I don't expect to be chosen, but I'm grateful to be considered." He stood up and walked Lucy to the door, which he opened and held for her. Taking a look at the sky, he grimaced at the dark clouds that were piling up, darkening the day. "Best get straight home. Looks like a storm's a-brewing."

"It sure does," said Lucy. "I know they say that if you don't like the weather in Maine, you should wait a minute, but don't you think it's gotten even more unpredictable lately?"

"Climate change." Brendan shook his head. "Don't get me started."

"Thanks for the interview," said Lucy, giving him a little wave as she hurried off to her car. The wind was picking up and blew her hair every which way, and she had to struggle against it to open the car door. Once inside, she smoothed her hair, deciding not to go back to the office but to head straight home, via a shortcut that she knew. With luck she'd be safe at home in ten minutes.

The road she had in mind ran in a mostly direct line through the county forest preserve, and it was well-maintained, but was only partially paved at either end. Most of the road was gravel, and it was sometimes closed to traffic in winter. It had only reopened recently, with the warning that some patches could be muddy, due to the recent thaw, but a sudden spattering of raindrops on her windshield convinced her that it was worth the slight risk. If she took the usual route on the highway, it would take at least half an hour to get home, even longer in heavy traffic now that it was getting on to five o'clock. And besides, she had new tires, and her car had all-wheel drive and could easily handle an unpaved country road.

She was keeping a nervous eye on the sky as she turned onto Old Forest Road and saw a fork of lightning split the dark clouds, causing her to press harder on the gas pedal in hopes of getting through the woods before lightning struck a tree or the rising wind knocked one down. Her decision to go off the main road didn't seem so smart now, especially since there seemed to be something wrong with her right front tire. She didn't hear the floppy sound of a flat, and she wasn't having trouble steering, but the warning light on her dash had gone on: LOW TIRE PRESSURE. She didn't always believe these indicators; the car's computer system was oversensitive, in her opinion, more often than not causing needless anxiety and concern. So she pressed on, fingers crossed, as the trees swayed forward and backward, threatening to fall onto the road, and thunder boomed overhead. She'd only proceeded a quarter mile or so when the car's indicator system went into alarm mode, and there was no denying that she had a flat since she could hear the whump-whump of the collapsed tire.

There was nothing for it but to stop and call AAA for help.

AAA was quick to answer her call, the dispatcher immediately asking if she was in a safe place before moving on to the business of her membership ID number and expiration date.

"Well, it's a little-traveled road in the woods, and I'm in the middle of a thunderstorm."

"Stay in the car and put on your flashers," advised the dispatcher. "It may take a while to get a service technician to you. There's been a rash of calls."

"I understand," said Lucy, resigned to her fate.

"I'll keep you posted. Is this the best number to reach you?"

"Yes," said Lucy, checking her bars and noticing that only one was left. No problem, she had plenty of gas and could use the charger in her car. It was always there, in the storage bin between the seats, except that today, the day she really needed it, it wasn't there. So trouble comes in threes, she thought: a thunderstorm, a flat tire, and a dying phone. What else could go wrong?

She adjusted the back of her seat so she'd have a bit more room and tried to relax, but the dispatcher's words kept playing in her head: "Are you in a safe place?" Suddenly the woods didn't seem so safe after all. She was alone and defenseless, and any crazed maniac could be wandering around, looking for a helpless victim. And then there were bears, emerging from hibernation with big appetites after their long winter's nap. And if that wasn't bad enough, it was growing darker by the minute, and rain was coming down in sheets, pelting the car. She clicked the button, locking her doors, and prepared to watch and wait, keeping an eye out for danger.

She was startled when her phone rang and almost dropped it before she could answer the call. "Good news," said the dispatcher. "There's a tow truck in your area, so we're putting you at the top of the list. Silver Cloud should arrive in ten minutes."

"Great," said Lucy, with a big sigh of relief. "It's really kind of scary out here in the woods."

"Soon you'll be back on the road," promised the dispatcher, and true enough, Lucy could already see the approaching headlights of the truck. When it had pulled up behind her, and the tech got out, she unlocked her door and climbed out of her car, pulling up the hood on her jacket.

"I'm really glad to see you," she said, producing her membership card.

"So what's the problem? A flat?" He was dressed for the weather in an oil-stained yellow rain slicker and was already walking around the car, checking the tires. "That is one very flat tire," he said, arriving at the front of the car and studying the situation. "Have you got a spare?"

"One of those itty-bitty ones," confessed Lucy.

"It'll have to do. I can put it on for you, but you've got to get to a service station promptly and get the flat repaired. These spares only last for fifty miles or so."

"Not a problem. I just want to get home tonight."

So, while Lucy watched, he jacked up the car and switched the tires, stashing the flat in the back of her car. Lucy signed the paperwork and was back on the road, bouncing over roots and avoiding potholes and vowing never, ever to do such a stupid thing again. From now, on she was sticking to main roads, not wandering off into the hinterland. When she finally turned out onto Red Top Road, she was only a few hundred feet from home, and she could see the old farmhouse perched at the top of the hill, windows blazing with light. She'd never been so glad to see the old place, never mind the electric bill.

She discovered that supper was well in hand when she walked into the kitchen and smelled the delicious scent of onions and peppers. "Sausage hoagies," Bill announced, shoving the veggies around in the frying pan with a spatula. "How does that sound?"

"Great," said Lucy, collapsing onto a chair at the big, round golden-oak table. "And it smells even better than it sounds."

"Tough day?" he inquired, pouring a glass of Chianti and setting it down on the table for her.

"I tried to take Old Forest Road and got a flat tire," she said, pausing to take a sip. "AAA came; the wait wasn't too bad." She shuddered. "Just a bit creepy in the woods."

"Any bears?" teased Bill, adding Italian sausage to the veggies and popping the rolls into the oven to warm.

"No bears; they're probably still hibernating. But I sure am glad to be home. And I've got to get the tire fixed tomorrow." She drank a bit more wine. "So how was your day?"

"That woman Catherine Klein called. She wants to get together with us; she says she's been waiting a long time to find her family."

Lucy stared at the wineglass, studying the way the kitchen light reflected on the surface of the red wine. "It's kind of pushy, isn't it? I mean, we have a family. Do we need more members? For all we know, she's crazy or some sort of criminal. She could be anybody."

"Aren't you the least bit curious?" asked Bill, pushing the sausage around in the pan.

"Not really," said Lucy. "I wish she'd go away."

"Not likely." Bill added a jar of spaghetti sauce to the pan and set a lid on top, then joined her at the table, where he'd set his beer. "The thing is, she could go around us and go straight to Mom. That's my worry." He took a long swallow.

"Has she threatened to do that?"

"Not in so many words, but it's out there. She was at the funeral, and she knows where Mom lives. And she's getting impatient; she mentioned that several times." He picked at the label on his beer bottle. "I really don't want Mom getting involved."

"What don't you want Gram getting involved in?" asked Zoe, coming from the family room, drawn to the kitchen by the heady aroma of sausage and tomato sauce. "Dinner smells so good that I can't concentrate on my reading."

"It'll be ready in a few minutes. Where's Sara?"

"She's having dinner with some friends; she won't be home for supper."

"Okay, ladies, I think we're ready," announced Bill, setting the pan on the table. Lucy got the rolls out of the oven, and Zoe quickly produced plates, napkins, and silverware. They were all digging in when Zoe spoke up. "You never told me why you're worried about Gram," she said.

"There's this woman who's decided she's related to us. She did some DNA test or something," said Lucy, talking with her mouth full.

"Really?" Zoe was intrigued. "That's amazing."

"It's not so amazing. It's a problem. She claims she's my half sister, that my father is also her father."

"But that means Poppop must've had an affair, right?" Zoe was thoughtful, putting things together. "And this is not a good time for poor Gram to learn that her husband was messing around with another woman," said Zoe.

"Exactly," said Bill.

"If there's ever a good time. So we've been trying to stall her, to put her off, but she's growing impatient," said Lucy, using her fork to pull a slice of green pepper out of her hoagie and nibbling on it. "I dread to think what she might do."

"I think you've got to head her off at the pass before she

decides to go and see Gram," said Zoe, in a matter-of-fact tone. "It would be better if she heard about this from you guys and knows you've got her back. Present a united front."

"That's a good point," said Bill, draining his beer and getting up to fetch another from the fridge. "That would give us more control of the situation."

"But your poor mother," protested Lucy. "I just don't see why she has to deal with this mess, not now."

Zoe covered her mother's hand with hers. "Gram is tougher than you think. And she was married to Poppop for almost fifty years. Do you think she really doesn't know everything about him?"

Lucy looked across the table at her husband, wondering if there was something he was hiding from her. He looked back, apparently reading her mind, and shook his head. "I'm an open book, Lucy. I've got no secrets, and I don't think my dad did, either." He uncapped his beer. "I'll call Mom tonight."

So while Lucy emptied the clean dishes from the dishwasher and filled it with the dirty supper dishes, Bill sat at the table and called his mother. Zoe hovered in the doorway to the family room, nervously fidgeting. "I hope I'm right and Gram's not too upset," she said, grabbing a sponge and proceeding to wipe down the stove top.

"Hi, Mom, it's me," said Bill, when his mother answered. "How's everything?"

He put the phone on speaker, and Lucy listened in as his mother launched into a long description of her recent activities, mostly centering around her friend Althea's fading memory, which was causing problems at their weekly bridge game. "She simply can't remember which suit is trump, and nobody wants to partner with her anymore."

"That's too bad," sympathized Bill. "Uh, Mom, something's come up, and I want to discuss it with you."

"That doesn't sound good," said Edna.

"Maybe it is, maybe it isn't." He took a deep breath. "Okay. Here goes. There's this woman who came to Dad's funeral who says that he was her father. She took one of those DNA tests. She's about my age, and she wants to meet with us all; she says she wants to be part of the family."

"What's her name?" snapped Edna.

"Catherine Klein. She calls herself Kate."

"Hmph."

"Any idea about this woman? Did Dad ever mention— you know, confess—to some, I don't know . . ."

Lucy and Zoe exchanged a glance, amused at Bill's difficulty expressing himself.

Edna, however, got straight to the point. "An affair, you mean?"

"I guess so."

"No." Edna paused, apparently thinking. "How old is this woman?"

"About my age, I guess."

There was a long silence. "I suppose it's possible," she finally said, speaking slowly and thoughtfully. "When I was pregnant with you, your father was working on assignment in San Francisco. He was gone for weeks at a time, and when he did get home, I wasn't myself. I didn't feel well, and I was cranky. I was mad at him for being away, even though it wasn't his fault, and I was scared. It was one of those rough patches that couples go through, but once you arrived, everything changed. He was thrilled to have a son, and I was glad to not be pregnant anymore."

"So you think this woman might be his daughter?"

"I suppose it's possible, but I'm pretty sure he didn't know about her. If he had, I think he would have made some provision for her and her mother. He was a good man, a decent man."

"So do you want to meet her and learn more?" asked Bill. "That's the question."

"I guess so. I've been thinking of coming for a visit anyway." She sighed. "I really can't face Althea, for one thing. I need a break."

Lucy found herself smiling. Here Edna was a recent widow suddenly confronted by her late husband's likely affair, and she was more concerned about her friend's memory loss.

"Oh, and by the way, Bill," continued Edna, "do you happen to have a copy of Dad's will. I can't seem to find it anywhere."

"I'll look, Mom. So when are you thinking of visiting?"

"Oh, I don't know," she answered, sounding uncertain.

"Make it soon," urged Bill. "You know we've always got a place for you here."

Not exactly, thought Lucy, thinking of the superhero décor in Toby's old room.

# Chapter Eight

The next morning, Lucy dropped off the car at the repair shop and walked over to the office, tightening her scarf and buttoning up her jacket against the blast of freezing wind that was blowing off the water. This was the time of year she found hardest, when it seemed as if winter would never let go and the weather would never warm up. When she got to the *Pennysaver*, she smiled to see that Phyllis had set a big pitcher's worth of Irish daffodils on her reception counter.

"Oooh," cooed Lucy, burying her nose in the flowers, inhaling their musky, springy scent. "I love daffodils."

"What's not to love," agreed Phyllis. "First sign of spring, even earlier than the pussy willows."

"Point taken. I'm going to look for some this weekend, back by Blueberry Pond. They're the earliest."

"Bring me some, too," said Phyllis, looking up to greet Rob as he entered. He seemed to be a man with a mission, giving them a curt wave and heading straight to Ted's desk, where he sat right down and grabbed the phone. Lucy and Phyllis exchanged a glance, and Lucy ambled over to her desk, where she kept an ear cocked, curious to learn what he was up to.

She didn't get much, however, as she missed his opening question, and the rest of the conversation was *hmms* and *oh reallys* and a final *got it, thanks.* Clearly dissatisfied, he got up and poured himself a cup of coffee, took it back to his desk, and swiveled his chair around to face Lucy.

"I don't suppose you know anything about this Melanie Wall case, do you?" he asked, peering at her over his coffee mug.

"Melanie Wall? What about her?"

"She accused this county jail guard, Gabe McGourt, of sexual misconduct, but the case was dropped because she never showed up."

"That was last summer, right?" asked Phyllis. "You must remember, Lucy. This girl got herself arrested for drugs and couldn't make bail and claimed one of the corrections officers at the county lockup got too friendly and groped her or something." She smoothed her sweater over her ample bosom. "Kind of a gray area, if you ask me. Half the time those women offer themselves, just to get drugs and stuff."

Lucy wasn't sure she agreed with Phyllis on this particular point; it seemed to her there was a clear difference between physically restraining a prisoner and sexual assault. But she also knew Melanie was the sort of girl who pushed the envelope. "Yeah, I remember Melanie. She worked with Sara and Zoe at the Queen Vic. They were always complaining about her, about how she'd leave a room half-cleaned and they'd have to finish the job. One time, Sara found her passed out on a half-made bed."

"Did she have family around here?" asked Phyllis.

"I don't think so, but I don't know for sure," admitted Lucy. "I could ask the girls what they remember." She turned to Rob. "Do you think there's a story here?"

"For sure," he replied. "Everybody knows the sheriff is corrupt . . ."

Lucy felt this was going a bit too far. "That's a big assumption," she began. "If Ted were here, he'd tell you to slow down. You're just beginning to develop contacts and figure out the lay of the land. You don't want to start off on the wrong foot."

Rob straightened his back and slapped his hand on Ted's rolltop desk. "That's the sort of attitude that enables corruption to flourish," he declared. "There is such a thing as right and wrong, and powerful people tend to abuse their power, and we have to stand up for the little guy. Or girl, in this case." He paused. "You know that Murphy's got his own private goon squad, otherwise known as deputy sheriffs, and the corrections officers, too. They're all beholden to him for their jobs, and he turns a blind eye on any abuses they commit. It's a perverted loyalty thing or something, a gang mentality. They all stick together."

"They do," admitted Lucy, "and that's why you need to be careful. There's a whole network of favors and kinship in these small towns, and you need to figure out the structure before you start attacking people. Believe me, I learned the hard way when I pressed a candidate for School Committee about a principal I suggested was incompetent, only to learn that he was her brother." Lucy shrugged. "Different last name. How was I to know?"

"What happened?" asked Rob, scratching his cheek.

"She won, he kept his job, and my son didn't get to go to the statewide moot court." She sighed. "I got off easy. I didn't get fired, but I did get a stern talking-to from Ted, who told me that in this town, everybody's related, and blood is thicker than water. A lot of families here go back for centuries, and newcomers don't count for much."

"Well, I don't plan to stick around for long," said Rob, pushing his chair away from the desk and standing up. "But I do plan to make a difference while I'm here." With that, he zipped up his jacket and headed for the door, looking a bit like a hound who'd caught the scent of a rabbit.

"Lord preserve us," sighed Phyllis, rolling her eyes.

At lunchtime, with her stories filed by the noon deadline, Lucy headed over to the repair shop to pick up her car. When she reached the lot, she saw her car was ready to go, with a brand-new tire. That was an expense she hadn't expected, so she had her credit card in hand when she presented herself to the cashier, Lynne.

"Hi, Lucy. Have you got a minute? Fred wants to talk to you."

Never what you wanted to hear, she thought, as Lynne disappeared into the service bay. She returned in a moment, with Fred in tow.

"What's the bad news?" asked Lucy, as Fred wiped his greasy hands on a towel. "Did I destroy the rim?"

"Nah, everything's fine, but I couldn't save the tire. It looked pretty new, too."

"It was," said Lucy, with a sigh. "I got new tires for Christmas."

Fred shook his head. "Funny thing. It looked like somebody shot at it with a nail gun or something. I found five of these." He reached into the chest pocket of his bib overalls and produced a handful of roofing nails. "They're short, but they did the job, eventually."

"That's why I didn't realize I had a flat until I'd gone some distance?"

"That's right," said Fred.

"A nail gun? I couldn't have just picked up the nails?" asked Lucy.

"It's all I can figure." Fred shrugged. "Seems like a mean sort of trick, but you never know with folks today."

"I suppose it could have been an accident," said Lucy, trying to think if she'd passed any construction sites. The only possibility, she thought, was the sheriff's office, where workers had been putting on a new roof. "Like maybe somebody dropped a nail gun?"

"It happens," said Fred. "My cousin got shot that way. He was lucky; it went into his butt, but the doc said it only missed his spine by an inch or so." He grinned, revealing a missing tooth or two. "He went online and found all these X-rays of people with nails in their heads, anywhere you can think of." He paused. "They really oughta make those guns safer, or train people better, or something."

"Well, thanks for fixing the car," said Lucy, turning toward Lori and the cash register and handing over her credit card. "I've gotta get back to work. Like those Disney dwarves used to sing in the movie, "I owe, I owe.""

"That's a good one, Lucy," said Fred, before going back to the waiting car in the service bay. Lynne gave her a slip to sign, and wincing at the total, Lucy signed on the dotted line.

That evening, when she was mixing up a meat loaf, both girls came home together and caught Lucy letting Libby the dog lick off her greasy fingers.

"Mom, that's gross," complained Zoe.

"No, it's not. The meat loaf is in the pan, and when Libby finishes I'm going to wash my hands." She wiggled her fingers. "It's just a little treat for her."

Libby agreed, wagging her tail as she thoroughly licked Lucy's hands, leaving them cleaner than clean. "Maybe I don't really need to wash . . ." suggested Lucy, displaying her hands and eliciting a chorus of groans from her daughters.

"I'm losing my appetite," complained Sara.

"Well, you can make the salad," suggested Lucy, sudsing up. When she'd finished washing and was drying her hands, she asked if they remembered Melanie Wall.

"Remember," groaned Zoe. "I wish I could forget."

"Yeah," agreed Sara, who was emptying a bag of salad greens into a bowl. "At first, we felt bad for her and tried to cover things up so Mrs. Bonaventure wouldn't fire her. But after a while, that got real tiresome."

"Especially since she didn't seem to care about keeping the job," added Zoe, slicing up a tomato. "All she wanted to do was get high."

"What was she like?" asked Lucy, putting the towel back on its hook. "I seem to remember her as rather quiet, like a little mouse."

"She was real quiet, like a little ghost. And when she wasn't high, she was a good worker. She had a funny little sense of humor." Sara shook her head. "You just knew she came from a messed-up home; she was one of those girls who never had a chance."

"She wanted to be friends so bad. She was always asking what we were doing after work or on the weekend."

"And then she got arrested, so we were real glad we never hung out with her," said Sara.

"You never heard from her after that?" asked Lucy, watching as Sara put a sheet of plastic cling wrap over the salad bowl.

"I don't think so," replied Zoe, with a shrug, heading up the back stairs.

"Why do you want to find Melanie Wall?" asked Sara, tucking the salad into the fridge.

"No reason," said Lucy, setting the oven at three-fifty and sliding the meat loaf inside. "Just curious, I guess."

"Sounds like trouble to me," said Sara, plopping down at the kitchen table and checking her phone. She glanced at Libby, who had settled on her doggy bed and was snoozing. "Let sleeping dogs lie. That's what they say."

"You're probably right," said Lucy, scrubbing up some potatoes.

Much to Rob's surprise, his photos of the elementary school kids making Valentines for Vets was a big hit, featured above the fold on the front page of both the *Gabber* and *Pennysaver* editions and posted as a photo essay in the online *Courier*. Lucy's story describing the grand-marshal candidates also got a lot of attention and sparked a number of office betting pools on the final choice. When the press conference announcing the grand-marshal selection finally came around a week later, it happened to be a Wednesday, deadline day, and Ted was holding the paper for the big announcement. Lucy got off to a slow start because she forgot to set the alarm and cast a longing glance at the shortcut but drove right by, staying on Red Top Road and sticking to the main roads even though it meant she might be late. Nothing ever started on time, she told herself, as she waited at the stop sign to make her turn onto Route 1, especially news conferences.

The Hibernian Knights had their own building, a modest but well-maintained, gray-shingled building that stood in the middle of a huge parking lot. When Lucy arrived, there were already quite a few cars in the lot, including a good number of official vehicles from the sheriff's department, fire department, highway department, and water department, as well as a plain black sedan with clergy plates that Lucy happened to know belonged to Father Bill, from St. Brigid's Church.

Stepping inside, she discovered that the lobby was empty and everyone was settling into their seats in the main meeting room. The podium on the stage was empty, but several board members were seated in the circle of chairs arranged behind the podium. They were all male, apart from the secretary, Lucy noted, and dressed in everything from business suits and ties to the retired man's uniform of flannel shirt, sweater vest, and chinos. She recognized their state rep among the group, along with an assistant DA. The three candidates were seated on the other side of the stage, chatting and doing their best to appear as if they were best buddies. Taking a seat near the front, Lucy noticed that Eileen Clancy was nervously twisting a handkerchief in her hands, and James Ryan was tapping one foot and glancing repeatedly at the podium. Only Brendan Coyle seemed truly unconcerned about the selection, focused instead on the conversation.

There was a bit of a buzz when Sheriff Murphy entered, accompanied by two of his uniformed deputies. The three men stood at attention as the fire department's color guard marched onto the stage and everyone rose for the Pledge of Allegiance. That was followed by "The Star-Spangled Banner," sung by the Singing State Trooper, Ed Corrigan. When that business was completed, the color guard marched into the wings, and the two deputies seated them-

selves with the other Hibernian board members. The candidates sat a bit straighter, and the sheriff took his place at
the podium.

"Thank you all for coming," he began, with an expan-
sive grin, which prompted a bit of a chuckle from the audience. Puzzled at first, Lucy realized that attendance was
probably required, especially if these local functionaries
wanted to keep their jobs.

"This year, we had an especially fine group of candidates for grand marshal, and if you will indulge me, I will
introduce each of them." He proceeded to do so, beginning with Eileen, who blushed furiously as he outlined her
contributions to the community, her business acumen, and
her devotion to her students. "She has dedicated her life to
perpetuating Irish culture through dance, and dozens—
nay, hundreds—of young people have a better apprecia-
tion of their heritage thanks to her efforts."

When the applause died down, he introduced Brendan
Coyle, launching into a long description of his various
good works. Brendan seemed amused by the account, occasionally shrugging his shoulders as if to brush off the ac-
colades. When Murphy described his efforts at community
organizing as "rabble-rousing" he smiled broadly and raised
his hand. "Anybody who's interested, meet me afterward,"
he invited, getting a big round of applause.

The sheriff's tone changed as he described James Ryan,
calling him a quiet man who worked tirelessly to benefit
the community, especially the Irish-American community.
He cited low-interest loan programs and involvement in
community projects, and cited him as a major fund-raiser
for St. Brigid's. "We might as well name that beautiful new
organ after him. He twisted a lot of arms and got us all to

dig deeper than we thought we could, right?" he asked, getting a roar of approval from the audience.

Lucy was beginning to get tired of all this jollity, which frankly seemed rather false to her. She'd covered lots of similar events when a check was given to a worthy cause; they called them "grin and grabs" at the paper, which is pretty much what they were. Some worthy would give a brief speech, a check would be handed over, and everybody would smile for the photo. She'd also covered prize presentations, MVP announcements, award ceremonies at the school, even a big lottery winner, but she'd never encountered an atmosphere this thick and ripe with forced bonhomie and self-congratulation. It was supposed to be about the candidates for grand marshal, but something else was happening: It was really all about the sheriff and the people to whom he granted his favors. These folks were the "in" crowd, they were determined to remain so, and the devil take the rest.

"Well, now I'll turn this over to the president of the Hibernian Knights board of directors, our very own assistant district attorney, for whom I see a bright future, Mr. Kevin Kenneally."

Kenneally was tall and skinny, with a thick thatch of red hair. He was dressed in a gray suit, starched white shirt, and green tie, and his shoes were highly polished. He had a big class ring on one finger but had not yet achieved a Rolex watch. He had a charming, "aw shucks" air about him, and got straight to business after thanking the sheriff for his kind words.

"As president of the board of directors of the Hibernian Knights, I am happy to announce that the grand marshal for the St. Patrick's Day parade will be"—he paused dra-

matically before saying the name that everyone expected—
"James Ryan."

Ryan, of course, had a few words to say, and Lucy duti-
fully jotted down them down, checking her watch. This
thing had gone on for more than an hour, and since it was
breaking news, she had to write it up immediately. She figured she could file the story in the old *Gabber* office in
Gilead, which would save her the drive back to Tinker's
Cove. How much of this back-patting self-congratulation
would Ted want, she wondered, aware that he couldn't
hold the paper indefinitely.

Finally, it was over, and people were gathering around
Ryan to congratulate him. Lucy saw Eileen Clancy standing by herself, looking dejected, and decided to offer a bit
of consolation and maybe get a quote.

"Too bad, Eileen," she said, with a smile. "Maybe next
year?"

"It just wasn't my year," she said, through clenched
teeth. "Jim Ryan's been waiting for some time to be chosen." She paused. "You've got to pay your dues, and I
guess I'm still in the debit column." Then, realizing she
might have misspoken, she added, "Of course, Jim is the
best choice. He'll be a fabulous grand marshal. I wish him
all the best."

Right, thought Lucy, imagining that Eileen was probably picturing Jim Ryan's float hitting a pothole and sending him flying.

"I've got to go and congratulate him," she said, stepping away from Lucy. "Thanks for coming, and have a
great day."

"You, too," said Lucy, turning to speak to Brendan
Coyle, who was chatting easily with Kevin.

"I was just telling Brendan that it was very close," said Kevin, slapping him on the shoulder. "Next year, I predict he'll be chosen."

Brendan smiled at her. "Maybe, maybe not. Times are changing, and people are becoming more open-minded. Even the Hibernian Knights are bound to change, to become more in step with society at large."

"Make that baby steps," said Kevin, shaking Brendan's hand and heading over to join the group around James Ryan.

"So you're not disappointed?" asked Lucy.

"You know that Woody Allen line about not wanting to belong to a club that would admit him as a member? That's kind of how I feel about the Hibernians."

"Off the record, I'm sure."

"Absolutely," said Brendan, with a wink.

Lucy had tucked her notebook in her bag and was headed for the door when she was hailed by the sheriff. "Grand day, isn't it?" he said, beaming at her.

"You must be very pleased."

"Indeed I am." He paused. "You'll be giving this the coverage it deserves, a major announcement and all?"

"Our deadline is usually noon, but Ted's holding the paper," said Lucy. "And the story will go online right away."

"That's great." The sheriff furrowed his brow. "By the way, I heard your car broke down last week? Is everything okay?"

"Just a flat," said Lucy. "How did you know?"

"Oh, all the breakdowns are reported to me." He bared his teeth in a grin. "Routine public safety policy."

"Well, Silver Cloud came quickly, and I was home before the storm got too bad."

"It was quite a blow, wasn't it?" He caught her eyes with his direct gaze. "You should be more careful in future, not go wandering off into dangerous territory."

"I will," said Lucy, wondering if the sheriff was offering a bit of kindly advice, or a threat.

# Chapter Nine

Leaving the Hibernian Knights hall, Lucy's eye was caught by the massive gray granite prison that squatted atop the tallest hill in the county and loomed over the little town of Gilead. Sun glinted off the razor wire that topped the tall chain-link fence that encircled the prison, and she wondered if daylight penetrated the small, heavily barred windows. Probably only briefly, if at all, she decided, calculating the angle of the sun and the thickness of the jail's granite walls.

The sheriff could have campaigned to replace the nineteenth-century jail with a modern facility, but had chosen not to. Maybe the idea hadn't even occurred to him, she thought, turning her back on the grim structure and walking to her car. It seemed odd, though, considering how he made sure the deputies had the latest, glitziest squad cars, painted with enormous enlargements of the sheriff's seal on the doors. He'd also modernized the county's emergency dispatch system, instituted annual fitness exams and weapons training for deputies and corrections officers, and, somewhat controversially, had changed the color of their uniforms from dark gray to a rather bright shade of blue. "Friendlier," he'd said, announcing the change, but keen observers had noticed that the new color flattered his baby-blue eyes.

Lucy was familiar with the jail; she'd been inside numerous times to interview locals charged with crimes and awaiting trial, and she always came away with a sense of relief that she could leave. The place gave her the willies, especially the sound made by the various doors a visitor had to pass through. They all closed with a resounding *thud* that made you wonder if they would ever open again.

It was telling, she thought, negotiating the route to the *Gabber* office, that when prison reform activists organized demonstrations protesting conditions in the county jail about a year ago, the sheriff had refused any suggestion that the prison could be modernized or improved. He had stubbornly refused to acknowledge the protestors, who had eventually given up and moved on in search of greener pastures, and had continued to resistany and all calls to humanize the facility. The women's wing was especially harsh, she remembered, and the slightest infraction resulted in solitary confinement. "For the ladies' safety," the sheriff had insisted, when questioned, quickly moving on to his decision to change the female prisoner's uniforms from gray to pink—a move that Lucy knew the women had not appreciated; one inmate had complained that they all now looked like bottles of Pepto-Bismol.

No matter what the sheriff did, thought Lucy as she parked her car, nobody ever opposed him. He always got exactly what he wanted, and after his veiled warning to her, she understood why. Thinking back, she tried to figure out how she had crossed him, what she'd done that had made him feel he had to assert his power over her, but she couldn't imagine what it was. All she'd done was ask some questions, which he'd easily brushed away. Maybe her reputation as a hard-hitting journalist had preceded her? Hardly, she thought, climbing out of the car. She'd covered a few big stories, she'd had some lucky scoops, but for the most part she wrote boring stories about town committee meetings and getting-to-know-you features about locals and their varying achievements: growing big pumpkins, sewing patchwork quilts, running in a marathon. All she'd done that might possibly have irritated the sheriff, she realized, reaching the doorway, was ask for the parade guidelines. That must be it, she decided. She'd asked for the guidelines, implying that he'd lied when he told her Rosie had applied too late, after the deadline. She'd confronted him with information that seemed to indicate there was no deadline, and he didn't like it. In fact, she wondered, reaching for the door, was it possible he had suggested to one of the roofers that he have a small accident with the nail gun? Stepping inside the overheated office, Lucy suddenly felt chilled.

"Hey, Lucy, you're finally here," called Ted, looking up from the huge steel desk, big as an aircraft carrier, that had formerly been occupied by Sam Wilson.

"Wow, some change from the *Pennysaver*," said Lucy, looking around the carpeted modern space, which even boasted a rubber tree plant. The newsroom, with its neat row of cubicles, was empty, however.

"Where is everybody?" she asked.

"Out. They're on the beat. Looking for stories, taking photos, building connections. You can't report local news from a desk; that's what I told them."

"How many of these keen newshounds have you unleashed on an unsuspecting public?" asked Lucy.

"Actually, there's just Rob and you, and Pete Popper.

Fran Croydon is still recuperating from her surgery." He gave her a little half smile. "Pete's over at the high school, covering a science fair."

"So much for beating the bushes for news," said Lucy. "I've got the grand-marshal announcement to write up for you."

"Don't tell me. Let me guess," said Ted, as if there was some question as to who was chosen. "Was it . . . James Ryan?"

"Darn," muttered Lucy, slipping out of her jacket. "You spoiled my surprise."

"Write it up. I saved twelve inches for you on the front page. You can go longer if you want for the online edition, which we can put up as soon as you're done."

"You'll post it?"

"Actually, no. I need Rob for that. Where is he?"

"Out on the beat, I suppose," said Lucy, choosing a cubicle and powering up the PC, which immediately obliged by lighting up. "So all this new equipment came with the *Gabber*?"

"Even the fake plant," said Ted, beaming at her.

She'd just finished a concise account of the grand-marshal announcement when the door opened and Rob came in, wearing dark sunglasses. He took his jacket off and hung it on the rack, but kept the sunglasses on when he seated himself in the farthest cubicle.

"What's up?" asked Ted, who hadn't looked up from the story he was editing when Rob came in.

Rob's answer was indistinct, but Lucy thought she caught the word "budget."

"Everything all right?" asked Ted, fixing his gaze on Rob. "Why are you wearing sunglasses indoors? And why can't you talk?"

Rob removed the sunglasses, revealing a very swollen, very black eye. His lip was also swollen, which Lucy hadn't noticed previously, distracted as she was by the Ray-Bans.

"That's quite a shiner," said Ted. "It looks painful."

"Id iz," mumbled Rob, through his teeth.

"Don't tell me you walked into a door," said Lucy.

"Id wuz a bar," said Rob.

"You got in a bar fight?" Ted didn't like the sound of that.

"Dat place out on Route 1."

"And they just didn't like the looks of you?" asked Lucy. "So somebody decided to rearrange your face?"

"I axed the wrong question," admitted Rob.

Lucy had a flash of inspiration. "Not the sheriff. You didn't go off about him, did you?"

"No." Rob shook his head, slowly. "I'm not stupid," he began, speaking with effort. "I very tactfully steered the conversation to Gabe McGourt and that girl, Melanie Wall. Like I was new in town, and I'd heard something about it and was just curious."

"Who were you talking to?" asked Ted.

"Just a bunch of guys, fishermen probably. They were real friendly, talking about the local talent, until I mentioned this McGourt guy. Then they hustled me outside, and one guy, the big one, socked me in the face. I remember the first hit. After that, it's all a blur."

"Did you go to the ER?" Lucy couldn't help it, her motherly instincts came to the fore. "You might have a concussion."

"Nah. I was only out for a minute or so. I drove home and found some frozen peas in the freezer. Not mine. Probably left by the last tenant." He sighed a long sigh. "Lucky, hunh?"

"Stupid, more like," said Ted. "What did I tell you? Everybody knows everybody around here, and even if they don't like them, they'll stick up for them against an outsider. You've got to be careful, do your homework, suss things out."

"That's what I was trying to do," said Rob, in a defensive tone.

"Ted's right," said Lucy, somewhat surprised to find herself agreeing with her boss. "It's worse than I thought. The sheriff is into everything; he knows every single thing that goes on. He's scary; you don't know if he's truly concerned about you or if he's threatening you. It's a little bit of both, and it's how he keeps everybody in line."

"Has he threatened you, Lucy?" asked Ted, concerned.

"I honestly don't know." She shrugged. "I'm probably just being oversensitive. I get a flat tire and I think the world is out to get me."

Ted was thoughtful, toying with his stapler. "This is new to me," he said. "We're in uncharted territory. Sam, bless him, was happy to be Murphy's official spokesperson, and I don't blame him; he had bills to pay and payroll to meet, and he kept the *Gabber* afloat in tough times. But that's not my way."

"So what are we going to do?" asked Lucy.

"We're going to go slow, we're going to build contacts, we're going to do research, and we're going to chip away and expose the truth. One morning, Sheriff Murphy is going to wake up and find the feds banging at the door with a search warrant, and he's going to wonder how it all happened." He nodded. "That's the plan."

"Sounds good," said Lucy. "Meanwhile, I've got this puff piece . . ."

"Post it, Rob." Ted grinned. "It's going to be a stealth

attack." He got up and fixed himself a cup of coffee, taking it with him and pulling up a chair next to Rob's desk. "So refresh my memory," he began, after taking a big slurp. "Who exactly is Gabe McGourt, and what makes him newsworthy?"

"He's a prison guard who was accused by a woman named Melanie Wall of sexual assault."

"And you want to follow up on it?"

"I do. But I can't find any trace of Melanie; the whole thing just kind of dissolved into thin air. Nothing happened, and McGourt, as far as I know, is still working at the jail."

"Do you remember anything about this, Lucy?" This was followed by another slurp.

"Not much," said Lucy. "Melanie worked at the Queen Vic with my girls last summer. She was a chambermaid, but they didn't stay in touch."

"Do you think you could ask them about her, Lucy?"

"I already tried," said Lucy. "They said she was nice enough, but kind of flaky. She came in late; one time they found her passed out on an unmade bed. I got the impression that they got tired of covering for her." Lucy shrugged. "And then one day she didn't come in. End of story."

"Well, maybe they'll think of something," said Ted, draining his mug.

As it happened, Ted was right. When Lucy got home that evening, Zoe handed over her cell phone. "I was cleaning out old messages, and I found a text from Melanie," she said. The message was brief and to the point: "Heading back to Boston. Let's stay in touch." There was also an address, somewhere in Quincy.

"Did you stay in touch?" asked Lucy, returning the phone. The address was easy enough to remember, 15 Granite Street, but Lucy jotted it down on a piece of paper, just to be safe.

"Nope. That was a busy time for me, I was still working at the Vic, and school was starting up. I probably swiped right past it."

"Well, this was a lucky find. Sara and I are going apartment hunting in Boston tomorrow. Want to come?"

"Wish I could," Zoe replied, with a sigh, "but I've got a paper due."

"We'll bring you something," promised Lucy, reaching for the refrigerator door. "Some chocolate from Phillips."

"Don't forget," she said, adding the name of the famous Boston candy shop to Lucy's note with the address. "I'm counting on it."

Lucy had been looking forward to this expedition with Sara ever since theylearned that Sara's internship had led to a full-time job in the geology department at the Museum of Science. She was thrilled and excited for her daughter, but she was also well aware of the advantages of having a place to stay in the city. She foresaw a future filled with visits to the Museum of Fine Arts, Italian dinners in the North End, sorties to Cambridge bookstores and boutiques, and even the occasional Broadway show that had taken to the road.

She was telling all this to Sara as they drove together down Route 1, but Sara wasn't equally enthusiastic. "Remember, Mom, I'm just getting a starting salary, and rents are crazy in Boston. I'm probably going to have to get a roommate, or else it's going to be really small, like a studio."

"Oh, your Dad and I are flexible. You can get one of those inflatable mattresses," said Lucy.

"Really?" Sara was skeptical. "Do you think you'd be comfortable like that?"

"Sure, for one night," said Lucy.

"I guess that might work," admitted Sara, with a distinct lack of enthusiasm.

"We wouldn't get in your way, you know," continued Lucy. "But we would want to visit every once in a while, make sure you're happy and all."

"I'm an adult, Mom," insisted Sara. "I can take care of myself."

"I know. You are very capable, but I'm your mother, and I'm going to be worrying about you."

"There's no need, Mom. Really."

"We'll see," said Lucy, philosophically. "You might be surprised to find that you miss us, and you'll be happy to see a friendly face. And we'll take you out to dinner. Anywhere you want to go. Just think of it."

Sara didn't answer, but looked glumly out the window.

The first appointment was for an apartment in a high-rise near the Museum of Science, handy for Sara's job.

"It's petite," admitted the real estate lady, unlocking the door, "but perfect for a young woman who's starting out."

She opened the door with a flourish, and Lucy popped in ahead of Sara, eager to see the apartment. It was small, really only one room with a mini-kitchen on one wall. The window gave a view of the opposite building, a similar brick high-rise. Opening one door, expecting a bath, she discovered a closet. Sara had found the bathroom, which Lucy discovered was actually a cramped space smaller than the closet.

"Well, it's doable, I suppose," she said brightly, "especially since the rent can't be very much."

"It's a bargain at twenty-four hundred a month," said

the real estate lady. "And you'll need first, last, and a security deposit. Oh, and no pets."

"There really isn't room for a pet," said Lucy, heading for the door.

"So you want a place that allows pets?" asked the real estate lady, unwilling to lose a potential renter.

"No," laughed Sara. "This is way beyond my budget, I'm afraid."

"You could get a roommate," suggested the woman.

"I think we'll have to keep looking," said Sara. "Do you have anything for around a thousand a month?"

"For that, you'll have to go out of town," said the woman, with a little sniff. "Quincy is supposed to be quite affordable."

"Oh, good," said Lucy, remembering the cute little studio there that Sara had borrowed during her internship. "We were planning to go there anyway."

"Do you have any properties there?" asked Sara, politely.

"Oh, no," said the woman, recoiling as if the idea was simply too ridiculous to even contemplate. "Definitely not in Quincy."

As they joined the usual traffic jam on the Southeast Expressway, Lucy suggested they might as well stop in Dorchester at Phillips for Zoe's chocolate and then continue back on the highway to Melanie's place to get the lay of the land. "If she's there, she might have some suggestions for you," she said."

They were past the giant gas tanks, with the colorful designs created by Corita Kent, when the GPS told them to exit the highway. Following its directions, they soon found themselves on a narrow street crowded with three-decker houses and were able to park right in front of number 15.

Like the other houses on the street, it boasted three porches stacked on top of each other, each one belonging to an apartment. There was a small lawn boasting a couple of rhododendron bushes and a patch of grass.

"This is obviously a working neighborhood," said Lucy, commenting on the availability of parking spaces. They climbed the steps to the porch at number 15 and studied the names handwritten next to the three doorbells; WALL was conspicuously crossed out next to the top bell, and replaced by SCHERMERHORN. Lucy pressed it anyway.

"Mom! What are you doing?"

"Maybe the Schermerhorns know something about Melanie."

"If they're even home," muttered Sara.

As it turned out, one of the residents was just returning from the Stop & Shop, coming up the short walk behind them, carrying a couple of bags of groceries. "Can I help you?" she asked.

"I hope so. We're looking for Melanie Wall."

"I guess she's moved," said Sara.

"She had the apartment before my husband and I got it," said the woman, who was in her early sixties, with a wild head of graying hair. She was dressed in workout pants and sneakers, topped with a Bruins sweatshirt and a quilted vest. "I never met her."

"When did you move in?" asked Lucy, figuring this was Mrs. Schermerhorn. "If you don't mind my asking."

"I don't mind. It was last September. The owner—she lives in the house, on the first floor—she said the previous tenant hadn't paid her rent in a couple of months, so we could have the place."

"What happened to her stuff?" asked Sara.

Mrs. Schermerhorn shrugged. "I don't know. You'd have to ask Carole."

"Do you think she's home?"

"Only one way to find out. It's the bottom bell," she replied, putting her groceries down on the porch floor and unlocking the door. "Have a nice day," she said, picking up the bags and stepping inside, careful to make sure the door closed behind her.

Lucy pressed the bottom bell, and a voice called out, "Coming." Some minutes later, the door was opened by an elderly woman in an aqua leisure suit, who was leaning on a cane. "If you're selling something, I don't want it," she said, stepping back and starting to shut the door.

"Not selling anything," Lucy said quickly. "We're looking for your former tenant, Melanie Wall. Did she leave a forwarding address, by any chance?"

"No such luck," the woman said, in a defensive tone. "Are you from the city?" she asked, suspiciously.

"No. We're old friends of Melanie's. We're from Maine."

"Well, that's all right then. I only asked because the city has all these rules that make it real hard to evict a tenant, even if they don't pay their rent."

"I understand," said Lucy, who suspected Melanie's belongings had found their way to the Salvation Army. "So you don't have any idea about what happened to Melanie?"

"Nope. She left in June; she already owed me for May, too, and she never came back. I tried her phone, no answers, and when September rolled around with no sign of her—that's when a lot of renters come back from wherever they spent the summer, and you get the college kids looking—well, that's when I decided enough was enough, and I talked it over with Bunchy—he's my nephew—and he said I should go for it, and he and a couple of buddies cleared the place out. If she showed up and made a fuss, well, he said he'd take care of it."

"Did she show up and make a fuss?"

"No." She glanced upward. "These new folks are nice, and they pay right on time."

"Good tenants are hard to find," said Lucy, agreeably. "My daughter here is looking for a place, she's got a job at the Museum of Science."

The landlord looked her over and nodded. "She looks like a nice girl."

"She is. I wonder if you know of anything that's available?"

"For not too much money," added Sara. "I'm just starting out."

"My sister's got a basement, a studio, really. She's two streets over, on Gilbert, number 45. I'll call and tell her you're coming."

"Thanks for your help," said Lucy.

"Yeah, I really appreciate it," said Sara.

They easily found 45 Gilbert Street, which was a Craftsman-style bungalow, with a well- tended garden in front. The owner, who looked like Carole's twin, greeted them with a smile, and they quickly concluded the arrangement, agreeing to rent the modest, but very clean, studio for $950 a month.

"Boy, that seems like a lot of money for a very small apartment," said Lucy, as they headed back on the Southeast Expressway for home. "And a basement, to boot."

"Yeah, Mom, but I can afford it. I won't have to share. And face it, I don't have much furniture."

"We'll have to start checking out some yard sales," said Lucy, slamming on the brakes to avoid rear-ending the SUV in front of her. "I'm glad you can take the T to work; this traffic is crazy."

"Yeah, I can walk to the station. That's good." Sara looked out the window, studying the glitzy new apartment buildings that had sprung up next to the highway. "I saw these advertised, right by the expressway. The rents are crazy."

"Your place is homey, and there's trees and a garden, more like what you're used to."

"Yeah." Sara sighed. "It's kind of upsetting about Melanie, isn't it? I know she had a lot of problems, but people don't just disappear, do they?"

"I think they do, especially if they owe a lot of money."

"But wouldn't she want her stuff? Even if she had to sneak in to get it?"

"Was she like that? Sneaky?" asked Lucy, as they descended into the darkness of the O'Neill Tunnel, which ran underneath downtown Boston.

Sara was silent, thinking, and didn't speak until they emerged into the light again at the stunning Zakim Bridge, with its triangular cables and support piers that echoed the nearby Bunker Hill Monument. "She was real evasive and edgy, always looking over her shoulder. She had this boyfriend, and she was terrified of him."

"Do you remember his name?" asked Lucy.

"Gabe, Gabe Mcsomething. We tried to tell her she could get a restraining order, told her to talk to Officer Sally, but she said it was no good. He had friends in the department. She said all she could do was get away, and one day I guess she did because she didn't show up." Sara was thoughtful. "I hope that's it. I hope he didn't, you know . . ."

"I hope she got away," said Lucy.

They stopped for a McDonald's supper on the way, and it was growing dark when they reached home on Red Top Road. Zoe's car was gone, but Bill's truck was in the driveway, but there was no sign of him when they went into the house. Only Libby greeted them, rising painfully from her doggy bed and wagging her tail.

"We're home," called Lucy, standing at the bottom of the stairs.

"I'm up here, in the office." Bill's voice came down from the attic, where he had carved out a tiny, cramped space to work on his accounts and blueprints.

"I'll come up," said Lucy, eager to tell him about the place they'd found for Sara.

She was slightly winded after climbing two flights, especially since the last was steep and twisty. "What are you doing up here?" she asked, ducking her head to step through the low doorway.

"I'm looking for Dad's will. Mom thinks I've got a copy."

"Do you?"

"I don't think so," said Bill, who was on his knees, looking through a box of old files. "I don't remember getting one. Do you?"

"Nope." Lucy leaned her fanny against his desk, mindful of the sloping ceiling. "If we had, I think we would have taken special care of it. Heck," she added, "we would have read it, wouldn't we? To find out if we were going to get something?"

"Too right," said Bill, "but I don't have a clue."

Lucy suddenly had a frightening thought. "Doesn't your Mom have a copy?"

"Uh, no. That's why I'm looking."

"The lawyer must have a copy," suggested Lucy.

"He died years ago."

"So if there's no will, your dad died intestate, right?"

"Right. And under Florida law, that means Mom won't

get the entire estate, like Dad wanted, but will have to split it with us, and maybe even Catherine Klein."

"Well, we wouldn't take our share," said Lucy. "Not if your Dad wanted your Mom to have it."

"Right, but there's no telling what this Klein woman will do."

"I hope that will turns up," said Lucy.

"Me, too." Bill sat back on his heels. "Otherwise, it's going to be a real mess."

# Chapter Ten

The little bell on the *Pennysaver* office door jangled, announcing Rob's arrival on Monday morning. "I've got a hot tip for you, Lucy," he said, giving Phyllis a little salute as he made his way somewhat painfully to Ted's antique desk. When he had passed and couldn't see her face, she rolled her eyes.

Lucy caught Phyllis's expression, which echoed her own emotions. She knew she should be grateful that Rob was offering her a tip; she knew it shouldn't bother her that he was using Ted's desk. Ted was working from the office in Gilead, where he was pleased as punch with the new computers, wall-to-wall carpeting, and fake plant. Nevertheless, Rob seemed terribly presumptuous to Lucy, who gave him the evil eye while he fussed about, trying to get comfortable by adjusting the chair height and shoving the keyboard and mouse aside to make room for the laptop he'd started using. Come to think of it, since he was working on a laptop anyway, why did he need to use Ted's desk at all? He would have a lot more room in the morgue, where he could spread out on the big conference table. And where she wouldn't have him constantly in view.

"So what's this hot tip?" she asked, wondering if she ought to tell Rob about the desk's exalted provenance, but decided against it. It would probably just give him delusions of grandeur.

"Uh, that Brendan guy and Rosie are organizing an all-inclusive Irish Festival," he said, getting up and limping over to the coffee station, where he filled a mug. The swelling on his face had gone down, but he was still pretty bruised.

"An alternative to the parade?" asked Lucy.

"In addition to, I think," he said, stirring in some powdered creamer. "Why can't we have real cream? This stuff sucks," he added, as his enthusiastic stirring caused some of the coffee to spill onto his hand.

"We used to, but we didn't use it fast enough. and it spoiled. Maybe they've got cream over in Gilead and you could work from there," suggested Lucy. "How do you know about this festival? I haven't seen a press release."

"I saw Rosie last night, and she told me." He made his way slowly back to Ted's desk, carefully carrying his over-full mug. "You'd better get right on it. It's breaking news, and we can put it online."

"I'm aware of that," snapped Lucy, "and just because you're using Ted's desk doesn't mean you're my boss!"

Rob was quiet for a moment, apparently taken aback by Lucy's reaction. "Oh, sorry," he finally said. "I didn't mean to tell you how to do your job."

"It's okay," muttered Lucy, somewhat ashamed of herself. She flipped through her Rolodex, looking for Brendan's number. "How's the budget story going?"

"Boring, really boring." He rolled his eyes. "I've got an interview with the school superintendent this morning."

"What time?" asked Lucy, checking the clock.

"Nine-thirty."

"Well, not to tell you how to do your job, but it's twenty-five past right now."

Rob pushed back the wheeled desk chair and stood up fast, knocking over his coffee. "Oh, crap!"

"I'll take care of the spill; you'd better get going. Superintendent Goring really hates tardiness. He's got a thing about it."

"Oh, great," muttered Rob, raising himself by leaning heavily on the desk and hobbling over to the coatrack, where he grimaced as he put on his coat. Then he made an effort to straighten himself up before heading out the door.

"Do you think he's really in that much pain, or is he putting it on for our benefit?" asked Lucy.

"Probably a bit of both." Phyllis had already grabbed the paper-towel roll that sat next to the coffeepot and had begun wiping up the sticky mess. "It's funny, isn't it, how coffee tastes so good and smells so good, until you spill it? Then it gets real icky."

"Yeah," said Lucy, carefully removing the sodden desk calendar and shoving it into the wastebasket. "I'll grab some cleaning stuff."

"Good idea," agreed Phyllis. "It might even ruin the finish if it's not cleaned off."

"I'm on it." Lucy trotted into the bathroom, which also served as a cleaning closet, and returned with a spray bottle of cleanser and a sponge.

Phyllis tossed the wadded paper towels into the trash and returned to her desk as Corney Clark came in, announced by the jangling bell.

"Cleaning day?" she asked, sniffing the pine-scented air.

"Small catastrophe—a spill, that's all," said Phyllis. "But a spring cleaning is definitely a good idea."

"Only if you do it," said Lucy, laughing. "Hi, Corney. What brings you here today?"

"Hot news—a press release. I thought I'd bring it myself to make sure it gets top priority." Corney was president of the Tinker's Cove Chamber of Commerce and took dressing for success seriously. Today she was wearing a navy-blue pantsuit with a cashmere sweater underneath the jacket, and she'd given the outfit a nautical twist by adding a red, white, and blue scarf printed with sailboats. Her blond hair was cut in a stylish short bob, and her makeup was hardly noticeable, except for the fact that her eyelashes were coated with black mascara and her lips were glossed.

"Tell me all about it," said Lucy, plopping herself down at her desk and inviting Corney to take the visitor's chair.

"Here's the copy," she said, producing a printed sheet of paper. "It's for the Cove's first-ever all-inclusive Irish Festival."

"I heard about this," said Lucy, studying the press release. "Rosie Capshaw and Brendan Coyle are the organizers, right?"

"It was their idea," admitted Corney, tactfully, "but the Chamber is really doing the heavy lifting, if you know what I mean."

Lucy knew that she really meant the Chamber should get the credit.

"You're not worried about a conflict with Sheriff Murphy and his merry band of Hibernian Knights?"

"I don't think so," said Corney, chewing thoughtfully on her bottom lip. "For one thing, the festival is after the parade, in the afternoon, and it's here in Tinker's Cove, not in Gilead."

"And I see you've made all that very clear. 'The fun continues after the parade in Tinker's Cove'...blah, blah, blah."

"They might not like the all-inclusive part," suggested Phyllis, from her corner by the door.

"Well, that's too bad for them," said Corney. "Times are changing, and we can't afford to ignore the LGBTQ community. We want to welcome them, and their discretionary income, to Tinker's Cove. Also, I don't know if you've seen the figures the state just released, but the arts are a big income generator for towns like ours. We need more creative people like Rosie, if we're going to get ourselves on the Arts Map the state tourism bureau is planning to put out. That would be a good story for you, Lucy."

"I'll file it for later," said Lucy, wondering why everybody was so eager to give her tips for stories all of a sudden. "And I'll get right on the festival, I was planning to call Brendan when you came in."

"Then I'll leave you to it," said Corney, standing up and slinging her designer bag onto her shoulder.

Lucy immediately reached for her phone and arranged for Brendan to stop by the *Pennysaver* office next morning, apologizing for asking him to come to her, but explaining that it was a big news week and she was running up against deadline. Hearing that, he offered to bring Rosie along, if she was available. She was just wrapping up the call when the police scanner began to cackle, announcing a motor-vehicle accident on Route 1.

"Last thing I need," muttered Lucy.

"You'd better go," advised Phyllis. "They're already calling for mutual aid, it must be big."

Lucy had barely gotten underway when she had to pull over for the town's ambulance, which was speeding down

Main Street with lights flashing and sirens blaring. She pulled out as soon as it passed, following as close behind as was safe. Experience had taught her that tagging along behind a rescue vehicle was the best way to get to an accident scene as quickly as possible. The siren on the ambulance was loud, but it didn't quite drown out the chorus of other sirens that indicated mutual aid was on the way.

As it happened, the accident was just outside town, on Route 1, the coastal region's main highway. Traffic was already backed up, but drivers maneuvered their cars and pickups to the side of the road to make way for the ambulance, and Lucy followed right along, hoping the PRESS placard she'd stuck against the windshield explained her audacity. Then the brake lights on the ambulance lit up, and Lucy braked, too, and pulled off to the side of the road, just before the bridge over Lumbert Hill Road.

Traffic was at a standstill because police cars were blocking both sides of Route 1, clearing a large area for rescue vehicles as well as a landing space for a Med-Flight helicopter, if needed. People had exited their cars, curious to see what was going on, and Lucy's friend, Officer Barney Culpepper, was stringing yellow caution tape to keep them out of harm's way. Since she didn't see any sign of the accident, she ran up to him.

"What's going on, Barney?"

"Oh, hi, Lucy. You made good time. I just got here a minute or so ago myself."

"I was right behind the ambulance. So where's the accident?"

"Oh, down there," he said, pointing to the side of the road, where there was a steep drop-off to Lumbert Hill Road. A sudden explosion—a loud pop, followed by a black cloud of smoke—indicated the crashed vehicle had caught fire. Lucy immediately ran to the side of the bridge and looked over, snapping photos of the burning vehicle. More engines were down there alongside a flaming pickup truck, which was surrounded by firefighters who had been sent flying by the explosion. As Lucy watched, they began picking themselves up and attempted to return to the cab of the truck with the Jaws of Life. The heat and smoke were intense; even standing on the bridge, Lucy could feel the heat and smell the acrid smoke, and she was horrified to think that the driver was still in the truck, trapped. One of the firefighters almost made it to the door, but he collapsed in a heap and was pulled back by two others. She realized the grim truth that whoever was in that truck was not going to get out alive, and she could only hope that that person, whoever it was, was already dead and past suffering.

"This is awful," she said, as Barney came to stand beside her. All color had drained from her face, and she looked terribly shaken.

Barney voiced his concern. "I don't think you should stay, Lucy. It's not going to be nice."

Firefighters had begun pouring foam on the truck, which quickly extinguished the fire, and some onlookers cheered, unaware that there was a fatality.

"Do you know who it is?" she asked. "Who does the truck belong to?"

"This is unofficial, mind, and I could be wrong; we have to wait for a positive ID, but Gabe McGourt drives a truck like that. I noticed the Harley decal on the rear window."

"He liked motorcycles?"

"To a fault," said Barney, rubbing his nose. "I pulled him over a couple of times, let him go with a warning. He went way too fast—in the truck, too." Barney sighed. "Some people just have a death wish, I guess. Or think they're immortal. Drive like it, anyway."

"There was some sexual harassment business he was involved in, too, wasn't there?"

"I did hear something along those lines, but it never amounted to anything. Never went to trial, anyway." He stared down at the charred hulk of the truck. "Lucy, they're not going to get the body out until that truck cools down," advised Barney. "And, even then, they probably won't be able to make an ID 'cause of the condition of the corpse . . ."

"You'll let me know . . ."

"Yeah." He made eye contact and squeezed her shoulder. "You should go."

"Thanks." Lucy started back to her car, but spotting fire chief Buzz Bresnahan, she changed course. "Chief!" she called, and he turned around, greeting her with a mere suggestion of a smile.

"Hi, Lucy. Terrible thing, this." He lifted his white helmet and wiped his head with a bandanna. "Car fires are the worst. I hate 'em."

"There's no doubt that someone was in the truck?" asked Lucy.

"Yeah." He shook his head. "We have to wait for the medical examiner to get here. Lumbert Hill Road is closed, of course, but as soon as we get all this equipment out of the way, the road can reopen." He snorted. "They're already starting to honk. I guess the show's over."

"Can you tell me who provided mutual aid?" she asked, notebook at the ready.

"Gilead, of course, and Sandringham. We didn't need either. Gilead got here before we could call them off, but

Sandringham got the message and returned to their station."

"How many firefighters were involved?"

"I'll have to get that to you. I'll put out a press release as soon as I can."

"Thanks. I've got photos, and we can get it posted on the online edition."

Someone was calling him, so the chief thanked her and went on his way to attend to business. His walk was slower than it used to be, she thought, realizing that he must be approaching retirement. He'd been the fire chief for as long as she could remember, so it would be quite a change to have somebody new.

It wasn't only the *Pennysaver* that was changing, she thought, climbing into her car and calling Ted, to let him know she'd covered the fire.

"Good work. Send me the photos," he said, adding, "Fires are always front-page stuff."

Some of the fire trucks were starting to leave, no longer needed at the accident scene, so Lucy did a U-turn and joined the procession that was returning to Tinker's Cove. She felt let down and discouraged; this story would not have a happy ending. She wondered who would replace Buzz as fire chief; she hoped it would be somebody she could work with as easily as she'd worked with Buzz. Not somebody like Rob, who she found terribly annoying. If she could have her wish, she wanted everything to go back to the way it was earlier: the cozy little office on Main Street, with just herself and Phyllis and Ted. She wished Ted had never bought the *Gabber*; she wished he'd never gotten that grant from the TRUTH Project; she wished Rob would go back to wherever he'd come from. He clearly did not understand local news, which, at bottom, meant you had to write about your friends and neighbors. He had few friends in town, and he wasn't interested in getting to know his neighbors; he just wanted to make a big name for himself by muckraking, which was a dangerous approach in a small town like Tinker's Cove.

Spotting a parking space on Main Street, Lucy quickly grabbed it, then sat for a minute, collecting herself. She finally reached for the door handle, releasing a whiff of smoky scent from her jacket, and found herself tearing up. Fires were the worst, she decided, blinking hard and getting out of the car.

"You look like you've seen a ghost," announced Phyllis, when Lucy entered the office.

"It was a pickup, burst into flames, and the driver was trapped inside." Lucy's voice was thick, and she was battling back tears.

"Oh, how awful." Phyllis passed her the box of tissues she kept on her desk. "Anybody we know?"

Lucy took a couple and gave her nose a good blow. "Only by reputation. Barney said he thought the truck belonged to Gabe McGourt."

"The corrections officer?"

"Yeah. Do you know him?"

"Yeah. He's been sniffing around lately, showing some interest in Elfrida's oldest, Angie. He's got a place just down the street from them and kept offering to take Angie for a ride on his motorcycle." She smiled a satisfied little smile. "Wilf told him to take a hike."

"When was this?" asked Lucy.

"Just the other day; he was out working on his bike when Angie walked by."

"But she was bothered enough to tell someone?"

"Yeah, she's a good girl. She told her mother, and Elfrida called Wilf, so he went over to talk to him. You know, man to man."

"And what happened?"

"Wilf said that at first he got all indignant and huffy, but when Wilf told him she's only sixteen, he lost interest real fast."

"That's good. From what I've heard he's"—Lucy paused, catching herself—"make that *was* kind of a jerk. Barney caught him speeding lots of times, but always let him off with a warning."

Phyllis smirked. "Professional courtesy, I guess."

"I guess," agreed Lucy, thinking that the sheriff's men, whether they were deputies or corrections officers, were above the law as long as they remained loyal to the sheriff. He would intervene if one of them got in trouble, and the accuser would pay the price, not the wrongdoer. She was pondering this situation when Rob came in, clearly furious.

"I was stuck in traffic forever, thanks to a crash on Route 1, which I should have been covering instead of talking to Mr. Goring, who should be called Mr. Boring!"

"No worry. I covered it," said Lucy.

Rob seated himself in Ted's chair, shoulders hunched in a sulk. "I saw smoke. Were there any fatalities?"

"Yeah. The driver was trapped." She shuddered. "It was awful; they couldn't get him out."

Rob was silent. Lucy wasn't sure if he was thinking about how awful it would be to be trapped in a burning car, or if he was upset about missing a breaking news story. "Who was it?" he finally asked. "Have they made an identification?"

"Not officially," said Lucy, "but my sources say the truck belonged to Gabe McGourt."

"Gabe McGourt?" Rob was stunned. "The guy I've been investigating?"

"The very same," admitted Lucy. "Of course, he could've loaned his truck to somebody else. It's not certain until they make an official ID."

"This smells to high heaven," said Rob, with a self-satisfied smirk. "Take my word for it, this accident was no accident. Not if the victim is Gabe McGourt." He drummed his fingers on Ted's desk. "I'd bet my life on it."

"I wouldn't, if I were you," said Lucy.

"What?"

"Bet your life on it."

# Chapter Eleven

When Lucy arrived at the office the next morning, she found Rob chatting with Rosie Capshaw. It occurred to Lucy that perhaps there was something going on between the two and wondered why she hadn't thought of it earlier. Perhaps because she considered Rob so obnoxious, that's why. She couldn't imagine that a nice young woman like Rosie would be the least bit interested in him.

"Hi, Lucy," he said, beaming with joy and apparently elated simply to be in Rosie's presence. "Rosie's here."

"I am indeed," agreed Rosie, with a chuckle, "and Brendan is on his way."

"Great." Lucy couldn't wait to break up this lovefest. "Let's meet in the morgue; that way we won't disturb Rob while he works."

Rob's expression changed to one of sadness, and Rosie gave him a sympathetic smile before she followed Lucy into the morgue. They had just seated themselves at the big conference table when Brendan arrived. "Good to see you," he said, full of enthusiasm as he took a seat. "I'm glad to be here, but all the credit goes to Rosie. The Irish Festival was her idea, after all."

"But you took my little idea and ran with it," said Rosie. "He's the one who started making phone calls and getting things moving. All I'm doing is bringing my puppets, that's all."

"She's too modest, this girl," insisted Brendan. "She was the one who said we should collaborate with the Chamber of Commerce . . ."

"And once Corney came on board, things really started to happen," said Rosie.

"She was already here, this morning," said Lucy. "She brought this press release."

"Oh, let me see!" Rosie and Brendan studied the sheet of paper, nodding along as they read.

"Anything you want to add?" asked Lucy.

"Yes, we're still looking for people who want to participate, with a talent, or food, or anything at all. We're open-minded, and everybody's Irish on St. Patrick's Day. All they have to do is call either me or Brendan," said Rosie.

"And we want to make it clear that the festival is not competing with the parade. The parade is a special and wonderful expression of Irish pride," said Brendan. "The festival is scheduled for the afternoon, after the parade, and is another way for folks to celebrate Irish heritage, even if they're not Irish."

"Point taken," said Lucy. "Mind if I snap a photo of you two?"

Rosie and Brendan had been gone a few minutes when a couple of uniformed state troopers, along with Assistant DA Kevin Kenneally, came into the office.

Wondering what had brought them to the *Pennysaver*, she was about to greet them when Kenneally began speaking.

"Rob Callahan," he began, "we have a few questions for you."

"No problem," said Rob. "Want to sit down?"

"Thanks," said Kenneally, taking the offered chair. The two uniforms remained standing behind him.

"So what's this all about?" asked Rob.

"I understand you've been inquiring about Gabe McGourt," began Kenneally. "Do you mind telling me why?"

"Nothing personal," said Rob, looking puzzled. "I'd heard some rumors that he was involved in a sexual harassment situation, and I was wondering if there was a story there. That's all."

"And have you had any personal contact with McGourt? Spoken with him? Had a disagreement of any kind?"

"No. Absolutely not."

"Are you sure? Because if you're lying, it could be a problem for you, and I notice you've clearly been in a fight."

"It wasn't with McGourt; it was some other guys," said Rob. "Look, am I under suspicion of something? Because I didn't hear you give me my Miranda rights." He turned to Lucy, who was standing by mutely, in amazement. "Did you hear them read me my rights?"

"Uh, no," said Lucy, giving Kenneally a puzzled look. Then her brain switched into high gear, and she asked, "Has McGourt been positively identified? Was he the victim in that crash yesterday?"

Kenneally looked at her. "Sorry, but we're not ready to make an official announcement," he said. "Maybe this afternoon." Then he directed his steely gray gaze to Rob. "No need to get all upset," he said, standing up. "Just a little chat, that's all."

"Yeah," said one of the troopers, looking Rob in the eye. "See you around."

"Not if I see you first," muttered Rob, under his breath, as the three made their way to the door.

Kenneally paused at the reception counter to speak to Phylllis. "Have a nice day, now," he said, before grabbing the doorknob.

So Kenneally, taking his cues from the sheriff, was following the playbook for ambitious young politicians, making friends with the receptionist, thought Lucy. She watched with amusement to see Phyllis's reaction and wasn't disappointed.

"Hmph," was all he got, as he and the two troopers stepped outside. Kenneally closed the door gently, and the little bell gave a quiet little *ting*.

"That was weird," Lucy said. "And scary."

"You're telling me," said Rob. "I hope they don't think I was involved in this accident."

"Never mind," said Phyllis, joining in. "Everything will be all right. Kenneally's just trying to stir things up."

"Well, I don't like it," said Rob. "I'm supposed to be covering the news, not making it."

For once, Lucy felt a slight sympathy for Rob. She'd been in his shoes, and she knew they weren't very comfortable.

As Kenneally had suggested, the DA released the name of the accident victim that afternoon, by which time practically everyone in the county had heard the news and concluded it had to be Gabe McGourt. Lucy immediately attempted to contact his ex-wife and other family members, which always made her feel a bit like a ghoul. She knew, however, that people were most honest when grief was fresh and they were emotionally vulnerable, and often gave the most memorable and touching quotes then. She also believed that survivors appreciated the opportunity to memorialize their loved one—at least, that's what Ted always told her. "You're helping them process their grief, Lucy," was his usual rejoinder when Lucy complained about writing obituaries.

This time, however, the survivors weren't taking calls. She called again and again, but the ringing phones were never answered, and the voice mails were not returned. When Ted asked how she was getting on, and she admitted not at all, he sent her out to knock on their doors. But even then, the doors remained shut, and the shades were drawn at McGourt's mother's and ex-wife's homes. In fact, both houses seemed deserted, as if the occupants had left town.

With deadline fast approaching, they had no option except to run the official laudatory announcement released by the sheriff, which cited McGourt's education, numerous citations for superior achievement in his work as a corrections officer, and complimentary quotes from his coworkers. The copy included a quote from the sheriff himself: "Gabe will be greatly missed by all of us in the department, for both his excellent work ethic and his unfailing kindness and generosity to everyone he worked with, inmates as well as colleagues." It ended with a notation that funeral plans would be announced shortly.

Ted wasn't happy about the situation and made it clear in an introduction that the obituary had been provided by the sheriff's department, and that while *The Courier* had made every effort to contact family members, those efforts had met with no response. "This is weird," he said, finalizing the story and sending it to the print shop. "I've never encountered anything like this before."

"It's the sheriff," said Rob. "You only get what he wants you to get."

"Maybe the family just wanted privacy," said Lucy. "It's possible."

"I don't think so," said Ted. "I'm beginning to think Rob is right, and that's why the *Gabber* never had anything except puff pieces about the sheriff and the county government."

"Well, it's up to us to change that," said Lucy. "We just have to follow the news and see where the stories take us. Go after the truth."

"You're right, Lucy," said Ted. "But be careful."

"Yeah," advised Rob. "Watch your back. Whatever you do, don't break any traffic regulations. Speeding, going through a stop sign, you could end up getting seriously harassed."

Ted's and Rob's words of caution haunted her on Thursday afternoon. That morning, Rachel, who had directed several little-theater amateur productions, had told her that rehearsals for the festival talent show were already beginning and had invited her to stop by to interview some of the participants. She didn't really think she'd end up in jail for running a stop sign, but then she remembered her flat tire on the lonesome road through the woods and began to think Rob might have a point, and she drove very carefully and mindfully as she made her way to the Community Church.

A busy scene greeted her when she stepped inside the church basement. Tables had been set up, where volunteers were busy making posters and costumes; others were working in the kitchen area, probably baking Irish soda bread, if Lucy could trust her nose to identify the buttery scent that was filling the hall. Performers were taking turns rehearsing on the stage, coached by Rachel.

"Hi, Lucy," Rachel smiled, greeting her warmly with a hug and air kisses. "This festival is going to be great. Just listen to this." She called out Sam Parris's name, and a young black man who had been waiting in the wings took the stage. "Sam, this is Lucy Stone from the *Pennysaver*; she's covering the rehearsal for the paper. Would you mind giving her a preview?"

"I'd love to," said Sam, with a big smile. He straightened his back, took a deep breath, and began singing an old Irish folk tune in the clearest, most beautiful tenor voice Lucy had ever heard.

"Can you believe it?" murmured Rachel, a blissful expression on her face. "Pitch perfect. And that tone . . ."

"Amazing," said Lucy, enjoying the song too much to remember to take a photo. It ended much too soon, Sam got a smattering of applause from the others, and she belatedly grabbed her phone. "Can I take your picture?" she asked.

"With Rachel, too?" Sam asked.

"Of course."

Rachel quickly grabbed two green cardboard leprechaun hats, which they slapped on their heads. Then they stood together, arms around each other, smiling broadly for the photo. Checking the image of the white woman and the black man, which neatly illustrated the inclusiveness of the festival, Lucy was delighted. She also suspected that Rachel had purposely chosen Sam for the photo to make that very point, which was further emphasized by the leprechaun hats. "Those hats were just what the photo needed," she said. "Good work."

Rachel announced a ten-minute break for the performers and sat down with Lucy, where she enthusiastically listed the various acts and Lucy jotted them down. "I cannot believe there is so much untapped talent, but people have been coming out of the woodwork, eager to strut their stuff. Sam is extraordinary, but he's not the only one." She smiled mischievously. "What about you, Lucy? Perhaps you could write a poem, or read one?"

"No way," she said, laughing at the idea.

"Well, what about one of your news stories? That account of the ropewalk fire, for instance. A bit of local history . . ."

Lucy was adamant. "I don't think so. But maybe Zoe and Sara could perform an Irish dance. They actually took classes from Eileen Clancy a few years ago, and every once in a while, they do a jig around the house. It's kind of funny, actually; they've added their own bits."

"Oh, that sounds perfect for the festival," enthused Rachel. "Do you think they'll do it?"

"I'll ask. I bet they'd get a kick out of it, pun intended!"

Rachel groaned. "Back to work for me," she said, getting up. "Check out the crafts people," she advised. "They're doing some interesting stuff. And there's going to be food, too. Irish stew and soda bread, corned beef sandwiches, fish and chips—even beer, if they can get a temporary license."

Lucy had her doubts about the temporary license, but didn't say anything. She knew the licenses were granted by the town's board of selectmen, but needed approval from the chief of police. The chief, Jim Kirwan, was known as a team player; he made a point of mentioning the cooperation his department received from the sheriff at every press conference. He was unlikely to oppose Murphy if he voiced an objection to the temporary license. Time would tell, but Lucy suspected the sheriff would do everything he could to pose hurdles for the festival planners.

Leaving Rachel to continue the rehearsals, Lucy briefly interviewed several volunteers who were making banners and posters, along with a jewelry maker known for his claddagh rings and Celtic crosses, a potter who was offering teapots and mugs glazed in a beautiful green color, and a knitter who made pot holders and baby clothes featuring intricate patterns adapted from traditional fishermen's sweaters. Spotting Rosie, who was just arriving with a banshee head on a pole, she went to greet her.

"Hi, Rosie. Who's your scary friend?"

"If you think he's scary now, wait 'til he gets his fluttery, ragged clothing. Pretty spooky, if I say so myself," she said, with a gleeful cackle. "Especially after dark, when I light him up."

"I guess he'll be in the noise parade, after dark?" asked Lucy, referring to the proposed schedule of events.

"Along with a bunch of his buddies: St. Patrick with snakes, Mother Jones, a couple of leprechauns, and a lot more screaming banshees."

"There'll be sound effects?" asked Lucy.

Rosie gave her a look. "It's a noise parade, right? Everybody makes noise however they can, pot lids, drums, kazoos."

"You've got me there," admitted Lucy. "But it seems this is more like Halloween than St. Patrick's Day."

"Ah, who do you think invented Halloween? I'll bet it was the Irish!"

"That's a bet I'm not taking," said Lucy, laughing. "But while I've got you, I was wondering if you know of any connection between Rob and Gabe McGourt? The cops were in the office questioning him . . ."

"About Gabe?" demanded Rosie, shocked to her core. "Like they think he had something to do with the crash?"

"They were certainly implying he had some sort of disagreement, some issue with Gabe, but Rob insisted he was only doing his job, investigating a sexual harassment accusation that he suspected was hushed up and might be worth a story."

"Is that what he told the cops?" asked Rosie, sounding dismayed.

"Yup." Lucy leaned in. "Isn't that right? Is there something more?"

Rosie grabbed one of the gray steel folding chairs that were scattered around the room and sat down, removing the pole and dropping it on the floor with a clatter and holding the banshee head in her lap. Lucy found the odd juxtaposition of a beautiful young woman holding a disembodied head slightly disturbing; it reminded her a bit of paintings she'd seen of Salome holding the head of John the Baptist. But Rosie wasn't wicked, she reminded herself; she wasn't a bit like Salome.

"I wish he'd told the truth," said Rosie, absentmindedly stroking the papier-mâché head. "Rob and I have become friends . . ."

Lucy interrupted. "Just friends?"

Rosie shrugged. "Right now we're just friends; we're both new here, we're outsiders. It's only natural that we'd be drawn to each other. We're both artists, I don't know if you know, but Rob is working on a novel . . ."

As is every young journalist, thought Lucy to herself.

". . . and I have the puppets. And I do some paintings. Rob and I have similar dreams." She paused. "Anyway, I told him I'd been having trouble with Gabe McGourt. He kept calling me, pestering me to go out with him, but I al-

ways came up with some excuse to say no. I was ac-
quainted with him. I'd chatted with him a couple of times,
but I didn't really like him. There's no night life in this
town except at the roadhouse. I tried going there a couple
of times, but as soon as I walked in the door, he'd be all
over me."

Lucy didn't like the sound of this. "Like physically?"

"He didn't grab me or anything, but he stuck with me,
wouldn't let me talk to anybody else. So I stopped going
for a while, but a couple of weeks ago, I thought I'd give it
another try. I thought he might have given up, you know?
And that's the night I met Rob, and we were talking and
having a good time when Gabe showed up. He immediately came over and tried to join us, but Rob told him to
get lost. That didn't go over very well, and Gabe was getting sort of aggressive, but Rob and I got out of there before it turned into a fight."

"I suppose quite a few people witnessed this scene?"

"I'd say most of the twenty- and thirty-something pop-
ulation of the town." She let out a big breath. "That's why
I wish he'd told the truth."

"I wouldn't worry too much," said Lucy. "Some words
in a bar hardly make for a motive."

"But there might have been more, I don't know. What I
do know is that Gabe could be real obnoxious, and he
might have kept after Rob." She picked up the banshee
head and stood up. "I've got to get his thing dressed; some
high school girls are coming by after school to help me finish up the banshees, and I want to have a finished one to
show them."

"Thanks for telling me all this," said Lucy, also rising
from her chair. "Maybe I can convince Rob to revise his
statement. I know one of the state police detectives pretty
well, and I think he'd understand."

"That's a good idea, Lucy. I hope he decides to tell the truth before the cops find out for themselves." She bit her lip. "Rob's a good guy. He would never intentionally hurt someone, and I can't believe he would ever do something as nasty as sabotaging someone's truck."

Lucy was stunned. "Do you think that's what happened? That somebody intended for Gabe to die?"

"It wouldn't surprise me," admitted Rosie. "And if the cops are asking questions, I'd guess they think that's what happened."

Lucy didn't want to go there. "I know how they work," she insisted. "I think they're just doing due diligence so they can close the case."

Rosie was bent over, taking an old sheet out of the large tote bag she'd brought with her. "I hope you're right," she said, cutting through the hem with a pair of scissors she'd also brought. Then she took hold of the sheet on either side of the cut and pulled, making a ripping sound.

Lucy left her to her work, reducing the sheet to long strips of white cloth, and began making her way slowly through the big hall, exchanging smiles and greetings with the people she knew, which was most everyone. She was chatting with Pam Stillings, her friend and her boss, Ted's, wife, when she noticed the county health agent, Terry McLaren, coming through the door. "Oh, gosh," said Pam. "Here comes trouble, and since I'm the only outreach committee member here, I'm afraid I'm the one who has to deal with it."

Pam hurried to greet Terry, who was a middle-aged woman with very short gray hair. She was wearing a bright blue windbreaker issued by the county, which had her name and job embroidered over her left breast. On the back, HEALTH AGENT was written in big block letters.

As Lucy watched, Pam shook hands with Terry, and the

two made their way to the kitchen area. Lucy decided to follow, wondering what was going on, and watched as Pam showed Terry the permit for food service that was tacked to a bulletin board.

"That's for the church," said Terry, pointing to the line where the permit holder was identified.

"Well, this is the very same church," said Pam.

"I know, but the church isn't sponsoring the festival; that's a separate group."

"The vestry voted to accommodate the festival," said Pam, "so I guess we're sponsors."

"No." Terry shook her head and opened a plastic folder, producing a printed sheet of regulations and giving it to Pam. "The church is only providing the venue; the festival is actually sponsored by the Gilead Community Action Committee, and that group needs to apply for a food-service permit, which they have failed to do." She glanced at the small group of bakers who had gathered at the opposite end of the kitchen island. "I may have to shut this down."

"Oh, please, no," said Lydia Volpe, known far and wide for her pizzelle cookies, which were always the first to be snapped up at any bake sale. "We've all worked so hard."

"Wouldn't you like some raffle tickets?" offered one of the volunteers, displaying a roll of numbered tickets and pulling off a long strip. "They're going to be five for two dollars, but these will be complimentary for you," she said, in a misguided attempt at bribing a public official.

"Uh, no, thank you," said Terry, in an affronted manner. "I'll give the GCAC twenty-four hours to get the food-service permit. No permit, no food service. Understand?"

"Yes." Pam nodded. "I'll call Brendan right away, I'm sure he'll get right on it."

"Good." Terry looked around the room. "So the festival is going to take place here, in this hall?"

"Not the entire festival," explained Pam. "Mostly we're using it for prep. A lot of the festival events will take place outside: the noise parade, musical performances, fireworks, things like that."

Terry pounced, reminding Lucy of a cat going after a mouse. "Fireworks?"

Pam knew she was in trouble. "I believe I heard something about fireworks." Like the mouse, she tried to evade the cat. "But I'm not sure."

Terry licked her lips. "If there are fireworks, the GCAC will need a special permit from the county fire marshal."

"I'll be sure to pass that information along to Brendan," said Pam, sensing the possibility of escape.

Terry bared her pointy teeth in something like a smile. "Unfortunately, permits for fireworks require an appointment with the fire marshal, and I'm afraid he's booked solid for the next few weeks." She again opened the plastic folder and produced yet another sheet of regulations, then shut the stiff folder with a snap. "Have a nice day," she said, then turned and marched off toward the door.

"My goodness," fumed Lydia. "That was quite a performance."

"Well," offered Lucy, "if you ever wondered what county government actually does, now we know."

"They're just a bunch of party poopers," exclaimed Pam, grabbing her phone and calling Brendan.

Rachel, who'd been observing the scene, joined the group of distressed women. "What's going on?" she asked.

Lucy explained the situation while Pam left a message for Brendan to call her immediately.

Rachel was immediately suspicious of the health agent's

motives. "This all sounds pretty fishy to me. I bet the sheriff made her do it."

"I think so, too, but what can we do?" asked Pam.

"I'm not sure, but there must be something," insisted Rachel. "I'll call Bob and ask him to look into it. Maybe it's harassment, or a civil rights violation."

Lucy had a high regard for Rachel's husband, Bob Goodman, who was a lawyer, but she doubted there was anything he could do. She suspected the sheriff was a master at manipulating the town's various rules and regulations for his own advantage, sometimes overlooking the fine points of the law and deciding at other times to enforce them. Sometimes, as when he informed Rosie she'd missed the deadline for applying to march in the parade, he made them up. That was how he maintained his power, and she was convinced he'd go to any lengths to keep it.

# Chapter Twelve

Lucy was thinking about the sheriff as she drove home, and trying to come up with a way to expose and break his hold on the county, when she got a call on her cell from Edna. Her mother-in-law rarely phoned, so her first thought was that Edna must be in some sort of trouble. "Hi, what's up?" she asked, bracing herself for a crisis.

Edna was slow to answer, and when she did, she sounded unsure of herself. "Um, well, I—I thought I'd take you up on your invitation for a visit—if it's still good, that is."

Somewhat relieved, Lucy was quick to reply. "Of course, it's still good. We'd love to have you come, and stay for as long as you want."

"Well, I don't want to be a burden . . ."

"Don't be silly. We've got plenty of room, and it will be a pleasure to have you—the girls were saying the other day how much they love your blueberry muffins, and I've still got plenty of those blueberries we picked last summer in the freezer. When can you come?"

"I'm not sure. I've been talking to Kate, you see, and it depends on when she can make the trip."

Hearing this, Lucy had a feeling that this conversation would demand her entire attention, so she pulled off the road into the parking area by the hospital thrift shop, just outside of town. "Were you thinking that Kate would stay here, too?" she asked, unwilling to entertain an uninvited guest.

"Oh, no. I never thought of such a thing," insisted Edna. "Kate has some business she needs to attend to in Portland, and since she knows that you all live in Maine, she suggested it might be a good time for us all to finally get together as a family."

"Are you sure that's a good idea?" asked Lucy, not at all sure she was ready to play happy families with Catherine Klein.

"Well, yes, Lucy. She's family, after all, and, wouldn't you know, I don't remember her at all from the funeral. I have no idea what she looks like." Her voice softened. "Does she resemble my Bill? You met her, didn't you? Did you think she looked like him?"

Lucy was floored. "You know, Edna, that was the farthest thing from my mind. She's nice enough looking, but I can't say I saw any family resemblance."

"Of course, you wouldn't have been looking for it, I suppose," said Edna, sounding disappointed. "Not unless the resemblance was very strong and striking."

"Well, it definitely wasn't," said Lucy, her suspicions about Kate Klein's motives growing. "Has this Kate been calling you a lot? Or emailing?"

"Oh, no. Not a lot. But she does check in with me every so often; she says she just wants to make sure that I'm doing okay." She paused. "I have to admit, I do enjoy talking with her. She always wants to know about my Bill—well, it's only natural since he's her father." Hearing Lucy's sharp intake of breath, Edna continued in a rather more assertive tone. "Well, I know that you and Bill aren't convinced; you think it's not definite or something. But they say DNA doesn't lie, and I have to say Kate is very interested in learning about her father, and I enjoy talking about him, sharing my memories."

Lucy knew the discomfort she was feeling was rooted in guilt. Why hadn't she and Bill been better about keeping in touch with Edna? They'd taken her at her word that she was doing fine and, relieved, had gone about their own business. They'd conveniently ignored the fact that she was really coping with terrible grief, and they should have been more caring and supportive. They'd left the door wide open for this Kate woman to insinuate herself with Edna, taking advantage of her loneliness and filling the enormous void left by her husband's death.

"We're looking forward to sharing those memories with you, too," said Lucy. "We have videos and photo albums, if it's not too soon . . ."

"I'd love to see them," said Edna. "And so would Kate."

*I'm sure she would*, thought Lucy, stifling the urge to bad-mouth Kate and focusing instead on the details of the visit. "Do you have any idea when you might come?"

"Now that I've spoken with you, I'll check with Kate, and we'll pick a date. How does that sound?"

"Absolutely fine," said Lucy, uncomfortably aware that Kate was now a force to be reckoned with and had a great deal of influence over Edna. "You're always welcome, you know." She paused. "By the way, have you found the missing will?" The devil seized her tongue, and she asked the question that had been lurking in the dark recesses of her mind. "Has Kate been asking you about it?"

"Oh, yes. She's been very helpful; she's offered a lot of ideas for places to look." Edna sighed. "I tell you, I've turned this house upside down, but I haven't found it. I'm afraid I'm going to have to do something pretty soon so I can access Bill's accounts, but I've been putting it off."

Lucy didn't like the sound of this at all, but didn't want to worry Edna. "We'll look here, too," said Lucy. "I'm sure it will turn up."

"That's what Kate says. She's convinced it will turn up," offered Edna. "I can't wait for us all to meet her."

"Me, too," said Lucy, hoping she didn't sound as insincere as she felt.

It was with some relief that she spotted Bill's truck in the driveway when she got home. He was in the kitchen, seated at the round golden-oak table and looking through the mail with a can of beer at hand.

"Oh, boy, we've got trouble" was Lucy's greeting, as she dropped her bag on the table by the door and went straight to the fridge to pour herself a glass of wine.

"Nice to see you, too," said Bill.

"I'm sorry, I shouldn't dump this on you the minute I walk through the door, but I'm so upset . . ."

He faced her, furrowing his brows in concern. "What's the matter?"

"It's your mom. She called to say she's coming for a visit." Lucy sat down and took a big swallow of chardonnay.

Bill was puzzled. "Is that a problem? It's never been a problem before."

"No, not her visit. I'm glad she's coming. But that Kate Klein woman is tagging along . . ."

Now Bill was alarmed. "Coming here?"

"Not to our house, but your mom is timing her trip to

coincide with this Klein woman's itinerary so we can all meet and get to know each other." Lucy was watching Bill closely to see his reaction, and so far, it didn't seem good. "She sounded as if she already believes that this Klein woman is really your dad's child, and . . . ?

Bill's face was stony. "And what?"

"And she's been helping your mother look for the missing will."

"Crap." He bit his lip and ran his finger around the rim of his beer. "She's really after money; she's working a con, and my mom is falling for it."

"I think so," said Lucy. She took another healthy swallow of wine. "Your mother said that DNA doesn't lie; she's really convinced that Kate is your father's child."

"Well, maybe that's true, about DNA. But people do lie, and I imagine a clever person could produce a pretty convincing and entirely fake Genious report. The question is, what do we do about it? Without the will, we're sunk."

"We have to discredit her, expose her."

"Easier said than done."

"And it'll kill mom, if she's really swallowed this woman's line."

"I know," agreed Lucy, staring at her glass and wondering why it was now nearly empty.

The weekend passed quickly, filled with the usual chores, which this week included clearing out the guest room and making it ready for Edna. The last occupant had been Lucy and Bill's grandson, Patrick, and Lucy had decorated it with superhero-themed linens for his visit. She wanted Edna to feel special, so she stripped away the superheros, including Bill's prized vintage Batman poster, and made the bed with rose-patterned sheets and coverlet. She re-

placed Batman with a framed Monet print and got busy
emptying the bookshelf and dresser drawers. As she
worked, she kept an eye out for anything remotely resem-
bling a will, on the off chance Bill Sr. had left it there during a visit, but there was nothing except the usual clutter
that tends to accumulate in any empty space. She lined the
dresser drawers with pretty floral wrapping paper and
filled the bookshelf with a selection of light reading: trav-
elogs, cozy mysteries, and historical fiction. She trans-
ferred the out-of-season clothes to other closets, and she
added a half-dozen padded hangers to the white plastic
ones that remained on the empty pole.

As she closed the door, she glanced across the hall to her
newly renovated master bedroom, which now included an
en suite bath, and smiled. It would be so much pleasanter
for everyone now that she and Bill had their own bath and
didn't have to compete with Edna and the girls for private
time in the old family bathroom.

By the time Monday morning rolled around, Lucy was
satisfied that everything was ready for Edna's visit, whenever she decided to come. She'd even placed an empty
water glass and vase on the nightstand, ready to be filled
when the time came, along with a couple of current maga-
zines.

She was thinking what else she might do—perhaps adding a small box of chocolates would be a nice touch, or a
tin of cookies, homemade cookies like lemon crisps—as
she fought the brisk March wind and arrived at the office.
The little bell on the door seemed to jingle-jangle quite
cheerily today, she thought, and she greeted Phyllis with a
bright smile.

"February's over," she declared, "and March is blowing
in like a lion."

Phyllis, however, did not react as expected. Instead of laughing at Lucy's nonsense, she frowned and shook her head. Her hair, Lucy noticed, was dyed green in honor of St. Patrick's Day. "Not a good morning."

Lucy was immediately concerned, noticing Phyllis's weepy eyes and trembling lips, and feared something terrible must have happened to Phyllis's husband, Wilf, or some other member of her family. Maybe her niece, Elfrida, or one of her kids. "What happened?"

"Cops were here and arrested Rob."

"Rob? Oh, no." She had a very bad feeling about this news, remembering Rosie's fears that Rob hadn't been truthful when he was questioned. "When was this? And why? Did they say why?"

"Just a few minutes ago; you just missed them." Phyllis sniffed and bit her lip. "They're accusing him of murdering Gabe McGourt."

Murder, thought Lucy, swallowing hard. This was a lot worse than obstructing an investigation by lying to the police.

"What was it like? Did they have guns drawn? Were you scared?"

"Nothing like that. It was Detective Horowitz and a couple of state troopers. They were real polite, told him the charges, and read him his rights. Rob seemed stunned, but he didn't protest. He let them cuff him, and he walked out." She sniffed again and pointed to the rolltop desk. "Oh, and they took his laptop."

For evidence, thought Lucy. They'd want to go through his emails, as well as his notes and the stories he was working on. "Does Ted know?" she asked.

"Not yet. I should've called him, but I've been sitting here in shock." Phyllis did look pale—the green hair defi-

nitely wasn't helping—and she also seemed smaller somehow. Her boldly colorful striped sweater and matching
reading glasses were in sharp contrast to her shaky, fragile
state.

Lucy sat right down at her desk, without bothering to
shed her jacket, and called Ted, only to get his voice mail.
Wouldn't you think the man would have call forwarding,
she thought, slamming the phone down. She really wanted
to talk to him, to hear his voice, but settled instead for a
quick text. Operating on automatic, her next call was to
the DA.

"Didn't take you long, Lucy," commented Phil Aucoin,
by way of greeting.

"What's going on?" demanded Lucy. "Are you really
charging Rob Callahan with murdering Gabe McGourt?"

"You know me, Lucy. I follow the evidence, and that's
where the evidence led—right to his door, so to speak."

"Look, I know he wasn't entirely truthful about that
spat at the roadhouse . . ."

"It was a little more than a spat, I'm afraid. A few
punches were thrown . . ."

"He told me there was no fight. They just had words."

"Well, I've got about five witnesses who say otherwise."

"And you believe them?"

"Why would they lie? These are solid citizens; they
don't even know Callahan, so I don't think they have any
grudges against him. They have no reason to lie."

"They could be pressured to lie by someone who wants
to frame Callahan." Like maybe assistant DA Kevin Kenneally, but she kept that thought to herself.

"Lucy, that's a terrible accusation to make against
public-spirited witnesses who were brave enough to come
forward and say what they saw. If you only knew how

hard it can be to get people to speak up in these situations. I have to tell you, it was quite heartening to me that they were willing to open up and relive what must have been a rather frightening situation."

"Okay, but it's still only hearsay . . ."

"Nope. We've got video showing Callahan near McGourt's truck."

Lucy's heart sank. "You have video of him actually tampering with the truck?"

"Well, not exactly, but we've got him in the right place at the right time."

"But it's crazy. He had no reason to kill McGourt."

Aucoin chuckled. "It's a tale as old as time, Lucy. They were rivals for Rosie Capshaw's affection."

"Again, that's not true. I've spoken to Rosie, and she insists she and Rob are just friends."

"Which bolsters my case, Lucy. He was in love with her, she wasn't reciprocating, and there was this other guy after her, too. Rob Callahan wanted to eliminate the competition and make sure he was Rosie's one and only."

"I don't buy it," said Lucy, "and neither will the jury."

"Well, we'll see, won't we," said Aucoin, putting an end to the discussion. "There's something I'd like you to do for me—well, it's really for Gabe's kids."

"I didn't know he had kids."

"Yup. Two boys, nine and six years old. He was devoted to them, made sure they got to Little League practice and karate and all that. He had joint custody with his ex, and nothing made him happier than having the boys for the weekend and taking them camping. He was well liked by his colleagues, you know, and they're holding a 5K race to raise money for the kids. I can fax over the details for you so you can write it up for the paper."

"Fine," agreed Lucy. "Any word on the funeral arrangements?"

"Next weekend, I believe. It takes a bit of time to organize these things. Gabe's fellow officers from all over the country will want to honor him. I've heard that a contingent from the California prison system is coming, along with several others from the West and Midwest."

Lucy was incredulous "All the way from California?"

"Yeah. In the last few years, there's been a real coming together of the law-enforcement community. When one of us falls, well, it's as if we've lost a member of the family, a brother."

"Or sister?"

Aucoin was quick to agree. "Right. Or sister." He paused. "And we all come together to grieve and support each other. There will be a big presence at the wake and the funeral, and, of course, a solemn motorcade to escort Corrections Officer Gabe McGourt to his final resting place."

"Any idea how many officers will be coming?"

"Oh, hundreds, easily. Maybe more."

"And the family is organizing all this?"

"Oh, no. It's Sheriff Murphy. He's in charge of it all, but with the family's blessing." He paused. "It's really for Gabe's boys, you know. So they will always remember their dad as the hero he was."

Lucy was about to choke, thinking this was really a stretch, and her thoughts returned to Rob. It seemed to her that it was going to be very hard for him to get a fair trial after the sheriff was done lionizing the victim. "What bail are you recommending?" she asked, figuring it would be high.

"No bail."

"Why? Rob doesn't have a record, he's employed, he's a good citizen . . ."

"He's new to the area, and he's a flight risk."

"Are you kidding me?"

"No. I'm serious. I'm recommending no bail, and I'm confident the judge will agree with me."

Lucy didn't like this at all; it seemed that Rob was not being treated fairly and that his rights were being violated. She'd always liked and trusted Phil Aucoin, considering him a fair and decent prosecutor, and she was saddened and puzzled by this behavior. It wasn't like him to pre-judge a case, and she suspected he was bending to the will of the sheriff.

"I hope the judge sees things differently," said Lucy.

"I wouldn't count on it, Lucy; this is a murder charge, after all," he replied, and Lucy thought there was a hint of cynicism in his tone. "Look, I've got another call . . ."

"Thanks for your time," she said, ending the call.

This was inconceivable, she thought, sitting at her desk in a state of shock. She'd always believed the justice system was fair, although she'd heard disturbing reports about private prisons and innocent people being framed and sent to death row, but those things didn't happen in Maine. At least, that's what she'd thought, until now. Her phone rang, and she grabbed it, relieved to hear Ted's voice.

"Where's Rob?" he demanded, in an angry voice. "I heard there's been an arrest in the McGourt case, and I want him to cover it, but he's not answering texts, phone, anything."

"Uh, he's the one; they arrested him."

"What?" Ted's voice was so loud that it filled the office, reaching even Phyllis without the benefit of speaker phone.

"I wasn't here, but Phyllis can tell you all about it. Horowitz and two troopers arrested him here at the office first thing this morning."

"It was just after eight," said Phyllis, activating the speaker feature.

"Where is he now?" demanded Ted.

"In custody, probably at the county jail," said Lucy. "Aucoin says no bail."

Ted was incredulous. "No bail?"

"Rob's not local, so he's considered a flight risk."

"This stinks."

"You said it." Lucy sighed. "What can we do?"

"The TRUTH Project has a legal defense team, but I never dreamed we'd need it. This is so outrageous . . ."

"Unless it's not," said Phyllis, in a quiet little voice.

Lucy turned her head and gave her a sharp look. From the phone, Ted roared, "What do you mean?"

"I mean, maybe he did do it. Maybe he's guilty."

There was a long silence as they considered the possibility. Then Ted spoke. "I'm calling the TRUTH Project folks right away."

"Good idea," said Lucy. She wanted to believe with her whole heart that Rob was innocent, but maybe he wasn't. Maybe he really was consumed by jealousy and tampered with Gabe McGourt's truck, sending him to a fiery death.

# Chapter Thirteen

The rest of the day passed in a blur as the depleted staff struggled to compensate for Rob's absence. Ted put Pete Popper in charge over at the *Gabber* office and took over the big story—Rob's arrest and the charges against him—squeezing in interviews and pounding out a paragraph or two between numerous, lengthy conference calls with the TRUTH Project's legal team. Lucy was given the job of writing up Rob's biography, based largely on his résumé, and also got stuck completing his unfinished school budget story. She found it difficult to concentrate on the tasks at hand, however, as she struggled to reconcile the Rob she knew, who she had to admit was rather conceited and even obnoxious, with the allegations against him. Maybe he wasn't her favorite person, but she would never have believed he was capable of murder. And the delightful Rosie Capshaw liked him, which Lucy found somewhat surprising but had to admit was a point in Rob's favor.

When she finally hit the SEND button on her last story, she was mentally and physically exhausted. "I'm done," she announced, pushing back her chair and grabbing her bag.

"Thanks, Lucy," said Ted, who was hunched over his keyboard. "Try to get some rest. Tomorrow's going to be a big day."

She knew he was referring to the arraignment, which was going to attract media from the entire region, maybe even the national networks. No doubt, white satellite trucks would surround the courthouse, and reporters would be attempting to interview anyone who was breathing.

"Do you have a plan?" asked Phyllis.

"I'm gonna be first in line at the courthouse; that's all I can do. I don't think I can expect any special treatment, not in this case."

"No. You'll be public enemy number two, right after Rob," said Lucy.

"Yup. Keep your phone on. I may need you."

"Will do," said Lucy, who was shrugging into her jacket.

"And, Phyllis, I don't need to tell you that you should firmly discourage any requests from the competing media. Don't give out any information, and don't let them in the door, not even to use the bathroom."

Phyllis chuckled. "You can count on me, boss."

"Well, I'm off," said Lucy, pausing to give Ted a pat on the shoulder. "Take your own advice: get some rest." She sighed. "Remember the immortal advice of Doris Day: 'Que sera, sera.'"

Ted looked up at her. "I gotta say, I was not prepared for this. This came out of left field."

"Look on the bright side," offered Phyllis. "You've got the inside scoop on a really big story."

"Yeah," admitted Ted. "So why does it feel so rotten?"

That was the word for it, thought Lucy, as she drove home. *Rotten.* This whole situation was rotten, no matter how you looked at it. It was rotten if Rob was actually guilty, if they'd been working alongside a cold-blooded killer, sharing coffee mugs and advice and trying to develop cordial working relationships. On the other hand, it was even more rotten if Rob was being set up by the sheriff in an attempt to cover up the truth—a truth, Lucy realized, that must involve others in the department. A conspiracy to protect the sheriff's power and those who were privileged to share it.

Just thinking about it had given her a headache, she decided, as she turned into her driveway. What she needed was a couple of painkillers and a cool washcloth on her forehead in a quiet, dark room. After that, she'd deal with dinner and whatever issues the girls were having. But first, twenty minutes of peace. That's all she asked, twenty minutes to concentrate on absolutely nothing but breathing in and out, in and out.

As soon as she opened the door, she realized it was not to be. Zoe was standing in the middle of the kitchen, waving a piece of paper, and Sara was beside her, clearly upset.

Lucy really didn't want to know, but she had to ask. "What's going on?"

"We got a cease-and-desist order from some lawyer," exclaimed Zoe.

"Cease and desist?" Lucy was puzzled. "What exactly are you supposed to cease and desist doing? Going to college? Driving? Wearing lipstick?"

"Dancing! We're supposed to stop dancing," explained Sara.

"Yeah. The letter is on behalf of Eileen Clancy, who claims that we're making unauthorized use of copyrighted dance choreography, which we intend to present in a—get this—'so-called multi-ethnic, all-Inclusive Irish Festival.' "

Lucy took the letter, then, on second thought, put it down on the kitchen table and poured herself a glass of chardonnay. She gulped down half the contents of the glass, then sat down to read the letter. "Is this true? Are you using her choreography?"

"Not really," said Zoe, seating herself at the table. "We did take a couple of classes from her, years ago, but didn't like it."

"That's when we started riffing on it; you know, we'd do a couple of the traditional steps, and then we'd start goofing around," said Sara, who was leaning her hips against the counter.

"It's only a minute or so of the traditional steps, since we only know two or three moves, just beginner stuff. I wouldn't call it choreographed. It's like a singer doing scales to warm up, that's all. Then we start throwing in our own stuff, modern jazz, hip-hop; it's kind of a mix."

"But we wear those really stiff skirts and the clunky shoes; everybody who's seen us rehearse absolutely loves it."

"It's really clever, and funny, if I say so myself," admitted Zoe.

"I'm sure it is; that's probably the problem," said Lucy, draining the glass and getting up to refill it, noticing that the level in the bottle had been dropping fast lately. "I wonder how she even knows about it."

"She must have spies," said Sara. "Undercover operatives at the festival rehearsals."

Lucy felt the hairs on the back of her neck rise, and it wasn't from the chill air emitted by the refrigerator. "You're right," she said, unscrewing the bottle cap. "The sheriff and the Hibernian Knights are doing everything they can to wreck the festival. They want to make sure their parade is the only show in the county." She filled her glass and replaced the bottle in the fridge. "They'll stop at nothing," she concluded, sitting down with her untouched wine.

"So what should we do?" asked Zoe. "Drop out of the show?"

"No way!" protested Sara.

Lucy took a sip of wine. "I don't see how she can stop you," she said, speaking slowly. "Not if what you say is true. I think basic dance steps must be like book titles. I don't see how any one person can copyright them. You can't copyright first position, or whatever the step-dance equivalent is, or nobody'd ever be able to dance a ballet."

"That's a really good point, Mom," said Sara.

"I'll check with Bob Goodman, see what he says."

"And I'll show our tape to the dance professor at Winchester; maybe she'll write a letter or something for us," said Zoe.

"That's a good idea, too," said Lucy, realizing she was now pain-free. Who knew chardonnay could cure headaches? "Any ideas about supper?"

The next morning, Lucy stopped by attorney Bob Goodman's office on her way to work to show him the cease-and-desist letter and get his advice. She knew he liked to get to the office early, before court went into session.

"Ignore it," said Bob, handing it back to her. "Throw it in the trash. It's not worth the paper it's written on."

"Why did Eileen Clancy bother with it then?" she asked.

"Intimidation, pure and simple. A lot of people get an official-looking letter from an attorney and get scared." He furrowed his brow. "I never heard of this outfit, Smith, Smith, and Jones, and I've been practicing for a long time. For all we know, she made the whole thing up."

"Do people do that?"

He grinned. "Oh, yeah. I tell you, Microsoft Word has a lot to answer for, giving people all those fancy fonts. Nowadays, anybody with a printer and some résumé paper can produce a good facsimile of almost any legal document."

"Or a DNA report?" asked Lucy.

He nodded. "You bet."

"Well, thanks," she said, folding the letter and putting it back in her bag. Stepping outside, she noticed a woman was exiting the adjacent law office, which was occupied by Linda Sparrow, who concentrated on family law. Since the two offices shared a walkway, she smiled a polite greeting at the woman, whom she recognized from the wedding photo in the *Pennysaver's* photo file as Gabe Mc-Gourt's ex-wife, Rosemary McGourt. She had a head of unruly, bleached-blond curls and had stuffed her excess poundage into a pair of tight workout pants.

"Hi!" exclaimed Lucy, "You're just the person I've been looking for."

Rosemary ducked her head and began walking faster, forcing Lucy to trot after her. "Honest, this will only take a minute. I'm Lucy Stone . . ."

"I know who you are," muttered Rosemary out of the side of her mouth, not missing a step.

"Well, I just want to say I'm really sorry for your loss," she began, feeling her way, in hopes of getting Rosemary's reaction to the elaborate funeral plans. "I know that Sheriff Murphy is planning an official departmental funeral, and I could use some information . . ."

Rosemary stopped suddenly, and Lucy narrowly avoided crashing into her. "Believe me, I don't have anything to say about that bastard or the sheriff's dog-and-

pony show that's fit to print—and that's off the record."
Then she was off again, marching down the sidewalk toward Jake's Donut Shack.

"Maybe we could have a little chat over a cup of coffee . . ." suggested Lucy, trotting alongside her. "I know I
could use one."

"Thanks, but no thanks." Rosemary didn't make eye
contact. "Go talk to his mother; she's the one who thinks
her darling boyo could do no wrong. I'd bet she'd love to
talk about him—and boy, does she love bagpipe music and
men in uniform."

"Okay," said Lucy, who was becoming breathless from
the effort of keeping up with Rosemary, who was surprisingly quick for such a large woman. "Thanks for the tip."

Rosemary snorted. "Don't bother to thank me. I warn
you, that woman is a piece of work." Then she hopped up
the steps to Jake's and yanked open the door, disappearing
inside.

Lucy considered following her, but decided against it.
She'd given it her best effort, but Rosemary didn't want to
talk. She remembered how she'd been unavailable immediately following Gabe's death and wondered if she was
under some sort of mandate from the sheriff to avoid the
media. If so, it seemed likely that Gabe's mother would
also be off-limits, but she figured it was worth a try.

Back in the car, she consulted an old printed telephone
book, which she'd found was the quickest way to locate
people who'd been living in the county before everybody
got cell phones and the phone company stopped issuing
the directories. Sure enough, there were a number of Mc-
Gourts, but M. C. seemed the likeliest, as she knew
women who lived alone often listed themselves with only

their initials. She suspected M.C. stood for Mary Catherine, which was a popular name among Irish-Catholics in Gabe's mother's generation. The address wasn't far, about ten minutes away, and it was still early, so she decided to take a chance and drop in unannounced.

The house, as she expected, was as neat as a pin. A white picket fence enclosed a neat patch of brown lawn, and a clump of snowdrops was blooming next to the doorstep. The front door had been freshly painted, and spotless white curtains hung in the windows, which appeared to have been newly washed; Mary Catherine apparently believed in getting her spring cleaning done early. As she prepared to ring the bell, it occurred to Lucy that she didn't do any spring cleaning last year and probably wouldn't this year, either, considering the way things were going. Come to think of it, as she pressed the doorbell button, she doubted anybody under the age of sixty bothered with such a thing anymore.

There was no immediate answer to the ring, and Lucy hesitated to ring a second time. She knew Mary Catherine might well be coping with arthritis or other issues of aging, as well as grief, and decided to wait a bit to give her time to get to the door. Sure enough, just as she was about to leave, the door opened, revealing a tiny woman with snowy-white hair and bright blue eyes. "Good day to you," she said, with an expectant expression. "How can I help you?"

Lucy hadn't really expected such a pleasant greeting and stammered a bit, identifying herself.

"From the paper? My goodness. It must be about my poor boy. Well, why don't you come in, and I'll tell you all about him."

"That's very kind of you," said Lucy, entering the hall-way, where she was immediately confronted with a large crucifix, with a dried palm leaf tucked behind it, that hung on the wall.

"Let's go into the parlor," invited Mary Catherine, lead-ing the way into a rather modestly sized front room that was comfortably furnished with a small sofa, a coffee table, and a corduroy-covered recliner. The sofa and re-cliner were lavishly provided with scatter pillows, and plates picturing JFK and Jackie hung on one wall; a photo of Pope John Paul II beamed at them approvingly from the opposite wall.

"Do sit down," invited Mary Catherine. "Can I get you a cup of tea?"

"Oh, no, thank you. I only want a few moments of your time," said Lucy, smiling and producing her notebook. "I know this is a difficult time for you, and I am so very sorry for your loss."

"Thank you." The old woman paused for a moment, gazing at a small statue of the Virgin Mary that stood on a side table. "It's times like this when a strong faith is such a support. As much as I miss my boy, I know he's in a better place, up there with his father and little brother, Michael. They're waiting for me, and soon, I hope, the good Lord willing, I'll be joining them."

Lucy nodded along, amazed at this woman's sincere conviction, which she couldn't quite share. "What can you tell me about your son, about Gabe?"

"Well, he was a dear boy. We named him after an angel, you know, and it was a prophetic choice, because he never got in trouble, never gave us a moment's worry or con-cern. He was a wonderful father, he loved his kids, and it's really too bad about the divorce, but I wouldn't want to say a bad word about Rosemary. He did marry out of the faith, but that doesn't really matter because in the eyes of the Lord they're still married, even if Rosemary doesn't think so."

"Did they have joint custody of the boys?" asked Lucy. "Did he spend a lot of time with them?"

"Oh, yes. And he'd bring them here, and I'd make sure I had some of their favorite cookies and videos. They loved sleeping over"—she paused, eyes twinkling naughtily, and added—"because I'd let them stay up a bit late."

"I suppose he played ball with them, took them to the playground?"

"Oh, yes. But, of course, he often had to work weekends or nights, and what with the alimony and child support, he could only afford a small studio apartment, so it was better if the boys came here with me. It was like reliving the days when I had my own boys, and I was always cooking and caring for them." She picked up a framed photograph from a side table that pictured a small boy in a white suit. "This is Justin at his First Communion. Doesn't he just look so proud? That was a few years ago; now we're getting Johnny ready for his First Communion."

Lucy wondered if Rosemary, who she occasionally saw at the Protestant Community Church, approved of all this emphasis on Catholicism. Or maybe, she thought, she appreciated having some time to herself that she could spend at the gym.

"It's a rare young man who doesn't get involved in some scrape or other," began Lucy, probing gently for more information about Gabe.

"Well, it's a shame those boys lost their Daddy," replied

Mary Catherine, misunderstanding the question. She clucked her tongue. "They'll be just fine, though. Gabe had lots of friends, and they've promised to look out for his boys. Even the sheriff himself told me that he would be keeping an eye on them, making sure they stayed on the straight-and-narrow path."

"I'm sure that's a great comfort to you," said Lucy, wondering if Gabe's mother had truly misunderstood or simply wanted to change the subject. It seemed she would have to be more direct in her questioning. "After the divorce, was Gabe interested in dating? Was he seeing anyone in particular?"

"Not that I know of. Like I said, he only got divorced because Rosemary demanded it. He was a good Catholic and knew they were married for all eternity."

"Even so, he might have had some female friends," suggested Lucy. "I believe he was involved with a woman named Melanie?"

"That is nothing but a vile, nasty rumor," snapped Mary Catherine, her eyes blazing. She stood right up, quivering with rage. "I think . . . I've just remembered . . . I have to see the priest about the funeral. I can't be late; he'll be expecting me."

"Of course," said Lucy, closing her notebook and getting to her feet. "I certainly understand, and I am grateful for your time."

Mary Catherine's face was stony; she was clearly struggling to maintain a polite façade as she opened the front door. "Have a nice day now," she said, glaring, as she yanked open the door.

Must have touched a nerve, thought Lucy, making her way down the path to the front gate. Mary Catherine was certainly not going to admit that her son was anything less than an angel, no matter what the truth might be.

Her phone rang when she reached her car, and she answered as she slid behind the wheel. It was Ted, calling from the courthouse. "So how did it go?"

"Fast, very fast. Over before it started."

That didn't sound good. "So no bail?"

"No bail."

"Did they set a trial date?"

"Not yet. The legal team from the TRUTH Project barely made the arraignment; they arrived just as court went into session. They did get a date for a pre-trial conference."

Lucy started her car. "Was the media coverage crazy?"

"Not too bad, actually. Boston and Portland papers were there, and two Boston TV stations, but that was it. The story hasn't gone national yet."

"I bet the sheriff was disappointed . . ."

"Yeah." Ted chuckled. "There were actually more cops and deputies than reporters."

Lucy shifted into gear and pulled out into the road. "How did Rob look? Is he holding up?"

Ted didn't answer right away. "He looked kind of lost," he finally said. "I was surprised. I thought he was this big-shot investigative reporter, the sort of guy who's prepared to pay the price for challenging the powers that be." He sighed. "He looked really anxious until the lawyers arrived."

"That's just natural," suggested Lucy, zipping along the road. "It's one thing to get arrested for refusing to reveal your sources, and quite another to be accused of murder."

A couple of harsh squawks shattered the quiet, and she checked her rear-view mirror, spotting flashing blue lights. "Darn. Now it's my turn to be harassed." She immediately put on her turn signal and pulled off to the side of the road.

"Keep your hands visible and be polite," advised Ted, "and keep your phone on."

Lucy braked and waited, watching as the Gilead cop approached her car.

"Do you have any idea why I stopped you?" asked the officer, a middle-aged guy with an amused twinkle in his eye.

"No, officer," said Lucy, in a very little voice. She had her suspicions: she had been talking on her cell phone for one thing; speeding also came to mind, as she really hadn't been paying attention to the posted limit. And then there was always the potential for harassment when her job put her at odds with the police.

"Your inspection sticker is out of date," he said.

A quick glance at the sticker on her front windshield revealed that it was three months overdue. "It sure is," admitted Lucy. "I'll take care of it right away."

The officer tipped his hat. "Good. Make sure you do."

Lucy couldn't believe she wasn't going to get a ticket. "Can I go?" she asked.

"Yes. Have a nice day."

"You, too, officer," she replied. Letting out a sigh of relief, she watched him walk back to his cruiser. When he was safely inside, she flicked on her signal and pulled out onto the road.

"That was unexpected," came Ted's voice from the phone, which she'd forgotten about.

"Yeah," said Lucy. "See you in the office."

"After you get that car inspected," reminded Ted.

"Right, boss." She couldn't believe it had slipped her mind so soon. She was definitely dealing with too much stuff. "I'll go straight to the garage."

# Chapter Fourteen

Lucy had a surprisingly expensive new set of windshield wipers and a fresh bright inspection sticker on her car when she drove to the airport in Portland a few days later to pick up Edna; Bill was tied up presenting an application to replace a defunct gas station with a three-unit condo at a planning committee meeting. While she negotiated busy Route 1 and the confusing highways around the city, her thoughts turned to Mary Catherine, who seemed stuck in the past by refusing to acknowledge her son's shortcomings. These days, women no longer turned a blind eye to their menfolk's bad behavior, but instead called it out. Every day it seemed that another high-powered, successful man was accused of sexual assault and hauled into court to face the women he had abused. Women no longer cowered in dark corners, ashamed to speak up when they were abused, but bravely recounted episodes of mauling, unwanted sexual advances, and even rape. Rape, it turned out, was a lot more common than Lucy had realized, and it occurred in unlikely places, such as the dressing rooms of fancy department stores, business offices, and conference rooms.

But even though there had been a huge change in attitudes toward sexual aggression, it seemed that a deceived wife still had to pay a price for her husband's infidelity. Simply sending a perpetrator to jail didn't help the wife, who had to endure public embarrassment as well as financial hardship due to the loss of her husband's income. It was one thing if your wandering husband was a top executive earning millions, but quite another if he was a teacher or a store manager and you lived paycheck to paycheck. There was no protection for these women, who might very well have had no idea what their spouses were up to.

That was the situation for Edna, who was left with the unenviable task of cleaning up the mess her husband had bequeathed her by dying intestate, a situation complicated by the arrival of a possible heir. Lucy couldn't quite believe that Bill Sr. hadn't made arrangements to take care of Edna after his death, but then she couldn't believe he'd been unfaithful, either. The old fellow had apparently been full of surprises, and not good surprises. Finally reaching the airport and parking the car, Lucy made a silent vow to be present for Edna, to listen to her concerns, and to offer support. What she didn't want to do was to argue or be confrontational, which she knew she had a tendency to do when she didn't agree with someone. Unfortunately, she had a feeling that she wasn't going to like what Edna had to say about Kate Klein, but she was determined to keep her emotions in check. The last thing Edna needed at this time was an argument. Given unstinted love and support, Edna would hopefully come to the right conclusion on her own.

The flight was delayed, of course, and Edna was apologetic about her late arrival and became increasingly agitated as the baggage carousel went round and round with no sign of her suitcase. When it finally appeared, the very last bit of luggage coming through the flap after an anxiety-producing gap, she was almost in tears.

"There, there," cooed Lucy, giving her a hug. "No reason to get upset. Even if it was lost, we can get you everything you need. No problem at all. I'm just so glad you came."

"Oh, Lucy, that's so sweet of you." Edna blinked a few times. "Where's Bill? Why didn't he come?"

"He wanted to come, but he has an important meeting to get approval for a condo development he hopes to build." Lucy tried to soften the blow by saying, "He'll probably be waiting for us when we get home. I know he's eager to see you."

"I see," said Edna, in a rather cool tone. "I certainly don't want to be an inconvenience," she added, grabbing her suitcase away from Lucy. "That's the last thing I want. You should have let me take the bus; there was really no need for you to come all this way and wait around to meet me. I can manage perfectly well on my own, you know."

"I was happy to do it," said Lucy, beginning to feel that her effort to give Edna a warm welcome was rather unappreciated as they made their way out of the terminal. "You've come all the way from Florida; making you take the bus was out of the question."

"I could have rented a car, you know. Then you wouldn't have needed to pick me up."

"We have cars, four cars; you don't need to rent one. And it's my pleasure to meet you and make you comfortable." They were at the curb, and Edna was struggling with her roller suitcase as well as her purse and carry-on bag. "Let me take something," begged Lucy, who was embarrassed to be seen unencumbered alongside this over-burdened elderly woman.

"Well, if you insist, you can take the carry-on," said Edna, handing over a brightly colored, quilted duffel. "But I can manage perfectly well."

"I insist," said Lucy, looping the carry-on over her shoulder. "The car's this way."

The light was fading as they walked through the parking lot, and it was dark by the time they had stowed the luggage and seated themselves in the car. "Well, Lucy," began Edna, as Lucy started the car, "I don't have to tell you that it is a great relief to be here. I thought for a time they were going to cancel my flight, and that would have been a disaster."

"How so?" asked Lucy, shoving the ticket in the machine and following up with her credit card.

"Because I'm meeting Kate Klein tomorrow," said Edna, as the striped wooden barrier rose and Lucy exited the parking lot.

"You are?" inquired Lucy, thinking this was news to her.

"Yes. And I'm hoping the whole family will meet her. You and Bill and the girls, we can show her photos of Toby and his family and Elizabeth, too. I know Kate wants to know all about us."

"I'm sure she does," said Lucy. "When and where is this meeting supposed to take place?"

"At the house, of course," said Edna. "Where else?"

"My house?" Lucy was flummoxed. "When exactly is this supposed to happen?"

"I thought lunch would be nice." Edna had folded her hands on her purse, which was on her lap, and was looking out the window. "It's a shame it's so dark and I can't see the view. I love those first glimpses of the coves, the blue water, the marsh grass, and the pine trees."

"Edna, I wish you'd told me about Kate, so I could have planned something. I don't know if Bill can take off work, or what the girls are doing tomorrow."

"Bill's his own boss, isn't he?"

"Yes, but sometimes he's made arrangements with sub-contractors, or is meeting a new client, or the bank . . ."

"Well, family is more important than that, isn't it? And the girls have to eat lunch, don't they?"

"They don't usually eat lunch at home. They're busy with classes and jobs and various commitments," said Lucy, keeping her eyes on the road. "And so am I," she added, thinking of her own job, which was becoming more demanding every day.

"Well, what do you suggest? Should I cancel?" There was a definite note of anger, or perhaps frustration, in Edna's voice.

"Let's see what Bill thinks," suggested Lucy, eager to pass the buck. She was only the daughter-in-law, after all. Bill would have to sort this out with his mother.

"Good idea," said Edna, patting her purse.

Lucy flipped on the radio, finding an oldies station, and the music filled the uncomfortable silence as they drove on through the night.

The old farmhouse on Red Top Road looked welcoming when they finally reached home, with all the windows alight and the porch light glowing. As soon as they turned into the driveway, the girls and Bill bounded out of the kitchen door to welcome Edna.

"Grandma, you're finally here," said Sara, giving Edna a big hug.

"It's great to see you," said Zoe, enveloping her grandmother in another hug.

"Mom!" was all Bill said, wrapping his arms around his mother and lifting her off the ground.

Then everyone pitched in to carry the bags and bring Edna into the house, where sandwiches, cookies, and cold drinks awaited on the kitchen table.

"Make yourself comfortable. Freshen up, if you want, in the powder room; the girls will take your things upstairs," said Bill.

"I think I will," said Edna, stepping into the downstairs bath.

Bill turned to Lucy and, in a lowered voice, asked, "How's she doing?"

Lucy rolled her eyes. "She's invited Kate Klein here for lunch tomorrow," she whispered in response. "She wants her to meet the whole family."

Bill's bearded jaw dropped. "What?"

"You heard me," whispered Lucy, as the door opened and Edna returned to the kitchen.

"Everything all right?" asked Edna, sensing that something was going on.

"Absolutely fine," said Lucy. "Why don't you have a bite? I know I'm hungry. I didn't get any supper."

"No supper?" Edna turned to Bill, who was getting a beer out of the fridge. "You're not taking very good care of your wife. You shouldn't have let poor Lucy make that trip to the airport."

"Not up to me, Mom," said Bill, joining them at the table. "Lucy insisted."

"And where are the girls?" demanded Edna. "I didn't come all this way so they could hide from me."

"They're not hiding; they're upstairs showering and getting ready for tomorrow. They've got demanding schedules, and they're rehearsing for a talent show. You'll see plenty of them, don't worry."

"What about you, Mom? Do you have any plans for to-morrow?" asked Bill, taking the bull by the horns.

"Well, as Lucy knows, I was hoping that we could all meet Kate Klein and welcome her into the family," said Edna, with a discontented shrug, "but Lucy didn't seem to think that was a good idea."

"Well, frankly, neither do I," said Bill, taking the seat opposite his mother. "We don't really know much about this woman or her motives. We need to be cautious, especially since there's the problem with Dad's will."

Edna's eyebrows shot up, and her chin quivered with anger. "Are you saying that Kate is some sort of gold digger?"

"I'm not saying that; I'm saying she might be."

Edna threw the sandwich she was eating back onto her plate and glared at Bill. "That's a terrible thing to say. And what am I supposed to do? I've already invited Kate. I can't just take it back. It's embarrassing, and hurtful. She's a very lovely woman."

"Bill is only trying to protect you," said Lucy, trying to smooth things over.

"Well, I don't need protection!" declared Edna, her chin quivering. "I'm a grown woman, and I can take care of myself."

"Of course, you can. But it's a fact that there are lots of swindlers out there who take advantage of seniors every day . . ."

"Now you're acting as if I'm some senile old lady and Kate is a swindler! Well, I never . . ."

"Mom, calm down," said Bill, in his father-knows-best tone of voice.

Amazingly, Edna responded by falling silent. Lucy wondered if Bill was simply repeating something he'd seen his father do when Edna got upset.

"This is what we're going to do. We're going to meet Kate Klein at some point soon, and we're going to do it at our friend Bob Goodman's office. Bob is an attorney, and he knows how to handle these family situations."

"Meeting at a lawyer's office doesn't seem to show much family feeling," complained Edna, sullenly.

"Maybe not. But if Kate isn't who she claims to be, I don't think she'll show up. And if she is truly interested in finding her family, she'll be happy to do it anywhere, lawyer's office or not."

"I suppose you're right," grumbled Edna. "I'll call her and put her off, tell her I'm working out the details."

"Great," said Bill, sounding relieved. "That will give us some time to get organized. And if this Kate is as wonderful as you say, we can all go out for ice cream afterward."

"That would be nice," said Edna, picking up her sandwich.

The next morning, Lucy called Bob Goodman to arrange the meeting Bill suggested but ran into an unforeseen obstacle. "No can do," said Bob, "I'm leaving today for a legal conference in Cincinnati."

"When will you be back?" asked Lucy.

"Not 'til Monday."

"Oh," said Lucy, with a sense of relief at this postponement. "I'll call your office and make an appointment for next week. Have a good time."

"I always do," said Bob, in a cheery voice. "I look forward to it all year."

Worried that Edna would be disappointed at the delayed meeting, Lucy decided it would be best to keep her busy and entertained. Since she had to work, she called her old friend Miss Tilley and asked if she would like company for lunch.

"I always love to see you, Lucy," replied Miss Tilley, in a spritely tone that belied her advanced age. Only her oldest and dearest friends dared to call her by her first name, Julia, and they were a sadly diminished group.

"I can't make it, unfortunately. I've got to cover Gabe McGourt's wake. I was thinking of my mother-in-law, Edna. She came in last night, and she's at loose ends, as everybody's busy today. I was hoping she could have lunch with you and then go on to the rehearsal with Rachel."

Rachel, Bob's wife, provided home health care for Miss Tilley.

"Then Edna could see Sara and Zoe's dance routine, and she could come home with them," finished Lucy. "I don't want to leave her moping all alone in the house."

"That sounds fine to me," said Miss Tilley. "Rachel and I have pretty much exhausted every topic under the sun, so it will be nice to have a guest with a fresh perspective. I hope Edna has a big appetite. Rachel made split pea soup yesterday and you know how that goes on and on; it seems to grow in the pot."

"Thanks," said Lucy. "I really appreciate this."

She was just about to leave the house when Edna made an appearance, washed and dressed and ready for the day. "I hope you don't mind, Lucy, but I peeked into your new bedroom and I have to say you've decorated it beautifully."

"I can hardly believe it's mine," said Lucy. "When I wake up I think I'm in a fancy hotel."

"Well, you and Bill deserve it, and a genuine master suite will certainly add to the value of your house." She sat down at the table and Lucy gave her a cup of coffee, then sat down opposite her and explained her plan. Edna willingly agreed, having met Miss Tilley and Rachel during past visits. She didn't mention meeting Kate Klein, and Lucy didn't bring it up, unwilling to reopen a sensitive subject. The girls hadn't awakened yet, and Lucy was running late, so she reluctantly left Edna to make her own breakfast and texted Sara with instructions to drive Edna to Miss Tilley's at eleven-thirty. Having completed those arrangements, she left the house to drive to work, her mind already turning to the day's news. The wake was scheduled to begin at eleven, so she hoped to finish up the school budget story and make a start on the Gabe McGourt profile.

When she reached the office, Phyllis delivered an update. "Ted called; the wake is huge, and you need to get over to McHoul's Funeral Home right away."

"But it's not even ten," protested Lucy.

"I guess he's got his reasons," said Phyllis, with a shrug. "I don't make the assignments, I just pass them on."

"Okay," said Lucy, turning on her heels and going back to her car to make the drive to Gilead.

As she approached Gilead, she noticed that black and blue ribbons had been affixed to each light pole on Main Street, and many businesses were flying BLUE LIVES MATTER flags. Passing the high school, she noticed the parking lot was filling up with police cruisers from cities and towns near and far. She'd driven past when it struck her that she was missing a photo op, so she turned around and took a few pictures of the scene. Back in the car, she observed a similar scene at the Department of Public Works facility DPW, where the parking area was rapidly filling with scores of police motorcycles. Again, she parked and was snapping photos when one of the officers approached her.

"Can I help you?" he asked, in an official tone of voice.

"I'm from the local paper," said Lucy, producing her press card. "I'm covering the wake."

"Right," he said, with an approving nod.

"Do you mind if I ask a few questions?"

"I'm not authorized to talk to the press," he said. "The sheriff's office is putting out a press release."

"I don't need to mention your name," said Lucy, noticing his badge, which read P. MAHONEY. "I just need a little background. I want to know why you came today, and did you come far?"

The officer considered. "I guess there's no harm in that. What I want to say is that no distance is too far when a fellow officer has fallen, and I'm here along with my brothers and sisters in blue to honor Gabe McGourt's sacrifice."

"Thanks," said Lucy, writing it all down in her notebook. "And off the record, how far did you come?"

"I'm from Jamestown, New York. We made it in fourteen hours, driving mostly at night."

"Wow," said Lucy, impressed despite herself. "And are they taking care of you? Do you get lodging and food?"

"Oh, yeah. We're good," he assured her, without providing details.

Lucy looked around at the large number of officers, which was growing by the minute. "Where are you all staying? And eating?" she asked.

"I'd better go," said Officer Mahoney. "Have a nice day."

"You, too," said Lucy, watching as he joined a group of officers who had gathered outside the DPW building and wondering how nice it really would be, considering he was going to attend a wake.

When she arrived at the funeral home, she was surprised to see that the walk leading to the neat clapboard building was lined with officers, all dressed in their blue uniforms, all holding American flags that fluttered in the March breeze. The parking lot was cordoned off, and so was the street, so she had to drive some distance before she was able to park on the side of the road. Then she had to hike back to the funeral home, where she found Ted and other reporters standing behind a line of metal barriers. The TV stations got better treatment; they were allowed to set up their cameras on the other side of the street, directly opposite, with a clear view of the street and the main door.

"How long have you been here?" asked Lucy, joining Ted and the others.

"Over an hour," said Ted. He tilted his head toward the line of flag-bearing officers. "They got here soon after."

"Any sign of the family?" she asked.

"Not yet," he replied, but it was only moments later that a siren was heard and the flag-bearing officers snapped to attention as a procession was spotted advancing down the street, blue lights flashing. It was led by the motorcycle officers, proceeding in a double line and pulling off, one by one, to park in the cordoned-off section of road. Then came the cruisers, representing police departments from near and far, which proceeded into the parking area. Finally, the sheriff's car arrived and stopped in front of the walk, blue lights winking. The driver got out and walked around to the passenger side of the car, where he opened the front door and the sheriff himself stepped out. He then waited while the officer opened the rear door, and Gabe McGourt's two boys popped out, dressed in miniature black suits. They waited on the sidewalk while the sheriff assisted their grandmother, Mary Catherine, out of the car.

The small group proceeded into the funeral home for a private viewing, which lasted for a good ten minutes, while the assembled officers fell into a double line. Then the doors opened, and the line advanced into the building, past the honor guard of flag bearers who were standing at attention on either side of the walkway.

Other mourners, friends of the family, formed a loose queue behind the officers. The line moved slowly, and it was well past one o'clock by the time everyone was admitted and allowed to express their condolences to the family.

"Any sign of his ex?" asked Ted, whispering in Lucy's ear.

"No. She's kind of conspicuously absent, if you ask me. I tried to get her to talk about McGourt, but she wouldn't say a word."

"Interesting," said Ted. He cocked his head at the clusters of officers who had exited the funeral home and were standing in scattered little groups. "I guess I'll see if I can get some quotes from these cops."

"Good luck. I tried earlier, but all Officer Mahoney from Jamestown, New York, told me was that the sheriff was going to issue a press release. They're obviously under orders not to talk."

"There's always someone who didn't get the memo," said Ted, with a grin. "You go on back to the office and track down that press release."

"Aye, aye, sir," said Lucy, who was tired of standing and glad to get moving. Besides, all these cops made her feel uneasy and slightly guilty, though she knew she hadn't broken any laws, at least not laws that she knew about.

Lucy left the office at four and headed over to the Community Church to meet Edna, who was watching the rehearsal. When she arrived, she found her sitting in a folding chair, smiling at her granddaughters, who were practicing their routine.

"Lucy, those girls are so clever and talented," enthused Edna, as Lucy took a seat beside her.

"They are pretty special. I'm going to miss Sara; she's moving to Boston in June to start her job at the Museum of Science."

"You've got to let your chicks fly," said Edna, with a resigned little smile.

"I know," agreed Lucy. "Did you enjoy lunch with Miss Tilley and Rachel?"

"Oh, yes. Miss Tilley is a card. She's got this pillow on her sofa that says, 'If you haven't got anything nice to say about anybody, come sit by me.' "

"I know," laughed Lucy. "I think it's a quote from Alice Roosevelt Longworth, Teddy's daughter, who was quite a wit in her time. But don't be fooled; Miss T is a sweetie, though she tries to hide it."

"I found her very interesting indeed," said Edna, clapping enthusiastically as the girls finished their routine. After taking a bow or two, they clattered down the stage steps in their clunky step-dancing shoes and joined their mother and grandmother.

"Did you really like it?" asked Zoe.

"Absolutely," said Edna, beaming at them.

"So, Mom, what's going on?" asked Sara. "The town is crawling with police. They're everywhere, and there's all these weird black-and-white American flags with a blue stripe."

"They're Blue Lives Matter flags to show support for the police; everybody knows that," said Zoe, eager to put her sister down. "Where have you been? Under a rock or something?"

"I've been busy finishing up my degree and getting a job," said Sara, defending herself as she sat down and started changing her shoes.

"Well, it's this movement, a reaction to Black Lives Matter," said Zoe, bending over to lace up her duck boots. "It's apparently okay for cops to shoot black people, and if they say they don't like it, the cops come back at them with this Blue Lives Matter thing."

Sara looked puzzled. "Don't all lives matter?"

"Some more than others, I guess," replied Zoe, dropping her dancing shoes into a bag.

"This is not the time to say anything that could be construed as critical of the police," advised Lucy, speaking in a low voice. "The county is full of cops who came for Gabe McGourt's funeral. I was at the wake today, and there were hundreds, maybe thousands. It was a pretty overwhelming show of solidarity."

"And you have to remember that this officer's family and his friends have sustained a terrible loss," said Edna. "Miss Tilley told me he died in the most awful way, in a fire. And he leaves two little boys. It's terribly sad."

"But it wasn't like he was a hero or anything," insisted Sara. "He was a prison guard, and he died because he crashed his truck."

"It's all a big fraud," insisted Zoe, as they began walking to the door. "This girl Allie—you know her, Mom."

"She was in your class in high school, wasn't she?" asked Lucy, remembering a tiny girl with a big smile.

"Yeah," continued Zoe, speaking rather loudly to be heard over the rehearsing Irish tenor. "Now she works in the bakery at the IGA. Well, she spent a couple of months in the county jail on drug charges. She said that this Gabe guy was one of the worst corrections officers. She was terrified of him."

Lucy's first reaction was shock that little Allie had been involved in drugs, and sadness that she'd gone to prison. Then, remembering they weren't alone but in a crowded rehearsal, she looked about, hoping no one was listening. "Lower your voice," she advised. "You're entitled to your views, but I don't think most people agree with you. I don't want to get into some sort of confrontation."

Zoe raised her eyebrows in astonishment. "Mom, you're a reporter. You're supposed to be interested in finding out the truth and printing it."

The words stung, like a slap on the face. "I know," admitted Lucy, as the group walked toward the exit. "I don't like it one bit, but right now I think we have to be cautious and wait for the right opportunity. A lot of people are caught up in this thing . . ."

"They're being manipulated," said Zoe. "The sheriff is playing on their emotions."

"That's true," said Lucy, holding the door for the others, "but if you saw the display I saw today, you'd think twice before mouthing off. I just want to keep you safe. I don't want to see you girls in jail like your friend Allie."

"Oh, Lucy, don't be silly," said Edna, chuckling, as they walked through the parking lot. "The police protect us from bad people, and they put their lives on the line for us." She turned to face Sara and Zoe. "Girls, you should always remember that. When your father was a little boy, I used to tell him that if he was lost and didn't know his way home, he should find a policeman. The policeman would hold his hand and bring him home."

"Right, Grandma, we'll remember," called Sara, as she and Zoe ran across the lot to Zoe's little Corolla.

"Kids today," said Edna, as Lucy used her fob to unlock

the doors of her SUV, which responded with a loud click. "They're so cynical."

"Aren't we all," murmured Lucy, as she slid behind the wheel.

"What did you say?" asked Edna, settling herself in the passenger seat.

"Just that it's nice to have you with us," said Lucy, starting the engine.

# Chapter Fifteen

Lucy tried to hang on to Edna's rosy description of the police as she covered Gabe McGourt's funeral on Saturday, but as the seemingly endless procession of police cars and motorcycles proceeded through the small town, she found it increasingly difficult. Complicating her emotions was the fact that she was clearly in the minority; the entire route to the cemetery was lined with grieving citizens, respectfully removing their caps and bowing their heads as the gleaming black hearse containing McGourt's body drove by. These folks, like Edna, believed the police were their friends, ready to protect them. As a reporter, however, she knew how easy it was for a formerly upstanding citizen to find him or herself on the wrong side of the law: a fight with a spouse that got out of hand, a drink too many at a party, a moment's distraction while driving. Her mother always used to comment on other's misfortunes by saying, "There but for the grace of God go I," and Lucy had taken it to heart and knew only too well that she herself was not without sin. It was perhaps that conviction that made her somewhat leery of the massed ranks of police that had gathered in Gilead. Truth be told, she found all those blue uniforms and holstered weapons awfully intimidating.

Admission to the cemetery was controlled, limited to the immediate family and high-ranking officials, while the masses of attending officers remained outside the gates, in parade formation. Lucy and Ted, along with other media reps, were allowed entry but were confined at some distance from the grave and the blue canopy provided to shelter the mourners from the capricious early-March weather.

No storms were expected, thought Lucy, noticing that the day was especially fine and unusually warm for March. A light breeze blew, and a few clouds flitted through the blue sky, but it seemed to her that even the weather was making a mockery of this elaborately staged event. A gray sky and light rain would have been more appropriate, allowing her to begin her story by noting: "Even the sky mourned the loss of Corrections Officer Gabriel McGourt, shedding copious tears on the assembled company . . ."

It was not to be, however, as the sun stubbornly insisted on shining, and even the bagpiped refrain of "Amazing Grace," played at a rather quick tempo, wasn't somber at all but lent a down-home, countrified air to the proceedings. The media area was unfortunately located too far from the gravesite for her to hear the priest's words, but Lucy divined that the service was ending when a gun salute was fired, followed by a lone trumpet sounding taps.

"Well," said Ted, as they exited the cemetery and once again encountered rank upon rank of uniformed officers, "if I were a criminal, this would be the perfect time to rob a bank."

"I'm in," said Lucy, "let's do it."

"Sorry, no can do. We've got to meet the TRUTH Project lawyers."

"It's a missed opportunity," said Lucy, calculating that it would take some time for the road to be cleared by the departing mourners. "But making a clean getaway looks like it might present a problem."

Ted assessed the traffic jam and sighed. "I'll call and tell the lawyers we'll be late."

When they arrived at the old *Gabber* office, which had a brand-new sign announcing that the paper had been renamed *The Courier* in gilded letters above the door, they found two people they assumed were the lawyers waiting for them. It was an easy assumption, since the woman and man sitting in the reception area were both wearing suits. His was dark gray, and hers was navy blue, and they both were accompanied by oversized briefcases, which sat at their feet like obedient little dogs.

That conclusion was reinforced by Hilda Neely, who, it was rumored, had been the paper's receptionist since shortly after the Civil War, and who seemed to grow tinier and more crooked every year. "There's some folks to see you," she told Ted, in a quavery voice. "They say they're lawyers."

"Hi, I'm Jason Boardman from the TRUTH Project," said the guy, who was rather short and had a full head of very curly brown hair. "And this is Nancy Porter-Fuchs."

Nancy extended her hand, which featured neatly clipped, unpolished nails and a wedding band that glittered with some sizable diamonds. She stood a full head above her partner; her blond hair was cut in a short pixie cut, and her squarish face was free of makeup except for lip gloss.

"Glad to meet you," said Nancy, grasping Lucy's hand in a strong grip.

"Same here," replied Lucy, amused that Nancy had greeted her first. "I'm Lucy Stone, and this is Ted Stillings, the publisher."

"Great to meet you, Ted," said Jason, shaking hands with both of them.

"So let's get down to business," urged Nancy. "We understand one of our TRUTH Project reporters is in a bit of a jam."

"Let's sit in the conference room," said Ted, leading the way down a short, carpeted hall and into an attractively furnished room, also carpeted, that was a far cry from the *Pennysaver*'s dusty old morgue. A large, gleaming table surrounded by padded chairs took up the center of the room, where a whiteboard hung on one wall and a bank of windows filled another, offering an admirable view of the fortress-like prison that loomed over the town. A beverage bar featuring a Keurig machine stood opposite the windowed wall. "Make yourselves comfortable," said Ted, "and uh, Lucy, would you make some coffee for everyone."

"None for me," said Nancy, giving Ted a disapproving stare.

"That would be great," said Jason, who had placed his large briefcase on the table and was opening it. "Two sugars and a cream."

Lucy's emotional barometer swung between amusement and resentment as she busied herself fixing coffee for Ted and Jason and fished bottled water out of the mini-fridge for everyone. Jason didn't wait for her to join them but cut right to the chase, asking Ted to explain the situation.

"As I told you on the phone, Rob Callahan, the reporter assigned to us by the TRUTH Project, is currently in the county jail, charged with murdering Gabe McGourt. McGourt worked at the county jail as a corrections officer, and the two were apparently rivals for the affection of a young woman, Rosie Capshaw. At least, that's what the DA contends." He paused. "As you have no doubt noticed, Gabe McGourt's funeral has attracted a lot of attention, as well as police from all over the country."

"We looked over your original application for the project," said Nancy, "and one of the factors you mentioned was the need to investigate the local sheriff, John P. Murphy. You suggested that this Murphy guy is—how did you put it?—'blocking any and all efforts to investigate his office.'"

Interesting, thought Lucy, waiting for the Keurig to go through its paces. No wonder Rob had wanted to focus on Murphy immediately and had no doubt been frustrated by Ted's insistence on taking it slow.

"That's true," said Ted. "That's why I was so happy when we got Rob. I was hoping to finally expose the corruption."

"Given all that, it looks like Rob is being framed. Would you agree?" asked Nancy.

"That's not entirely accurate," said Lucy, delivering the hot coffee to Ted and Jason. "Rob lied when he was questioned by the police about a fight in a bar with Gabe McGourt. He said it never happened, but there were witnesses who claimed they saw the two men fighting."

"And these witnesses are credible?" asked Jason.

"They're local people," said Lucy, "which makes them a lot more believable to folks around here than some troublemaker from Cleveland."

Nancy and Jason turned to Ted, looking for his take on the situation. "Lucy's got a point," he admitted. "Rob didn't exactly fit in with the bar crowd, and the sheriff is a master manipulator. They've had this huge funeral for Gabe McGourt, with crowds and the flags and all. He's now officially a fallen hero, and his death has become a tragedy affecting the entire community."

"What about the case against Callahan?" asked Nancy, unscrewing the top of her water bottle. "Do they have evidence? Did anybody see him tampering with McGourt's vehicle?"

"There's video showing him near the truck, but not actually meddling with it," said Ted.

"I think the case is mostly built on the witnesses and this supposed rivalry over Rosie Capshaw," said Lucy, finally taking a seat and joining the others at the table.

Jason was thoughtful, chewing on his mouth. "Looks like we've got our work cut out for us," he said.

"Yeah," agreed Nancy. "We'd better get started and hear what Rob Callahan has to say for himself. Looking on the bright side, it's not far to the prison."

"Just up the hill," said Ted, glancing at the window.

"Well, we're off," said Nancy, standing up.

"Nice to meet you all," said Jason, closing his briefcase.

"We'll keep you posted," said Nancy, before exiting the room.

When they'd gone, Ted let out a big sigh and turned to Lucy. "What do you think? Does Rob have a chance?"

Lucy gazed out the window, unable to take her eyes off the gray stone prison, surrounded by chain-link fencing and tall watchtowers. "I don't know. I'm not too optimistic, but we've got to keep the faith. Best justice system in the world, right? Innocent until proven guilty."

"I hope so," said Ted, leaning heavily on the table as he stood up.

"You know, Ted, my daughter told me about a high school friend who spent a couple of months in the county jail on drug charges. She said this Allie Shaw was terrified of Gabe McGourt; she said he was one of the worst corrections officers."

"It's no secret, Lucy. The guy was trouble."

"Well, do you want me to talk to Allie and see what she has to say? Maybe do a little opposition research?"

"Not now," said Ted, shaking his head. "Better not speak ill of the dead, at least not until his body's cold."

"The sooner the better, if you ask me. The way this is going, Gabe McGourt is going to be our next saint. We need to get the truth out, and fast. That's our job, isn't it?" she said, realizing she was echoing her daughter's argument.

"No." Ted shook his head. "Let's wait and see what the lawyers advise. Meanwhile, you've got that school budget story to write. That's top priority, and there's a School Committee meeting Monday night."

"Monday?" Lucy had been looking forward to a quiet family dinner, followed by catching the final episode of her favorite TV mini-series.

"Monday. And I want your story by ten on Tuesday morning, so I can post it online."

Lucy sighed, grateful for the invention of the DVR. "Aye, aye, sir." She saluted and marched out the door, deciding to head for home to salvage what was left of her weekend.

The School Committee met in the administration building, a small one-story clapboard structure located behind the high school. The meeting had just started when Lucy arrived, joining the handful of concerned citizens, mostly parents, who bothered to attend the bi-weekly meetings. As she took her seat, she got a smile from the committee chairman, Lydia Volpe, who was a retired kindergarten teacher and had taught all of Lucy's kids. Although she was definitely getting on in years, she'd remained slim and dressed in bright colors that flattered her olive complexion.

"We're hoping to finalize the budget tonight," said Lydia to the assembled committee, "then we'll submit it to the selectmen for their approval. A positive response from them will go a long way toward convincing the town meeting to vote in favor." She glanced at the thick sheaf of papers on the table in front of her, then continued, "Most of our work is done; tonight we're just hearing about a handful of new initiatives. First up, Maureen Clawson, who heads the phys ed department. I see you're asking for an additional twenty-five thousand. Can you tell us what that's for?"

Maureen was a very tiny, very fit woman who tied her hair back in a ponytail and always dressed in a track suit. Tonight's suit was bright green, with a strip of white piping on the sleeves and legs. "It's for an eighth-grade sex-ed program we feel is urgently needed. The money will pay for materials and a part-time educator."

"Urgently needed?" inquired Phil Botts, the newest board member. He was a realtor and frequently pointed out that quality schools boosted property values.

"Yes," said Maureen, with a wry smile. "So far this year, we have five pregnant students."

"I see the need for sex ed," said Francine Dewicki, a supermom who was a fervent booster of the school, "but isn't eighth grade a bit young?"

"One of our moms is fourteen," said Maureen.

"My question is why does the town need to fund this program?" asked George Wells, a middle-aged man who had a flourishing accounting business. "Isn't funding available from the state?"

"Oh, yes," said Maureen, who had been waiting to get this off her chest. "The state legislature did indeed vote last year to fund sex ed in public schools, but the funds are administered by the county health department. I spoke to the director, requesting that she apply for the funds, and she told me it is unfortunately against her religious principles. She's been quite vocal about her belief that sex should only take place within the bonds of matrimony and recommends we offer abstinence training instead of filling our children's innocent heads with filth."

"But that doesn't work, does it?" asked Lydia, her dark eyes flashing. "I mean, human nature being what it is."

"Research shows that abstinence training is ineffective," offered Maureen, with a smirk. "Not that research was actually needed on the subject."

"Not if you'd seen what these girls wear to school," observed George. "Pajamas, short shorts, ripped jeans, flimsy T-shirts . . ." He stopped, aware that Maureen and Francine were both giving him withering glances.

"So are we ready to vote?" asked Lydia, eager to change the subject.

Receiving nods all around, she called the question, which Lucy was pleased to see passed unanimously.

When the meeting finally ended, sometime after eleven o'clock, Lucy sat right down at the kitchen table and finished up the school budget story on her laptop. She only made brief mention of the fact that the county health director was blocking available state funding for sex ed, but planned to take up the matter with Ted in hopes of investigating further. If the health director was blocking funds for sex ed, what else might she be doing? Cutting off funds to combat opioid addiction? What about HIV testing? It seemed something that readers would be interested in.

When she arrived at the office the next morning, Ted announced he was pleased with her work on the school budget and had already posted her story.

"Thanks," she said, hanging her jacket on the coat stand. "What did you think about the county health director trying to block the state funds for sex ed?"

"What?" inquired Phyllis, looking up from the classifieds she was entering into the computer. She was wearing one of her favorite sweatshirts, which was scattered with glittering sequined shamrocks.

"She has religious objections. She wants abstinence education, believes sex should only take place within the bonds of matrimony."

"Who is this woman?"

Lucy was flipping through the county government directory. "Her name is Martha Dodd," reported Lucy. "Anybody know her?"

Phyllis and Ted both shook their heads.

"Well, I think we should investigate Ms. Dodd and the conduct of her office," said Lucy. "She tried to throw a monkey wrench in the Irish Festival, sent one of her agents, who threatened to shut it down if they didn't apply for a bunch of permits."

Ted didn't seem thrilled by the idea. "I guess we've got to do it," he said, reluctantly, staring down at his shoes. "It seems like a blatant misuse of power."

He looked so miserable that Lucy began to have second thoughts. "I don't have to do it; there's plenty of other stories." She hadn't noticed until now how he suddenly seemed to have aged and always seemed tired.

"I guess I didn't realize what I was getting into," said Ted. "It all seemed so noble, tackling abuse and corruption, restoring the democratic values our nation was built on . . ." He let out a long sigh. "I had no idea it would be so depressing and exhausting, or that the corruption would be so widespread . . . It seems like the sheriff has the whole county government in his grip."

"Buck up, bucko," said Lucy, causing Ted to smile. "We can't do it all at once; we have to chip away, one story at a time. It doesn't always have to be a big spotlight investigation; it can simply be an accurate account of the truth, like the paragraph in the school budget story about Dodd's refusal to apply for state funding. We can leave it at that for now, and see if readers respond."

"Good idea, Lucy," said Ted, obviously relieved. "Let's focus on getting Rob a fair deal."

"I'm certainly on board with that," said Lucy, deciding that she was definitely going to have a little talk with Allie Shaw. It might not make the paper, but could possibly provide new information that could help Rob's defense. Checking her watch, she realized she had to dash, or she was going to be late for the big family meeting with Kate Klein at Bob's office.

When she arrived, Bill and the girls, and Edna, were all sitting in Bob's nicely appointed waiting room. Bill and the girls were on the roll-arm sofa, and Edna was perched on the edge of a wing chair upholstered in crewel fabric. Bob's secretary, Dilys Lori Hemmings, was clicking away on a keyboard, but gave Lucy a warm smile when she arrived.

"Where's Kate?" asked Lucy, aware that she herself was ten minutes late.

"I do hope she's not lost," fussed Edna. "She's not familiar with Maine, and she's coming all the way from Portland."

"Everybody's got GPS these days," offered Sara. "It's really hard to get lost."

"Could be traffic," said Bill, philosophically.

"Or maybe she's chickened out," said Zoe.

"That wasn't very nice, Zoe," chided Edna. "I think once you all meet her, you'll see what a lovely, kind person Kate is."

"Sorry, Mom," said Bill, "but I just don't see why you're so keen on her. It's just complicating everything, especially since you can't find Dad's will. Meanwhile, the clock is ticking, and we've all got better things to do."

"Shame on you, Bill," said Edna. "You know family is more important than anything . . ."

"My real family," began Bill, stopping mid-sentence when the office door opened and Kate Klein arrived. Unlike her subdued appearance at the funeral, today Kate was dressed in a bright red coat and shiny black, high-heeled boots. She was carrying an expensive designer handbag, and her hair had been freshly highlighted with blond streaks.

"I'm so, so glad to be here," she began, breathlessly, going straight to Edna and taking both her hands. "I've dreamed of this day," she continued, drawing Edna to her feet and enfolding her in a big hug. She turned and surveyed the room. "My family, at last," she cooed, arms outstretched. Then she went around the room, greeting each person individually. "You must be Bill, my brother," she said, attempting a hug, but desisting when she saw Bill recoil. "And dear, dear Lucy," was her next attempt, rather more successful since Lucy submitted to a light hug and an air kiss.

"And these are the wonderful girls I've heard so much about," she exclaimed, getting stony looks from Sara and Zoe. Undeterred, she continued, "Now which is which? Who is the scientist, and who is the linguist?"

Zoe rolled her eyes and muttered, "I'm Zoe."

"I'm Sara," said her sister, reluctantly.

"Well, well, isn't this just amazing," enthused Kate.

"Uh, it sure is," said Bill. He turned to Dilys and asked her to tell Bob that they were all here and ready to proceed.

There was an awkward pause as they stood up and gathered outside Bob's office door, but he was quick to admit them, urging everyone to seat themselves in the captain's chairs he'd arranged in a half-circle in front of his desk. He then seated himself behind the desk and introduced himself to Kate and Edna.

"We're all here today because Kate Klein has presented DNA evidence that she is the daughter of the late William Stone and wishes to be acknowledged as such by the Stone family. Is that right?" began Bob.

"Yes," said Kate. "I recently did one of those gene tests, and that's what the results showed." She pulled a couple of sheets of paper out of her black alligator bag and leaned forward, passing them to Bob.

Bob studied the papers, then turned to Kate. "Was this the first you knew of your father? Did you have a relationship with him? Did he visit? Did your mother ever mention him?"

"No." Kate shook her head and looked very sad. "It's something I regret very much. You see, my mother died when I was very young, and I was raised by an aunt and uncle . . ."

Edna gave a little gasp, followed by a sympathetic, "Oh."

"And I'm afraid they weren't very nice people. They made it very clear that I was an unanticipated and unwanted responsibility."

This time Edna's "Oh" was louder, and she shook her head.

"I see," said Bob. "And now, I must ask, are you planning on making any financial claims against the Stone family?"

"Absolutely not, I wouldn't dream of it," exclaimed Kate. "As it happens, I'm alone in the world; my aunt and uncle have passed, and I have no other relatives. Well, until I got this DNA report and discovered I really do have a family, and I'm just so happy to meet them all and hope they'll welcome me." She turned and gazed briefly at each member of the family, one by one. "I know it's a lot to ask, but blood is thicker than water, and I'm sure that when you get to know me, you'll realize we have a lot in common."

"Oh, yes," said Edna, hopping to her feet and going to Kate, reaching out to her, and clasping her in a hug. "You've been through so much, my dear, but now that's over, and you have a family!"

Lucy and Bill glanced at each other in shared dismay, then turned to Bob. He responded with a wry smile and a shrug.

"Well, I guess we're done here," said Bill, standing up. "Let's all get something to eat."

"And a stiff drink," added Lucy, under her breath as she took his hand.

# Chapter Sixteen

Looking back on the meeting and subsequent luncheon with Kate as she left the office, free for the afternoon now that it was past deadline and the paper had been put to bed, Lucy had mixed feelings. Kate seemed nice enough, but perhaps rather more vivacious and openly emotional than Lucy was used to, now that she'd lived for so long among her reserved Maine neighbors. It almost seemed that Kate was putting on a show for them, knocking herself out to win them over. So far, Edna was the only family member who was falling for it, grieving for her lost husband and embracing Kate as the daughter she'd always longed for. Kate neatly filled the void in Edna's life, but the others were doing just fine without her. For them, it was a question of whether this new person was going to add something to their family life, and so far as Lucy could see, the answer was no.

Bill clearly saw her as a rival for his mother's affection and attention, but more importantly, he felt responsible for Edna. He was the man of the family, now that his father was gone, and was committed to securing his mother's welfare and protecting her assets. He was naturally suspicious of Kate's motives and wasn't convinced they were entirely honorable.

The girls couldn't care less about Kate. For one thing, she was of a different generation, too old to be a friend, more like an aunt. They'd never had an aunt, however, since Lucy and Bill were both only children, and didn't feel the need. They were both busy with friends and plans for their future; it wasn't at all clear how Kate would change anything for them. Now, if she'd boasted of important connections who could help them with their careers, they might be more interested, but since she was presenting herself as a needy, friendless orphan, they didn't see any advantage in getting involved.

As for herself, Lucy was trying to keep an open mind. She wasn't as suspicious of Kate as Bill was, but she wasn't taken in by her overblown show of family feeling, either. She didn't want to be mean, and perhaps Kate and Edna could develop a genuinely positive relationship that would benefit both of them. A relationship like that would benefit her, too, because Kate would share responsibility for Edna, a responsibility that Lucy knew would only grow more demanding in the coming years, as Edna aged. Nevertheless, Lucy couldn't rid herself of a niggling little doubt about Kate, a feeling that something was off, that she was pretending to be someone she wasn't. That didn't necessarily mean that she wasn't actually Bill's half sister; maybe she was just trying too hard to gain acceptance as a member of the family.

Or was she, wondered Lucy, recalling yesterday's luncheon at Murley's Family Restaurant. Kate had sat next to Edna and had pretty much ignored the rest of the family. At Bob's office, she'd spoken of her intense desire to join the family, but over a plate of Cobb salad, she hadn't shown much interest in Bill's antique home restoration business, Lucy's work as a reporter, Sara's new job at the museum in Boston, or Zoe's decision to change her major once again. The only member of the family that interested Kate was Edna.

Passing the IGA, where the parking lot was mostly empty this early in the morning, Lucy switched mental gears and impulsively decided to see if Allie Shaw was working in the market's bakery. She could pick up some fresh muffins to take to the office, and maybe learn a bit more about Gabe McGourt. The bakery was on the side of the store farthest from the door, so Lucy gave Bert, the deli guy, a big wave, smiled at Carrie behind the fish counter, and chatted a few minutes with Ralph about the sudden disappearance of New York sirloin from the beef offerings. They agreed that those newfangled petite sirloins were tough, and T-bone, porterhouse, and rib-eye steak were all too expensive, and Lucy confided that Bill really missed his Saturday night sirloins. "I'll get you a T-bone. I can label it a manager's special, just for you," promised Ralph.

Lucy wasn't sure this was entirely aboveboard and questioned him. "Are you sure that's okay? I don't want you to get in trouble."

"No problem, Lucy," said Ralph. "I'm the new meat manager."

"Congratulations, and thanks," said Lucy, smiling broadly. "I'll grab it on my way back."

Continuing past the dairy cases, where Maggie Poor was stocking the yogurt shelf, Lucy finally arrived at the store bakery, where the delicious scent of baking bread filled the air. Allie Shaw was busy decorating a birthday cake, but looked up to ask if she could get something for Lucy.

"What a good job you're doing," said Lucy, admiring the pink roses and green leaves that Allie was applying to the chocolate sheet cake. "Whenever I try to decorate a cake, it sure doesn't come out looking like that."

"You need to know the tricks of the trade," said Allie. "Also, good equipment helps."

"Yeah," agreed Lucy. "I just get those squeeze tubes of icing . . ."

"They're really hard to control," said Allie. She was still petite, but had filled out a bit and was no longer the emaciated high schooler Lucy remembered. She had a pair of cat's-eye glasses perched on her pert little nose, her long hair was tucked in a net, and she had a butterfly tattoo on her neck.

"I thought I'd get some muffins to take into work," said Lucy.

"I just stocked the case," said Allie, with a nod at a glassed-in display in the shape of an old-fashioned wheeled cart. "The blueberry ones are fresh out of the oven."

"Great," said Lucy, looking over her shoulder to make sure the coast was clear before stepping closer to the counter and lowering her voice. "Allie, there's something I want to ask you about. I know you spent a little time in the county jail, where you had some interactions with Gabe McGourt . . ."

Allie's eyes practically popped out of her head. "Look, I don't want to talk about that. They took me back here with no questions asked; it's all in the past. I'm not looking for trouble."

"I understand," said Lucy, nodding sympathetically. "I'm not judging, and I don't want to get you in trouble . . ."

Allie's face was quite red, and Lucy didn't think it was from the heat of the oven. "But you'll put my name and that I'm an ex-convict in the paper!"

"I don't have to use your name, and I don't need to put anything in the paper. That's not why I'm asking. I'm just looking for some background on this guy that might help Rob Callahan. He's the new reporter at the paper, and he's been charged with murdering McGourt." Lucy paused for breath. "They're making McGourt out to be some big hero, and you and I know that's not true."

"You can say that again," muttered Allie, squeezing out a perfect border of green leaves.

"And maybe this trial will reveal the truth about the sheriff and the jail he's running," said Lucy, hoping she'd managed to convince Allie to open up to her.

Allie was quiet, seemingly trying to decide what to do. Finally, she let out a big sigh and put down the pastry bag. "I don't think any of this is news; everybody knows it, they just don't want to talk about it or think about it. You take away people's rights, put them in a situation where they have no power but are under the complete control of those in authority—well, what do you think is going to happen? The ones with all the power are going to take advantage of the ones with no power, and that's what happens at the county jail."

"And when you throw in sex . . ." suggested Lucy.

"It's always there, the threat," said Allie. "And if you don't do what they want, they can punish you. You can end up in solitary, or cleaning toilets; they can do whatever they want to you."

"What about Gabe?" probed Lucy.

"He was the worst. Some of the others were strictly professional and played it by the book. Others would give you stuff if you were nice to them: that's how they put it: 'If you're nice to me, I'll be nice to you,' they'd say, and some of the girls would do stuff with them. But Gabe McGourt was scary, menacing. There was always violence, kind of lurking under the surface."

This was a hard question to ask, but Lucy had to know. "Did he rape you? Or hurt you?"

"Actually, no," said Allie, with a shake of her head. "I'm not very big, and I worked real hard at not attracting attention. I kept my head down, kind of hid behind the larger women." She let out a laugh. "Honestly, I don't think he knew I was there. I don't think he ever noticed me, he was so busy with the big, busty girls." She picked up the pastry bag. "That doesn't mean I wasn't terrified of him."

"Thanks for telling me all this," said Lucy. "I know it couldn't have been easy."

Allie smiled. "Actually, I feel a little better talking about it. I've been keeping this all in too long."

"You take care, and stay out of trouble," advised Lucy, grabbing one of the flattened boxes from the shelf beneath the muffins and opening it up. She used the provided tongs to fill the box with a half-dozen blueberry muffins.

"I intend to," said Allie. "Enjoy your muffins."

"They look delicious," said Lucy, before retracing her steps through the store, back to the meat counter. There, Ralph had her manager's special wrapped and ready to go. "Say hi to Bill for me," said Ralph. "And by the way, I've got a window casing that's rotted. Do you think he could take a look at it for me?"

"I'm pretty sure he could," said Lucy, taking the wrapped meat that she was shocked to see was priced at ninety-nine cents a pound. She'd expected a bit of a break on the price, but not this much. She considered returning it, saying she really couldn't accept such a big reduction, but didn't want to embarrass Ralph. He'd only been trying to be nice. So she smiled at him and said, "Thanks."

Walking to the checkout, Lucy grew more uncomfortable about the steak, which was only compounded when Dot, the cashier, eyed the package doubtfully. "Chicken gizzards?" she asked.

"For stock," lied Lucy, promising herself that she would never again accept one of Ralph's manager's specials. It reminded her too much of the tit-for-tat situation at the county jail, and she didn't want to be indebted to Ralph in that way, or to anyone.

Ted wasn't in when Lucy arrived at the office the next morning, but Phyllis was at the reception desk, decked out in kelly-green reading glasses and a green-and-white-striped sweater, with some rather large shamrocks dangling from her ears. A huge bunch of Irish daffodils bloomed on her desk. "You've got the spirit, I see," said Lucy.

"Erin go bragh," she announced, with a big smile.

"And what, might I ask, does that mean?" teased Lucy.

"Haven't got a clue. My husband's family came from Sweden, and mine is from Germany and Holland."

"Well, everyone's Irish on St. Patrick's Day, right?"

"Look, it's March in Maine," said Phyllis. "It's cold and gray, and the snow is filthy, and there's mud everywhere. Truth be told, I'm dying for a glimpse of green and just trying to avoid falling into depression."

"Point taken," said Lucy, realizing that Phyllis was on to something. January was a big letdown after Christmas. February brought Valentine's Day, which was a decidedly mixed blessing, depending on the state of one's love life, and March offered the promise of spring, but usually failed to deliver. No wonder people threw themselves into St. Patrick's Day festivities like shipwrecked sailors piling onto a lifeboat.

When she sat down at her desk and powered up her computer, Lucy found herself experiencing writer's block. She had plenty of assigned stories to write, but couldn't get started. Her emotions were unsettled, and somehow the picky details in the town budget and the upcoming town meeting with several contentious articles on the warrant didn't grab her attention. Her mind kept wandering, and she couldn't focus on her work. She was thinking instead about Kate Klein and wondering about her motives, and about how easy it was to step onto that slippery slope and become dishonest, even about something as small as a piece of steak. She thought about power and how it corrupts, about Gabe's burning truck and the hundreds of officers at his funeral. Were they mourning or presenting a show of intimidating force? Were they expressing genuine grief or issuing a warning? Or both?

Lucy eventually found herself hitting the keyboard, but she was only putting down random thoughts. What did the funeral actually have to do with Gabe McGourt, she wondered? It was no secret that he was not exactly Mr. Right, especially when it came to his relationships with women. He was divorced, and his wife steadfastly refused to talk about what happened, but the divorce took place around the same time that Melanie accused him of sexual assault. Were the two connected? There had certainly been gossip at the time, which had only died down when Melanie left town and the case was dropped. Gabe hadn't learned his lesson, however, if Allie and Rosie were to be believed, and Lucy didn't see why they shouldn't be. It all added up to a picture of an abusive, violent man who was unfortunately in a position of power—someone whose death probably came as a big relief to a number of people. So why did the sheriff organize this huge funeral, making a hero out of a man who was flawed and deeply troubled?

The only reason that came to mind was to create a cover-up, a lie so big that it smothered the truth.

Looking back over her notes, Lucy realized she had a story, a story that had flowed out of her mind, down her arms, and through her fingers as they flew over the keyboard. The text flowered on the screen, growing inch by inch, until she suddenly ran out of words. It was all there, the whole stinking mess, and before she could change her mind, she hit the SEND button.

It didn't take long for Ted to respond. Lucy had just come back from a bathroom break when she saw his email. "Lucy, you know I can't use this. Needs corroboration and named sources."

She immediately picked up the phone and called, angrily defending her story. "You're as bad as the rest of them; you're complicit in a cover-up!"

"Calm down, Lucy," he advised. "I know you're on to something, but it's too soon, and you need more evidence. It's a great story," he said, emphasizing the word *story*, "but right now that's all it is. It's what you think is the truth, not necessarily actually the truth. You need more facts to back up these accusations."

"You know I'm right, Ted," grumbled Lucy.

"Maybe." Ted paused. "Probably. But I don't want to risk the future of *The Courier* on a story that's going to get me hauled into court on a libel charge." Another pause. "You know what, I think you should send that story to the lawyers, to Nancy and Jason. It might help them."

"Okay," said Lucy, somewhat mollified. "What about the health department stuff? The sex ed and harassing the Irish Festival?"

"Yeah, play that up. Get some more quotes, beef it up. You know what to do. Okay?"

Lucy found herself smiling. "Okay."

Around lunchtime, Lucy's mind began to drift. She was hungry, and she felt a bit guilty about abandoning Edna. Work was her first priority, but there came a point when it was also an escape from difficulties at home. She had a demanding job, and she'd been busy, but she couldn't help feeling she'd been neglecting Edna. No wonder the poor woman was falling under Kate's spell; she had been left all alone day after day.

There was nothing keeping her at the paper; it was the nature of the job that she made her own hours, taking the time she needed to cover nighttime meetings, to interview sources when they were available, and then to write it all up. That meant she could come and go as she wished; she was no nine-to-fiver. Now, after putting in a long morning, she was well ahead on her assignments and could take some time to attend to her other responsibilities, among which Edna topped the list. Wouldn't it be nice, she thought, to take Edna out for lunch? The Queen Vic was open year-round, and it would be a nice treat for them both.

She picked up her cell and called Edna, but her call went to voice mail. A minute or two later, Edna called back. "I couldn't find my phone," she said, somewhat breathlessly, causing Lucy to smile. She'd seen Edna go through her frantic little pantomime several times, as she tended to leave her phone wherever she'd last used it. Most often, however, it was buried in the bottom of her roomy purse.

"Well, as it happens," began Lucy, "I'm pretty much finished for the day, and I wondered if you'd like to go out to lunch with me? The Queen Vic does a lovely club sandwich . . ."

"Oh, Lucy, aren't you sweet! I'd love to have lunch with

you, but Kate's already called. She'll be here any minute; she's going to take me to some new place in Rockland that she says everybody is raving about, and then we're going to see the Wyeths at the museum. She says we might even be able to take a side trip to see the house in that famous painting, the one with the woman lying on the hill."

"*Christina's World,*" said Lucy.

"That's the one!" exclaimed Edna. "Have you been?"

Lucy admitted she hadn't. "I've heard it's a very powerful experience," she added. "Sounds like you're going to have a lovely afternoon."

"Best of all is spending it with Kate," enthused Edna. "I know it must seem weird, since she's the product of my husband's affair with another woman, but we do seem to have a special connection. I suppose she reminds me of him. After all, half her DNA came from him!"

It occurred to Lucy that, as far as she knew, Kate was only making a brief visit to Maine, supposedly for business; making contact with the Stone family was an extra. "How long is she here for?" asked Lucy. "Doesn't she have to get back to Florida soon?"

"Oh, Lucy! Didn't I tell you? It's wonderful news," trilled Edna. "She's got one of those Airbnb's, right outside Tinker's Cove. She's rented it for a month, and from what she tells me, it's gorgeous and has fabulous views. Right on the water, with a fireplace, and there's plenty of room if I want to stay with her for a bit." She giggled. "We could have an overnight, like the kids do."

Oh, boy, thought Lucy. "Sounds wonderful," she said, trying to sound as if she meant it. "Have a good time, and I'll see you at dinner."

"Oh, don't set a place for me. I don't think we'll be back before eight or so. I'll probably eat with Kate; she mentioned something about a farm-to-table restaurant. She knows this place that cooks locally sourced sausage over an open fire."

I just bet she does, thought Lucy, wishing she could consign Kate to the flames. "I guess we'll see you when we see you."

Ending the call, Lucy considered calling Bill with the news about Kate, but decided there was no rush. He was bound to be upset, and he'd find out soon enough. Soon enough came at dinner when he asked where his mother was.

"She's out with Kate Klein," said Lucy, passing the mashed potatoes.

He helped himself to a big serving. "Wasn't Kate supposed to go back to Portland? Or Florida?"

Lucy sighed, preparing to face the worst. "She's got herself an Airbnb. She's staying for a month."

Bill set down the gravy boat. "She's here for a month?"

"Talk about a smooth operator," commented Zoe.

"Really nervy, if you ask me," offered Sara.

"All that and more," grumbled Bill.

"She's obviously making a play for Mom's affection," said Lucy, spearing a bit of lettuce with her fork. "She took her to Rockland today for lunch and the museum, and they're having a farm-to-table dinner. Wood-fired."

"Oh, at that cool place out on Route 1?" inquired Zoe.

"I think so."

"We should try it; it's supposed to be really good."

"That's a good idea," suggested Lucy. "If Edna likes the food, we could take her there, too. Like it's her idea, make her feel good about sharing something new and exciting." She cut into her pork chop, sourced from the IGA. "If you think about it, we've kind of taken her for granted. We haven't done anything to make her visit special; we've all been busy and have left her here all alone."

Bill was miffed and quick to defend himself. "Well, I'm

sorry, Lucy, but I have an anxious client who wants his job done on time!"

"I know, Bill. I've got commitments, too. We all do. But we could have made more time for your mother, that's all I'm saying."

"I think you're right, Mom," said Zoe. "I'm free tomorrow afternoon, and there's a movie at the library. I could take her."

Sara nodded approvingly. "What is it?"

"It's about an English woman who was a dedicated Communist. I missed it when they showed it at the college."

"I'm not sure that's the sort of thing that Edna would enjoy," said Lucy, thinking that this was going to be harder than she thought.

"No, I suppose not," admitted Zoe. "And I was going to go with this guy, anyway."

"Which guy?" asked Sara, very interested.

"Oh, no one you know." She paused. "He's just a friend."

Dinner had been over for an hour, the table was cleared, and the dishwasher was humming when Edna came home, looking very tired. She dragged herself across the family room, where the family was gathered so Bill and the girls could watch Duke versus Michigan, and plopped down on the sectional without bothering to take off her coat. "That was quite a day," she said.

"Did you have a good time?" asked Lucy, looking up from her crossword puzzle. She had no interest at all in March Madness.

"Oh, yes. It was a lot of fun, but Kate is quite a bit younger than I am, and that windswept hill out by Christina's house—well, it took quite a bit out of me."

"Can I get you something, Grandma?" asked Zoe, eager to do her part in the family's decision to pay more attention to Edna. "Shall I take your coat?"

"Thanks, dear. That would be lovely." Edna shrugged out of her coat, with Zoe's help, and asked for another favor as Zoe carried it off to hang it up. "Would you mind getting me that navy sweater from my suitcase? I'm a little chilly."

"Happy to," said Zoe, zipping out of the room. A few minutes later, she was back, with the sweater and a thick manila envelope. "Is this the will you were looking for?"

Suddenly, Bill didn't care about his brackets. "Did you find the will?" He snatched the envelope and opened it, unfolding the enclosed document. "You did. This is it. Where was it?"

"In the suitcase," said Zoe, helping her grandmother put the sweater on.

"My suitcase?" inquired Edna. "Really? I had no idea?"

"It was under the lining. When I took the sweater out, I noticed the zipper on the lining was partly opened, so I went to close it, and I felt something bulky under it, and I knew the will was missing, so I took a peek, and there was this envelope, along with a couple of passports."

"Of course." Edna dabbed at her eyes with a crumpled tissue she had extracted from the sleeve of her blouse. "Bill put it there when we took that Caribbean cruise in December. I remember him doing it, saying you never knew when it would be needed and we'd better have it with us. It's been there all this time." She blew her nose. "I don't know how I could have forgotten."

"Just the sort of thing Dad would do," said Bill.

"So like him," agreed Edna. "He always did it, whenever we traveled." She sighed and seemed to shrink into the sofa. "Now you'll all think I'm, you know, developing memory problems."

"Nothing of the kind," said Lucy, giving her mother-in-law a hug. "We're just glad it's turned up." She paused, glancing at Bill, who was holding the folded document. "Can we read it?" While she was pretty sure she knew what to expect, there was always the possibility of a surprise. A bequest for Bill, perhaps. Or maybe even the very thing she dreaded: some sort of provision and acknowledgment of Kate as his daughter.

"Sure." Edna shrugged. "It's very straightforward, the same as my will. We left everything to each other." She gave Bill a weak little smile, signaling he should commence reading.

"Okay, here goes," he began, scanning the first page. "There's some legalese about paying debts and taxes . . .'"

"That's the first part?" interrupted Zoe, sounding surprised. "The first part of the will is about debts and taxes?"

"Always," said Bill, with a nod. "You can't escape those, even by dying." He turned back to the will. "After paying state and federal taxes and any outstanding debts, we get to the monetary bequests. 'I'—that's Dad—'give, devise and bequeath all the rest, residue, and remainder of my estate, both real and personal and wherever situated, to my wife, Edna P. Stone, if she survives me.'" He then scanned the remaining pages. "That's all that's really relevant now."

Lucy found herself letting out a long sigh of relief.

"Tell them the rest, Bill," said Edna, in a resigned tone. "They're probably dying to know what happens when I go."

"Not at all!" exclaimed Lucy, squeezing Edna's shoulders. "We don't want to think about losing you."

"And it doesn't really matter, because you could change it. You could write another will," said Sara, always the realistic one.

"I won't. I wouldn't do that. My Bill's the one who earned the money, and he wanted it to go to his son after I die." She twisted the tissue she was holding in her hands and raised her teary face, looking straight at Bill. "And I'm trying not to spend too much, so there'll be plenty for you."

"Well, that's completely unnecessary," said Bill. His head was down, and he was replacing the will in its envelope, and when he spoke his voice was thick. "Dad wanted to provide for you; you were his everything, and that's the way it should be. You should have everything you need," he said, pausing, and then adding, "or want. It's your money now to spend as you see fit."

"That's right," said Lucy, standing up. "And I think we're all agreed, right?"

Both Sara and Zoe chimed in. "Absolutely," said Sara.

"For sure," agreed Zoe.

"Well, that's one problem solved," said Lucy, standing up. "I'm going to make a cup of chamomile tea. Would anyone like one?"

"Sounds lovely, dear," said Edna, somewhat mechanically.

Lucy went off to the kitchen, where she filled the kettle and set it on the stove, then got out a couple of mugs and dropped in the tea bags. While she waited for the water to boil, she couldn't help wondering why Edna wasn't ecstatic about the discovery of the will, and wondered how she could have forgotten that it was in the suitcase. Edna must have known—she said it herself—that Bill Sr. always took the will along when they traveled. It seemed odd that the suitcase wasn't the first place she had looked for the will.

Even odder, why didn't she notice the hidden documents when she packed the suitcase to come to Maine?

The only answer that Lucy could come up with was that maybe on some deep psychological level she hadn't wanted the will to be found. But why? Because it would mean that her husband was really gone forever? Or maybe because she wanted Kate to have a claim on his estate, since she believed wholeheartedly that Kate was his daughter and she knew she wasn't mentioned in the will. Of course, as Sara had pointed out, Bill Sr.'s will wasn't the last word. Edna could decide to write a new will of her own at any time and could leave every last cent to Kate.

Her thoughts were interrupted by the kettle's whistle, and she filled the mugs with boiling water and placed them on a tray, along with spoons and the sugar bowl. Proceeding into the family room, she had to admit she was relieved that the will had been found. Now they'd see if Kate was genuinely interested in establishing a relationship with Edna and the rest of the family, or if she was simply after the money.

# Chapter Seventeen

By noon the next day, Phyllis was literally tearing her green-tinted hair out, trying to keep up with the phone calls and drop-in customers who wanted to take advantage of Ted's latest brainstorm: one week of free classified ads. Everyone, it seemed, had simply been ignoring the amazing items they no longer wanted that they'd stored in their attics, basements, and garages. Yesterday's trash was today's treasure, and that rusty old Radio Flyer wagon was now a vintage collectible, offered for $100 or best offer.

Lucy was helping out, amused at the sudden eagerness to get rid of a size 14 wedding dress, never worn; a set of Japanese knives, never used; and a genuine, bright red English phone booth, described as a "unique decorative accent and conversation piece," offered for $995. "Why on earth have people been storing all this stuff?" she mused aloud, thinking it might make an interesting feature story, when the phones suddenly fell blessedly silent.

"Why did they ever get it all in the first place?" countered Phyllis, leaning back in her chair and fanning herself with a manila folder.

Lucy stood up and stretched, then went over to the water cooler and filled a cup for herself and one for Phyllis, who she suspected was in the early stages of menopause. "Here you go; you've got to stay hydrated."

"Thanks," said Phyllis, draining the paper cup and then heading directly for the bathroom. Her phone rang, and she paused, sighing as she reached for it, but Lucy stopped her.

"I'll get it," she said, plopping herself down in Phyllis's desk chair. The caller wasn't a customer, however; it was Ted.

"Lucy, I want you to get an interview with Rob Callahan."

"At the jail?" Lucy wasn't keen on the idea; she'd conducted a few jailhouse interviews in the past and always found it a deeply depressing and upsetting experience. The corrections officers were always officious, she had to submit to a pat-down before they'd admit her, and the sound of those numerous doors clanging behind her made her fearful that she'd never get out again. Worst of all was the smell, which she guessed was a mix of sweat, fear, and Lysol, and which clung to her clothes and hair after she'd made her escape. But she always did get out and then felt a bit ashamed of herself for being so squeamish.

"Yeah, where else?"

"Are you sure that's a good idea?" she asked. "We're not very popular with the sheriff right now, and I've got this great idea for a feature about the stuff people are advertising in the free classifieds."

The phones were ringing again, and Phyllis was still in the bathroom. Lucy tried to ignore them, straining to hear Ted's voice.

"If you've got time for the feature, go ahead. Rob takes

priority right now. You're on his visitor list, and the lawyers tell me you have every right to see him. Besides, they want to get his side of the story out. They want photos, a big spread. I've got Fran researching other jailed journalists all around the world. We want to plant the seed that this is part of a worldwide move on the part of authoritarian governments to stifle the free press."

Lucy found this a bit hard to swallow. "He's charged with murder, Ted. This isn't one of those 'I refuse to reveal my sources' situations."

"Well, from what Fran tells me, journalists get jailed every day on all sorts of bogus charges, ranging from spying to heresy. And sometimes there's no legal process at all; they just lure the poor sap into an embassy and bring out the bone saws. The guy walks in whole and is carried out in a bunch of black plastic garbage bags."

"Okay, okay. Your intrepid girl reporter is on the job, shining the light of public scrutiny into the darkest corner of our community."

"And tell Rob that we haven't forgotten him, that we're working hard on his case, and the lawyers think there's a good chance we can get the charges reduced and then he'd be eligible for bail, which the TRUTH Project would pay."

Lucy didn't think this was realistic and said so. "I don't want to raise his hopes for nothing," she insisted, as Phyllis reappeared with her hair neatly combed and a fresh slick of Amazing Apricot lipstick.

"No. Hope is the thing that will help him cope, even if it is a bit of reach."

"Well, I'll play it by ear. Any questions you want me to ask?" She was standing up, ready to cede Phyllis's desk.

"Mostly, let him proclaim his innocence, in as many ways as he can express it. Don't worry about giving away too much; the lawyers are going to vet the story before we print it, so there won't be anything damaging that the prosecution can use against him."

"Okay, boss," said Lucy, resigned to her fate. She hung up, and Phyllis settled herself, immediately taking the next call.

Lucy grabbed a couple of reporter's notebooks from the stack on her desk and dropped them into her purse, checked that her cell was charged, and put on her jacket.

"Where are you going?" demanded Phyllis, her hand over the phone receiver.

"To the jail, to interview Rob."

"Say hi for me," she said, with a sympathetic smile, then returned to her call. "Unh-hunh. Red vinyl, reclines, and also massages. A bargain at sixty dollars."

Smiling, Lucy gave her a little wave and reached for the door, setting the little bell to jingling.

That cheery sound was a distant memory when she pulled into one of the visitors' parking spots at the county jail. She climbed out of her car reluctantly, but straightened her shoulders and marched up the path to the heavily studded gray-metal door. She took a deep breath of moist spring air, then pulled the door open and entered.

The reception area was a small space. The walls were painted avocado green, the floor was covered with industrial vinyl tile, and a counter was staffed by a uniformed guard. Her frizzy hair was dyed blond and cut in a short, mannish style that exposed her heavy jaw and double chin, her ample bosom was covered in a baby-blue polyester blend shirt, and she peered suspiciously at Lucy through a pair of tiny, granny-style, wire-rimmed eyeglasses. Lucy thought the poor woman could certainly benefit from some of Sue's fashion advice, then immediately felt ashamed for being so catty. She was certainly no fashion plate herself in her ancient puffy jacket and duck boots.

"I'm here to visit a prisoner, Rob Callahan," said Lucy, summoning a big smile. "I'm Lucy Stone."

"I know who you are," said the guard.

Slightly unnerved, Lucy offered another smile. "Great. I believe I'm on the visitor list."

"Doesn't matter."

"Pardon?"

"Callahan's not allowed any visitors."

Lucy was puzzled. "How come?"

"Disciplinary matter."

"Oh." Lucy thought for a minute. "For how long?"

"I dunno."

"Well, is there some sort of protocol? A usual amount of time?"

"Depends on the infraction."

"Can you tell me what infraction Rob committed?"

"Nope. Prisoner confidentiality."

"Can I leave a note for him?"

The woman shrugged. "Sure."

Lucy quickly wrote a brief note to Rob, telling him she had tried to visit and would come again, and that the lawyers were working hard on his case. Folding it, she handed it to the guard. "Will you make sure he gets this?"

"I think his mail's on hold."

"Disciplinary matter?" asked Lucy.

The woman shrugged. Lucy started to reach for her wallet, thinking that a ten- or twenty-dollar bill might ensure delivery of the note, then decided an attempt to bribe a guard might only make things worse for Rob. Or herself. Instead, she decided a better course of action would be to go directly to the sheriff and demand some answers from him.

It was only a short walk to the sheriff's office, and as she marched along, Lucy organized her thoughts, preparing the questions she wanted answered. Her attitude was purposeful but polite as she entered the neat little brick building, with its brand-new shingled roof, and asked to see Sheriff Murphy.

"Of course," said his receptionist, Nora, giving her a friendly smile. "He's in a meeting, but should be free shortly. Can I get you something while you wait? Coffee, tea, a soft drink?"

"Nothing, thanks," said Lucy, seating herself in a comfy wing chair by the window. Outside, she noticed, little clumps of snowdrops were bravely poking through a lingering clump of snow.

She pulled out her phone and checked her messages; then sent a text to Ted, informing him that she hadn't been able to see Rob and was now waiting to talk to the sheriff. She'd just pressed SEND when the door to the sheriff's office opened and he stepped out, along with a man in a suit whom Lucy didn't recognize. The sheriff acknowledged her with a nod, took the guy's hand, and shook it firmly while clapping his shoulder. The man gave the receptionist a little wave and departed, allowing the sheriff to focus his attention on Lucy.

"Ah, now, it's Lucy Stone, our own Lois Lane," he said. His blue eyes twinkled, his perfect teeth gleamed, and his handshake was warm and firm. "What can I do for you?"

In spite of herself, Lucy found herself responding to his charm. "I just have a few questions for you. Clark Kent couldn't make it."

Murphy beamed at her. "Well, come on down, like the

game show host says, and I'll see if I can help you." He turned to the receptionist. "Hold my calls, darlin'."

Nora smiled and nodded, and Lucy stepped through the door the sheriff was holding for her, waiting politely until he invited her to sit. When he did, she ignored the cozy seating area and chose one of the visitor's chairs facing his desk, and he seated himself behind the desk in his big leather executive chair. "How's the family?" he asked.

"Fine, just fine," said Lucy, attempting to resist what she was certain was a calculated attempt to disarm her.

"I understand you've got two that have flown the nest, and two lovely lasses still at home."

Lucy decided resistance was futile, and that it was better to play along. "I'm going to lose another one soon. Sara will be moving to Boston to work at the Museum of Science."

"Congratulations. She must be a clever girl." He smiled approvingly. "But, of course, you'll miss her."

"True," agreed Lucy. "I still have one little nestling."

"Ah, they grow up too fast," said the sheriff. "Now, what can I do for you today?"

Startled, Lucy remembered the purpose of her visit, which was not to make small talk with the sheriff, no matter how friendly and flattering he seemed. "Actually, I came over to visit Rob Callahan, in the jail, but was told he is not allowed visitors because of a disciplinary matter."

"Oh, dear." Sheriff Murphy knitted his brow, expressing concern. "Discipline, of course, is the responsibility of the prison superintendent, Michael Harrison. You would have to ask him, but as you no doubt know, we take the rights of our prisoners very seriously. Any disciplinary infractions and punishments are confidential, unless a court judge decides otherwise."

"Well, I guess it's a matter for Rob's lawyers, then," said Lucy.

"Ah, the lawyers. I understand your friend has some very high-powered legal representatives who have come all the way from Washington, D.C."

"Yes. Rob is fortunate that his employer, the TRUTH Project, provides legal counsel for journalists who find themselves in legal jeopardy."

The sheriff was on it, like a dog seizing a juicy bone. "So he doesn't actually work for Ted at *The Courier*?"

"Not directly," explained Lucy. "This TRUTH Project provides experienced journalists to small-town newspapers to give advice and improve coverage in areas that are in danger of becoming underserved."

"And is that the situation here? We've always had a fine paper, the *Gabber*, and now Ted has taken over and named it *The Courier*, which I admit does sound more professional." He paused, propping his elbows on his desk and tenting his hands. "As for me, I miss the *Gabber*'s folksy, small-town approach. For the life of me, I can't see why Ted thought he needed to bring in an outsider, a big-city fella who doesn't understand our country ways. Where does this Rob come from anyways?"

"Cleveland," admitted Lucy.

"Ah. My point exactly. Why, he's probably used to all sorts of violence and shooting. Those big cities are infested with crime and rats, they're nothing at all like our safe little towns here in Maine. Here, we're not quite so diverse, everybody knows everybody, and we pretty much share the same traditional values. Good wholesome values."

Lucy thought this was a shameless exaggeration. She knew only too well that Gilead and Tinker's Cove both had plenty of drug addiction, domestic violence, and poverty.

The towns were picture-postcard pretty, and people often left their doors unlocked, and some even left their car keys in the ignition, trusting in their neighbors' honesty. That trust was sometimes violated, however, as her friend Barney Culpepper often reminded people in his role as community outreach officer.

She wasn't about to argue with the sheriff, however, so she returned to the reason for her visit. "We are indeed very lucky to live in such a safe community," she said. "And I'm sure we're all very grateful for the police and first responders who keep us safe. But I have to say, I am concerned about Rob Callahan and would very much like to see him and be reassured of his well-being. Is going to court the only way I can do that?"

The sheriff nodded along sympathetically as she delivered this little speech, then reached across the desk and took her hand. "You are to be commended for caring so deeply about your colleague, Lucy. Your concern is admirable, but unnecessary. Believe me, we're taking very good care of him." He shrugged. "I think you should leave this to the lawyers, let them earn those big hourly billings, which is probably what they're really after anyway."

"I don't . . ." began Lucy, only to be interrupted by the sheriff, who was still maintaining eye contact and was definitely not smiling. "Now, you and I know that justice will be done, and that process takes time. In the meantime, I think *The Courier* should focus on the good news and the wonderful strength of our community. We've got a big celebration coming up, including a marvelous parade, and I think that's the story you should be covering."

"Point taken," said Lucy, deciding it was time to go. "If only my boss felt the same way." She stood up and slipped the straps of her bag onto her shoulder. "Thanks for your time."

"No problem. I'm always happy to have a chat with an attractive young lady." The smile was back, but Lucy felt it wasn't genuine, it was a cover-up for the sheriff's frustration and anger about Ted's approach to the county news. "Now you drive safely; you've got a family that depends on you, and it can be dangerous out there what with all these cell phones and whatnot."

"I'll do my best," said Lucy, not quite believing the sheriff was truly concerned for her welfare. His words, she realized, and even his interest in her daughters could be interpreted as a sort of threat.

Back in the car, Lucy found herself driving extremely cautiously, not letting her mind drift, as she often did when driving on these familiar roads. She gripped the steering wheel tightly, watching for erratic drivers and preparing to avoid them; she braked well in advance of stop signs and flipped on her turn signals long before she actually needed to. She also kept an eye out for speed-limit signs and scrupulously obeyed them, even slowing to the posted fifteen mile an hour limit in front of the elementary school, although it was still in session and there were no children to be seen.

When her hands began to ache, she realized she was being somewhat paranoid and, feeling rebellious, switched on the radio. She was well out of town now, driving on Route 1, and she decided it would be much safer to keep up with the flow of traffic rather than continue to fight it. A couple of cars had passed her, pulling out dangerously into oncoming traffic, and she didn't want to be one of those poky drivers that other drivers cursed.

She was bopping along to the music when her cell

phone rang. It was Ted, informing her that he'd heard on the police scanner that a dog walker had discovered a body in the Great Bay conservation area and instructing her to get to the scene of the discovery ASAP. "Right, boss," she replied, feeling the familiar surge of adrenalin that came whenever she was put on a big story. And bodies were always big stories.

She quickly signaled and did a fast U-turn, speeding up a bit and heading for the Great Bay Reservation, which was only a few miles away. Paths in the conservation area, which surrounded a large, shallow saltwater bay that was actually an estuary, were popular with dog walkers and bird-watchers. Lucy was familiar with the area; she had often kayaked there with Bill and the kids, enjoying the calm water and frequently sighting great blue herons and kingfishers. Today, however, the parking area was filled with several police cruisers and the medical examiner's van. She parked alongside and headed on foot down the trail toward the little cluster of officials gathered in the marsh grass a few feet from the trail.

As she drew closer, she identified State Police Detective Lieutenant Horowitz, whom she knew well from covering other stories, along with some uniformed troopers. The ME was bent over, studying the ground, and a young woman was seated on a large rock with a black Lab lying on the ground beside her. As she drew closer, she realized the young woman was carrying a small baby that was snoozing against her chest in a carrier.

Assuming the young woman was the dog walker who had discovered the body, and since she was the first person Lucy encountered, she identified herself and asked for a brief interview. "What's your name?" she began, producing her notebook.

"Mickey Woods, and this is Sophie, only two months," she replied, seeming quite happy to talk. "My dog is named Connor. He's the one who found the body."

"Isn't that always the way?" sympathized Lucy. "Sometimes it makes me wonder why anybody walks dogs, considering the stuff they find."

"I know," laughed the woman. "He brings home all sorts of stuff. The other day, it was my neighbor's shoe; she left them on the porch because they were muddy."

Lucy smiled encouragingly. "So, did you see the body?"

"No, I just saw bones at first. I thought it was a bird or something, but then I realized it was a hand."

"The dog didn't . . ."

"Oh, no. It was sort of poking out of the ground. And there was a ring, one of those big silver skull rings." She paused. "That's all I saw, really. Connor was starting to dig, and I pulled him away and called nine-one-one."

"How long before the police came?" asked Lucy.

"I don't really know. I nursed the baby a bit, so the time passed."

Lucy remembered those days, and how time stopped when she was nursing her babies, marveling at their perfect little fingers and sweet cheeks. "Your baby is beautiful, by the way," she said, looking up as Lieutenant Horowitz approached.

"That was fast work, Lucy," he said, giving her a rather disapproving look. He was wearing a tan raincoat, which hung open over his usual gray suit, and a pair of black rubber boots.

"Ted heard it on the scanner," Lucy told him. "He sent me right over, since I happened to be in the neighborhood. Have you got an ID?"

"Not yet. It's a young woman; the ME thinks she's been in the ground for eight to ten months. That's all I've got."

"I understand she was wearing a ring?" pressed Lucy.

"Yeah, but we're not releasing that information just yet."

Lucy was surprised. "But wouldn't it help identify her?"

"It's up to the DA to decide what information to release to the public. He'll probably hold a press conference tomorrow. Meanwhile, all I'm prepared to say is that the body of a young woman was found buried in a shallow grave in the Great Bay Reservation, and according to the ME, she's been there for about eight to ten months. Period."

"Okay, thanks for that," said Lucy. Horowitz wheeled around and went back to the gravesite, leaving Lucy alone with Mickey.

"I hope you're not too upset," said Lucy, who knew the months after childbirth were often an emotional minefield, fueled by raging hormones.

"I have to admit, I'm kind of excited about the whole thing. I love mysteries. I read them and watch them on TV." She bent her neck and nuzzled her baby's silken head. "I especially like true crime."

"Well, it seems you've found a crime, since I don't think she buried herself."

"I know. I'll be looking for the story in the paper. Will I be in it?"

"Sure, if you don't mind. Can I take your photo?"

"Yeah, and be sure to put the dog in, too."

"Got it," said Lucy, snapping the photo.

The baby was beginning to stir in the carrier, and Mickey started jiggling a bit, in hopes of soothing the child. "Do you think I need to stay?" she asked Lucy.

As far as Lucy could tell, the investigators were ignoring Mickey. "Did you give your name and contact info?"

Mickey nodded, now swinging back and forth from her hips as the baby's cries grew louder.

"Then I don't see any reason why you can't go."

They walked back to the parking lot together, where Mickey carefully placed the baby into a car seat and drove off in an aged Subaru wagon. Lucy settled herself in her SUV and sat for a moment, chewing her lip. She hadn't heard of any missing girls, at least not officially, but she wondered if Melanie Wall might be the young woman buried in the marsh. Everyone had assumed that she had simply moved on in her life, but maybe her life had ended. Lucy decided to ask Sara if she remembered anything special about Melanie, and whether she had any distinctive jewelry like a big silver skull ring.

Sara didn't answer, and Lucy's call went to voice mail, so she put her phone down and started the car. She'd just turned out of the parking area when it rang and Sara cheerfully asked, "What's up, Mom?"

"I was just thinking and wondering if you remember whether Melanie Wall had any special jewelry. Do you remember anything in particular?"

"Oh, yeah, Mom. She had this big old silver skull ring; she always wore it. She was into a rock-and-roll sort of look, chokers and leather, some lace, too. And she had some major tattoos." She paused. "Why do you ask?"

"Well, they've found a body in the Great Bay Reservation, and I think it might be Melanie."

"Really?"

"It's not official, so maybe it's someone else."

"I hope it's not her, but I guess I shouldn't say that. It's terrible. I feel bad for whoever it is."

"So do I, sweetie. And it goes without saying, you stay safe, okay?"

"You bet, Mom."

Back on the road, Lucy suddenly felt tearful and let out a huge sob. She didn't know Melanie, not really; she'd only seen her around, but she certainly didn't deserve to end up in a shallow grave. What really bothered her, she decided, was the way Melanie had seemed to drop off the face of the earth and nobody seemed to care. The girls had gotten that email after she'd left town, but hadn't followed up. They simply weren't that close, and they were busy with school and their own lives.

It seemed that something had brought Melanie back to Tinker's Cove, and whatever it was had resulted in her death. It was horribly depressing to think about, the way these girls on the margin of society were practically disposable. They broke free from their families for whatever reason, ended up with crappy jobs and dabbled in drugs, were taken advantage of by predators, and, all too often, ended up dead.

She felt overwhelmed by it all, starting with her failure to see Rob. She didn't believe for one minute that he'd done anything that required discipline in prison; he was smart enough to realize that it would be much better for him to behave himself and be a model prisoner. This whole discipline thing was simply a screen, a way to keep family and friends from seeing him. But why? Was he being mistreated, or were they simply toying with him, letting him know who was in authority? It gave her a queasy feeling, and she remembered her interview with Allie Shaw.

*The ones with all the power are going to take advantage of the ones with no power . . . It's always there, the threat . . . they can do whatever they want to you.* That's what Allie had said, and she was right, unless a more powerful agent, like a judge, could be persuaded to intervene. The sheriff was all about power, getting it, keeping it, and using it, and he wasn't going to give it up without a fight.

That was the challenge, she decided, reaching the crest of Red Top Hill and turning into her driveway. But how on earth were they going to expose the truth about him?

An unfamiliar car was occupying her usual spot by the porch stairs, so she parked next to it, wondering who it belonged to. Maybe one of the girls had a visitor? Or was it Edna?

When she entered the kitchen, she discovered the visitor was Kate, and she was engaged in giving Edna a very warm embrace.

"It's been so lovely. Thanks for having me," said Kate, giving Edna a squeeze.

"Oh, it's been my pleasure," enthused Edna, beaming at Kate. "I hope we can see each other again soon."

"Absolutely, I'll be in touch," said Kate, turning to Lucy. "I hope you don't mind my dropping by to see Edna . . ."

"Oh, no," said Lucy, who minded a whole lot. "This is her home while she's visiting, and she's welcome to have visitors."

"I knew you'd feel that way," said Kate, giving Lucy's hand a squeeze. "Well, I must run. Hope to see you all again real soon."

The door had no sooner closed behind Kate when Lucy turned on Edna. "Really? Don't you see what she's up to? She's like a cuckoo, trying to replace us, your real family."

"My goodness, Lucy," said Edna, growing rather agitated. "That's a terrible thing to say. She's not trying to replace you all; she wants is to join us and be part of our family. She never had a father or a real family. She told me that when she was a little child in school, she used to make up stories about why she didn't have a father. He was a soldier, she'd say, pretending, or even a superhero, saving civilization."

"I'm not surprised," sneered Lucy. "From what I can see, she's a very good storyteller indeed, and you shouldn't believe everything she tells you."

Edna stared at her, her cheeks glowing, but she didn't say anything. Instead, she turned and walked out of the kitchen and went upstairs, straight to her room. Standing below, in the kitchen, Lucy heard the door click shut.

Damn, it had to be said, she told herself, throwing her bag down on a chair and taking off her jacket. It was too bad if Edna didn't want to hear the truth. Seniors got swindled every day, and Edna was a tempting target for a con artist, and that's what Lucy suspected Kate really was. It wasn't the possibility of losing a small fortune that bothered her, she told herself; it was the hurt that Edna would endure when she realized she'd been taken advantage of and realized that Kate hadn't really cared for her at all. Of course, she admitted with a sense of shame, it really was about the money, too.

# Chapter Eighteen

The next morning, Lucy was surprised when Edna dragged her suitcase down to the kitchen and announced that Kate had invited her to stay with her in her vacation rental.

"She has plenty of room, and I don't want to be a burden," she explained, with a brave little smile, buttoning up her coat. "It seems as if I'm a bit in the way here."

Lucy felt as if she'd been gut-punched. "That's not the case at all, Edna. We love having you here."

"I know, dear, but you are all so busy with your lives. With Kate, I'll be able to get out and about; she's eager to see all the sights, so it will be more interesting for me. She's got a whole itinerary planned—trips to Camden and all sorts of wonderful places. Why, today we're going to have lunch at the Whitehall Inn, where Edna St. Vincent Millay worked as a girl. She tells me they have a display there with photos and things. I'm really looking forward to that. You know, I was named after her. My mother adored her poetry."

"I know we've been neglecting you," admitted Lucy, as Edna went over to the window to see if Kate had arrived yet. "I guess we've taken you for granted."

"Nonsense, dear. I've enjoyed being here." She took in a sharp little breath and raised her shoulders. "Ah, she's here, and I'm off." She pulled up the handle on her roller suitcase, slipped the straps of her handbag onto her shoulder, and yanked open the door. "I"ll stay in touch," she promised, zipping out onto the porch.

Lucy looked through the curtained window on the door and saw that Kate was already hurrying up the path with a big grin on her face, ready, willing, and able to help Edna with her suitcase. Lucy opened the door, not willing to let Edna leave without a proper good-bye.

"Here already," she said, greeting Kate with a big smile that was actually painful. "Have a great time, you two." She gave Edna an awkward hug. "I'll give you a call tonight to see how you're settling in, and remember, you've always got a place here."

Edna looked as if she was about to cry, blinking and pressing her lips together. She took Lucy's hands and patted them. "I know, dear, and thank you for everything."

"Oh, you're welcome. It's been lovely having you. Now go on and have a wonderful time," she urged, wishing she actually meant it. "See you soon," she sang, waving as Kate and Edna negotiated the porch steps. She watched as they went down the brick walkway to the drive, where Kate helped Edna into the passenger seat and stowed the suitcase. She gave Lucy a triumphant smile and a wave, then got into the car and drove off.

Still somewhat shocked, Lucy closed the door and turned, surprised to see that Zoe was standing behind her. "What's going on?" she asked Lucy. "Grandma's room is empty; she's folded the sheets and left them on the bed."

"She's going to stay with Kate," said Lucy.

"No way," exclaimed Zoe.

"Way. They just left. Kate came and picked her up,"

replied Lucy, accepting a huge sense of guilt like her grandmother used to slip on the old gray cardigan she kept handy on the back of a kitchen chair. "We should have treated her better, taken her places, fussed over her."

Zoe had a different take. "Or she could have taken more of an interest in our lives. She never once asked me about my job or college or anything. She just sat in front of the TV with her flip phone in her hand, waiting for Kate to call."

"Somehow that doesn't make me feel better," said Lucy, slipping on her jacket and grabbing her bag. "I've gotta run. Would you take that hamburger out of the freezer for me? I'm going to make meat loaf for dinner."

"Dad will love that," said Zoe.

"You know what he isn't going to love? His mother trotting off with Kate," said Lucy, grabbing the doorknob.

"I sense a storm's a-brewin'," said Zoe. "Have a good day, Mom."

Lucy had reached town and was parking her car on Main Street when she noticed Rosemary McGourt on the sidewalk, dressed in workout clothes and headed toward the Move! Gym that had recently taken up occupancy in the old Slack's Hardware store on Main Street. She hopped out of the car and hailed her, hoping to get more information about Gabe.

"What do you want?" asked Rosemary, not missing a step and walking on.

"Just a bit of information," said Lucy, walking alongside Rosemary.

"Look, I've told you, I don't want to talk about my ex. I don't want to think about him. That was a bad part of my life, and I'm moving on." Which is exactly what she did, brushing past Lucy.

"Please," begged Lucy. "You know they've discovered a body that's probably Melanie Wall, and it's no secret she was involved with Gabe . . ."

"Stupid girl. I could've told her he was trouble."

"Did you know about her?"

"Honestly, I didn't pay attention. I was over Gabe. We'd been separated for over a year, and I was counting the days until the divorce came through."

"So you weren't living together?"

"No. And even before that, I mostly tried to pretend he wasn't there. I didn't pay attention to what he did or where he went or who he saw. My therapist says I had the worst case of denial she's ever seen. I was married, but I wasn't, if you get my meaning. He was like a piece of furniture . . . more like an unreliable old furnace or hot water heater that you think might explode at any minute. Getting myself and the kids through the day in one piece was all I thought about."

This was going nowhere, thought Lucy, deciding to try another tack. "What about friends? Did he have buddies? Anybody who can tell me about him?"

"I dunno. I don't care. I'm just glad I never have to see his ugly face ever again."

Lucy had a sudden inspiration. "What about the pall-bearers at his funeral? Do you know who they were?"

"I didn't go to the funeral. Gabe's mom wanted to take the boys, and in a moment of weakness, I let her." She let out a huge sigh. "And, boy, were they impressed with all the cop cars and motorcycles. Now they think he was some sort of hero instead of the abusive monster he really was!"

"I guess that was the point of the whole show," said Lucy, thinking she should try contacting Mary Catherine again. "Thanks for your help. Have a great workout."

Rosemary finally smiled. "You know what? I've lost twenty-one pounds."

"You look great; divorce must agree with you."

"Not divorce, death," said Rosemary. She raised her eyes toward heaven and adopted a phony Irish brogue. "'Twas a blessing, to be sure."

Lucy found herself smiling in response. So Rosemary had a sense of humor—good for her. She'd finally been able to escape Gabe McGourt's abuse, once and for all. But her smile vanished when she remembered Melanie Wall, whose decayed body had been found in a shallow grave. It didn't seem as if Melanie had been so lucky, she thought, standing at the curb and waiting for a car to pass. Looking at the old office, she glanced approvingly at the new sign with *The Courier* picked out in gold letters.

"Top o' the mornin' to you," said Phyllis by way of greeting. She was continuing the Irish theme with her green-tinted hair, green reading glasses, and a green sweatshirt picturing a leprechaun along with his glittering pot of gold sequins.

"You've sure got the spirit," said Lucy.

"And why not?" replied Phyllis. "A bit o' fun never hurt anyone."

"Fun," mused Lucy, thinking of Edna's abrupt departure this morning. "What a concept. I haven't had much of it lately."

"Well, you've just got to pick yourself up and start over. Today is the first day of the rest of your life. Remember, when one door closes, another door opens."

"Is this National Cliché Day or something?" asked Lucy, who was sitting at her desk without bothering to take off her jacket and pawing through the recent issues of the paper. At last, she found what she wanted: a photo of the pallbearers carrying Gabe McGourt's casket into the church.

"Nothing wrong with a good cliché," countered Phyllis. "They wouldn't be clichés if people didn't believe in them, right?"

"Well, I'm outta here," said Lucy, tucking the paper into her big tote bag. "It's the early bird that catches the worm."

"Make hay while the sun shines," said Phyllis, with a little wave.

As she drove over to Mary Catherine's house, Lucy wondered if she was on a fool's errand. After all, when she'd interviewed her before the funeral, Mary Catherine had practically thrown her out of the house, insulted when she'd inquired about Gabe's relationships with women. She'd considered her son an angel and wasn't about to admit anything to the contrary. Nevertheless, thought Lucy, she had to try to make peace with the woman since she was probably the only one who could identify all the pallbearers. Arriving once again at the neat little house, which had a shamrock wreath with a black bow on the door, Lucy took a deep breath and got out of the car. She squared her shoulders, dug the newspaper out of her purse, and marched up the walk to the door and rang the bell.

"Oh, it's you," said Mary Catherine, only opening the door a few inches and peering at Lucy through narrowed eyes.

"It's me," said Lucy, with a wry smile. "I want to make amends, and I brought you a copy of *The Courier* with all the details of Gabe's funeral, just in case you wanted to save it, maybe something for his boys to remember their father by."

"Now that was very decent of you," admitted Mary Catherine, opening the door a bit wider. "It was a lovely tribute to my poor boy, now wasn't it?"

"It certainly was," said Lucy. "I don't think we've seen anything like it around here. It was a first."

"It was all due to the sheriff, lovely man that he is." Now the door was fully open, and Lucy saw that Mary Catherine was dressed in a gray track suit with a black stripe down each leg. Her snowy-white hair was neatly permed, and she was wearing tiny little shamrock studs in each ear. "I was just about to have a cup of tea, dear. Will you join me?"

"I'd love to," said Lucy, determined not to blow this opportunity. "Thank you so much."

Mary Catherine stepped back, admitting her, and directed her to the living room, where she was invited to take a seat on the sofa. Then Mary Catherine disappeared into the kitchen, leaving Lucy to admire the plates hanging on the wall that pictured JFK and Jackie, the large photo of a smiling pope, and the porcelain statue of Mary in her blue robe. There were also a number of framed school photos of Gabe's boys, progressing through the grades.

"You must be so proud of your grandsons," began Lucy, when Mary Catherine arrived with the tea tray and set it down on the coffee table. "They're very handsome boys."

"And so smart, like their daddy," said Mary Catherine. "Now how do you take your tea, dear? Sugar? Milk?"

"Just plain, thanks."

Mary Catherine filled the Belleek cup with steaming brown liquid and passed it to Lucy on its matching saucer.

"Beautiful china. Did you get it in Ireland?"

"I did. I went back a few years ago to see the family, the ones that stayed." Mary Catherine poured a splash of milk into her cup, then filled it with tea and sat down in an armchair that was catty-corner to the sofa. "Now, I can't help wondering, did you come for anything in particular, or was it just to bring the paper?"

"Well, actually," began Lucy, winging it as she spoke, "my boss, the editor, wants to do a sort of follow-up piece about Gabe and how his death has affected his friends and colleagues. It would include memories and how people are coping, now that they've lost him, and a good bit about the Blue Lives Matter movement."

"I think that would be wonderful," said Mary Catherine, her cheeks growing a bit pink. "Of course, the funeral was a beautiful tribute—all those wonderful men and women in their blue uniforms. And some of them came so far, just to honor my boy." She paused and took a polite sip of tea, her pinky finger raised. "But it would be nice to have something a bit more personal, about what a wonderful father he was, and how unfairly fathers are treated by the divorce courts. I hope you'll put in something about that."

"Well, it all depends on what information I can gather," said Lucy, "and his friends' memories." Lucy took another sip of tea. "I will need your help to find contacts. I thought I'd start with the pallbearers, since they're usually the ones closest to the deceased."

"Oh, let me see," said Mary Catherine, picking the paper up off the coffee table and slowly turning the pages until she found the photo of the pallbearers. "There's the sheriff himself, of course; he was a pallbearer. Imagine! What an honor for my Gabe! And his cousin Bobby, but Bobby's away now, in rehab. He overdid it at the wake, and not for the first time, I'm sad to say. I don't think they'll let you talk to him."

"That's a shame," said Lucy, somewhat shocked at Mary Catherine's frankness.

"He's always had a bit of trouble in that department, but at least he's trying to mend his ways. I take comfort that he's not the only one who's fallen; there are plenty of others, but they're not getting the help they need, which is terribly unfortunate."

"So true," said Lucy, with a sad little nod. "We mustn't judge, lest we be judged."

Mary Catherine gave her an approving nod. "I see you're a good girl who goes to church. Which parish, might I ask?"

Lucy took a fortifying sip of tea and resisted the temptation to say she attended the Catholic church in Tinker's Cove. "I go to the Community Church," she confessed.

"Well, at least you go somewhere, and now they do say you don't have to be Catholic to go to heaven." Mary Catherine sniffed, then managed a little smile. "That's one thing that comforts me, you know. Gabe went to confession just before the"—she paused and took a steadying breath before continuing—"the accident. It was the first time in a long time; he'd been fretting about something." Mary Catherine leaned forward and whispered, "I think he felt guilty about skipping Mass and not taking the boys, which was his Christian duty, and I told him that if his conscience was bothering him, he should go to confession. He did"—she nodded and dabbed at her eyes—"and he told me, 'Ma, you were right. I really got a load off my mind, and I know what I have to do.' If only he'd lived and started going to Mass . . ." She blew her nose, tucked the hanky into the sleeve of her sweater, and took another look at the photo. "Three of these men are corrections officers, like Gabe. They're all in uniform, but I'm afraid I don't know them. Gabe kept his work separate from his family, because of the criminal element, you know."

"No matter. I can get their names from the sheriff's department."

"Of course."

"Isn't there one more?" asked Lucy. "Do you know that tall fellow with the fine head of hair?"

"Oh, my goodness. How could I miss him? That's his friend Jimmy; he lives in Chicago now. They're best buddies, always have been. He's a dear fellow, and so handsome. A heart of gold has Jimmy; you should definitely talk to him."

"I'd like to," said Lucy. "Do have his address, or phone number?"

"It just so happens that I do." Mary Catherine popped up and went straight to a tall secretary that stood beside the door. She lowered the desk flap and began sorting through papers in the little cubbyholes, eventually finding the one she wanted. "Ah, here it is! He wrote it himself, told me to call him if there was anything he could do for me. Anything at all, he said, he'd come running." As she spoke, she bent down over the desk and began copying the information onto a bit of notepaper, then folded it and gave it to Lucy.

Opening it, Lucy saw the notepad had been a gift from Catholic Charities, and Mary Catherine had written out the information in a lovely, flowing cursive script. "What beautiful penmanship you have," she said.

"We used to hate those penmanship classes at school," she remembered. "Sister Angela was a devil with that ruler of hers."

"No pain, no gain," said Lucy, realizing she was falling into Phyllis's penchant for clichés. It was definitely time to go. "Well, I must thank you for this lovely visit, and the tea," she said, standing up.

"It's been very nice," said Mary Catherine, blinking back a tear or two. "I do get a bit lonely and sad—missing him, you know."

"I'm sure you do." Lucy squeezed her hand. "You have your memories."

"And they'll have to do, that's what Father O'Byrne says."

"Bless you," said Lucy, wondering where that came from. She headed for the door, feeling she had to escape before she found herself attending confirmation classes at St. Brigid's.

"Take care now, and come again," invited Mary Catherine, opening the door for her.

Lucy stepped out and made her way down the path, wondering how many sins she'd committed, how many lies she'd told, all to get Jimmy's phone number. Once in the car, she immediately dialed his number, figuring the sooner the deed was done, the better.

Jimmy answered on the first ring, in a crisp, professional tone, stating his name as James Cunningham.

"Hi, I'm a reporter with *The Courier* paper in Maine. I'm working on a story about Gabe McGourt, and I wondered if you might share something about your reaction to his death. His mother gave me your name, and said you were good friends."

"How's his mother doing?" he asked, concern in his voice.

"Pretty well, I guess. She takes a good deal of comfort from his boys, the grandkids."

"She was wonderful to me when I was a confused kid. I owe her a great deal of thanks. She's the one who encouraged me to go to college." He seemed to be slipping into a reminiscent mood, and Lucy remained silent, not wanting to spoil the moment. "We were best friends as kids, that's true, but in recent years we kind of grew apart, the way people do. He stayed in Gilead and worked at the jail; I went to college and got a law degree. The last time I heard from him was sometime last summer." He paused, apparently remembering he was talking to a reporter. "I certainly don't want to go on the record about Gabe, no way."

Lucy wasn't about to give up. *Sometime last summer* could have been the time of Melanie's disappearance. "I'd appreciate anything you can tell me, completely off the record. He's kind of a black hole; I can't get any sense of who he was. Nobody wants to talk about him."

"That's not surprising; he was trouble, and he had a knack for making enemies. I loved the guy, but I couldn't take him, if you know what I mean."

"I guess we all have friends like that. People who are self-destructive," said Lucy, realizing that he felt a great need to talk about his childhood friend.

"Yeah, I definitely got the sense he'd gotten himself in some kind of mess. He called late, actually woke me up, and he sounded terrified; he wasn't really making much sense. He said he'd done something dreadful that would damn him to hell, but he wouldn't say what. He asked if I'd defend him if it went to court, and I said I'd do what I could to help him and make sure he got a good defense, but I needed to know more before I could commit myself. He didn't give me any details; he just got mad at me, which was pretty typical for him. He said I was like all the rest, and hung up. I was relieved and tried to forget all about it, but a couple of days later, I gave him a call, to check on him. He was joking around, insulting me the way he used to do, and said no worries, everything had been taken care of."

"That's really interesting," said Lucy. "They've found the body of a girl he was involved with, and she was killed last summer. Do you remember when he called you?"

"Oh, God. I think it must have been August, maybe early September . . . something like that, but I can't be definite." He sighed. "I wish I could say there was no way he could be involved in something like that, but I really can't. He had a terrible temper, and he was absolutely awful to his wife. I was happy when she finally left him."

"His mother told me something was bothering him and he went to confession just before he died. She said he seemed at peace with himself and told her he knew just what to do."

"Oh, God, I wish he'd called me, I would've advised him to lay low, not to do anything rash. We could have managed the risk."

Lucy was puzzled, "What do you mean?"

"I've seen it happen before. Guy gets the guilts, confesses, and next thing he's dead because his associates didn't appreciate being ratted on."

"Oh," said Lucy, with sudden comprehension.

"Yeah." He sounded sad. "What a waste."

"Well, thanks for your honesty. I respect that you want to stay off the record, and I won't print a word, but it might help me get to the bottom of the story. Somebody killed him, and the police have arrested an innocent man, one of my colleagues, in fact."

"I wish I could be more help," he said.

"Me, too," said Lucy, looking up as a police car approached on the street. "If you think of anything that might help, would you give me a call?" She gave him her phone number, watching as the car stopped in front of Mary Catherine's house. The door opened, and the sheriff got out, hitched up his gun belt and straightened his cap, then strode up the walk and rang the bell.

Lucy wondered if Mary Catherine had reported her visit to the sheriff and decided she'd better get a move on. "Thanks again," she said, ending the call and starting the car. A moment later, she was on her way, wondering if she'd been paranoid or if the sheriff was keeping an eye on her.

She spent the rest of the day working on the usual features that appeared every week—the Town Hall Almanac, the Citizen of the Week, the Events Calendar—and analyzing the warrant for the upcoming town meeting. She left a bit early, in order to get that meat loaf in the oven, and it was filling the kitchen with a wonderful meaty aroma when Bill came home.

"Hey! Meat loaf!" he exclaimed, wrapping his arms around Lucy's waist and hugging her as she stood at the sink, peeling potatoes.

"With gravy and mashed potatoes," she said, naming his favorite dinner.

"Mom's recipe?" he asked.

"Of course."

"She'll love that," he said, opening the fridge and taking out a can of lemon-flavored seltzer. He popped the top and took a long drink, then sat down at the golden-oak table and asked her about her day.

"Not great, actually. Your mom left with Kate first thing this morning."

"A day out?"

"Uh, no. She's gone to stay with Kate in her vacation rental."

"What?"

"Yeah. She said she felt she was in the way here, and Kate was going to take her sightseeing . . ."

"She's seen all the sights; she's visited lots of times. It's March, for Pete's sake; who wants to go driving around in the rain and wind and mud? And even snow! It's not safe at her age. What if Kate's rental car breaks down? Hunh? Has she thought of that? And what about us? Why doesn't she want to be with us?"

"I don't know, Bill. I think she was unhappy; maybe we reminded her too much of visits here with your father."

"No. I'll tell you what's going on. That Kate is trying to get her teeth into Mom, for her own purposes. She's after her money, I just know it. And when the will turned up, she figured she'd switch to Plan B and use a charm offensive to con Mom into believing she's the daughter she always wanted."

"So what should we do?" asked Lucy.

"Maybe I should call her, tell her what I think the truth is about Kate."

"No, don't do that. She won't believe you. Just ask her about her day; tell her you miss her and want to make sure she's okay. Ask if there's anything she needs."

"Really?" Bill was skeptical.

"Yeah. And tell her about the meat loaf and how even

though I try real hard, it's never as good as when she makes it."

"Okay," said Bill, pulling his phone from his pocket and making the call. "It's worth a try."

"Like my mom used to say, you catch more flies with honey than with vinegar."

Bill groaned, then shifted gears, responding to his mother's hello. "Hi, Mom," he began. "It's kind of quiet around here without you . . ."

# Chapter Nineteen

Lucy listened to the phone conversation with one ear while she prepared dinner and learned that Edna had had a wonderful day with Kate, but complained that she'd found it a bit difficult to keep up. She was looking forward to visiting Camden tomorrow but had begged off Kate's plan to climb the mountain to see the famous view described in Edna St. Vincent Millay's poem "Renascence," since the forecast was for wind and rain, and besides, her arthritis was acting up. She also fretted that while the vacation rental was absolutely lovely, there was only one bathroom on the first floor and the bedrooms, very luxurious to be sure, were both upstairs. Bill didn't pressure his mother, but let her know that she was missed and reminded her that their house did have an upstairs bathroom.

Lucy was smiling, actually gloating a bit at Kate's missteps, replaying that conversation as she drove off after dinner, leaving the house to cover a Board of Health meeting in town. She didn't usually cover the meetings, which tended to involve routine approvals of plans for septic systems and such, but she'd spotted the county health agent's name on the agenda and speculated that the board might be questioning her about her refusal to pass along the state funds for sex education. And if the board didn't bring the subject up, she planned to question the agent herself.

Her thoughts were running along on a track of their own as she turned out of her driveway and into the dark night, beginning to follow the familiar route she took several times every day, so she was shocked when she noticed flashing blue lights suddenly appearing in her rearview mirror. What on earth? The car had just been inspected; she hadn't broken any traffic laws, and there was plenty of room for the police car to pass her. She knew the law, however, so she began to pull over, but when the following car didn't pass but pulled behind her, she found her foot pressing down on the gas instead of continuing to brake. It wasn't a conscious decision but some sort of primal, instinctive reaction.

Bouncing from the shoulder and back onto the pavement, she switched on her flashers and continued along the road, driving just below the speed limit. Somewhat puzzled at her own refusal to stop, she rationalized her behavior by reminding herself that she'd attended Officer Barney's safety presentations for women and had absorbed his lessons: Don't get out of your car, don't get in someone else's car. Stand your ground. Yell as loud as you can for help. Don't be fooled by a flashing blue light at night; anybody can buy one from police supply outlets. If followed, put on your flashers and drive to the nearest police station; actual, legitimate officers have been trained to recognize what you're doing and will follow at a safe distance.

The problem, however, was that she was still on Red Top Road and was several miles from town and the nearest police station. The road was deserted; there were only a few homes besides their own, and they were clustered together in a small development on adjacent Prudence Path. She'd passed them some time ago and was now proceeding through a dark and lonely wooded area. She hadn't seen a single other car since she'd started out, except for the police car, which was now right on her tail, too close for comfort. The flashing blue light illuminated the inside of her car, and she felt exposed and vulnerable as she stubbornly drove on at twenty-nine miles an hour.

The flasher also made it possible for her to identify the following car, which she was dismayed to see was from the county sheriff's department. That didn't mean the sheriff was inside; the driver could be one of his deputies. It didn't matter much, she decided, since she didn't trust any of them. Not the sheriff himself, and none of his deputies or corrections officers, all of whom were loyal liege men to their boss.

The one ray of hope lay just ahead, she decided, at the Route 1 stop sign. Route 1 was the main coastal road and was well-traveled, even at night. Whoever was following her would be observed by passing vehicles and would be unlikely to try any shenanigans there. Her heart lifted as she approached the bend before the stop sign—only a few more feet and she'd be in a safer situation.

It was then that the following car suddenly swerved around her car and abruptly stopped, blocking the narrow two-lane road. She slammed on the brakes to avoid a collision, looked in vain for an escape route on the nonexistent shoulder, then slammed the gearshift into reverse and hit the gas. Since she had had no time to straighten out the steering, the car lurched backward right into the woods, where she got hung up on a fallen tree. The motor roared, and the wheels spun vainly in thin air, leaving her high and dry. She was trapped. Her only option now was to lock the car doors and call for help on her cell phone. She reached for it, trying to control her trembling hands, and began to punch in 911, but it slipped away, and she watched it disappear into the dark floor well.

Whatever happens, she told herself, don't get out of the car. It was her only protection from her pursuer. Heart pounding, her hands gripping the wheel, she waited for the driver to step out of the squad car. The flasher lit up the area around the two vehicles in a rhythmically pulsing blue light, one moment bright as day, the next complete darkness. It dazzled and confused her, and prevented her from seeing inside the squad car. Its driver's-side door was away from her, and she didn't see the driver exit the car; the sheriff seemed to materialize out of thin air right next to her car door. He seemed huge, looming above her seated position, standing only inches from the car.

"Step out of the vehicle," he said, his voice muffled by the closed window but audible.

"There's no need. I'm not going anywhere," said Lucy, raising her voice to be heard. "Call nine-one-one for me."

"You're resisting arrest," warned the sheriff. "I'd be within my rights to use force."

"I haven't done anything wrong," said Lucy. "I'm not resisting arrest. I accepted your escort and was driving to the Tinker's Cove Police Department when you swerved ahead of me and caused this accident."

"I'm warning you. Get out of the car, and raise your hands above your head."

Lucy stared straight ahead, mute and still, like a frightened rabbit.

The sheriff bent down and pressed his face close to the

glass window. "I've got all night," he snarled. "You can't get away. We might as well get this over with."

"Is this how you dealt with Gabe McGourt?" she asked. "Did you pull him over? He probably figured he didn't have anything to fear from you, so he would have pulled off the road, figuring you were going to have a nice, friendly chat. But you were two steps ahead of him; you knew he was guilt-stricken about killing Melanie, so you decided it was too dangerous to keep him around. He was slipping away from you, getting out from under your control. What if he confessed? Then the whole cover-up would be exposed, and you'd be finished."

"Gabe was killed in a terrible accident when his truck was booby-trapped by Rob Callahan," said the sheriff.

"Rob is innocent. You're the killer. You killed him and set his truck on fire to cover up the evidence. It worked; there wasn't enough of him left to determine a cause of death, and you had a handy fall guy in Rob Callahan, the new guy in town."

He smiled and shook his head. "Nonsense. It's well known the two were rivals for Rosie Capshaw's affection."

"Not according to Rosie," said Lucy. Her attention was caught by a gleam of light in the rearview mirror, and she realized it came from her house, up there on top of Red Top Hill. She hadn't gotten very far at all before the sheriff stopped her. From the yellowish cast, she thought it must be the bug light on the porch, the light they left on all night for kids coming home late, to welcome friends, and for anyone in need of help.

Playing the rabbit wasn't working for her, she decided. It certainly hadn't worked for the rabbit she'd spotted on the lawn a few days ago, frozen in place as a red-tailed hawk swooped down and grabbed it in its talons, carrying it away.

The sheriff's radio was cackling, and he shifted his weight uneasily, aware that failing to respond would cause concern back at the department. "Get out now," he growled, reaching for his gun.

It was now or never, decided Lucy. She had to act. Grabbing the door handle, she flipped the lock and threw all her strength into the door, slamming it into the sheriff's gut and knocking the gun out of his hand. She caught a glimpse of him scrabbling around to retrieve it as she ran as fast and hard as she could, running for her life, not looking behind her. She could hear him grunting and groaning, his feet thumping on the blacktop. She tried to zig and zag, fearing that he would shoot her in the back, and praying that he was smart enough to know that the sound of a shot would alert the neighborhood.

She was breathing hard, her chest hurt, and her legs were cramping as she fought her way uphill, but she kept on, one foot at a time, inching closer to home and safety. Her eyes were fixed on the yellow light, and she began yelling—yelling for help. It was then that she hit a muddy patch and began to slip, and the next thing she knew, she was flat on her face. Her hands stung, her shoulder was on fire, she was completely winded and couldn't catch her breath. She couldn't get up.

The sheriff was grabbing her arm, attempting to lift her, and she shrieked in pain. He didn't stop; he grabbed her harder and pulled her to her feet, attempting to pull her hands behind her back to cuff her. She twisted and wriggled; she kicked his shins, she spat in his face. He whacked her with a baton, and she fell to her knees, unable to resist. Every part of her hurt; she was struggling to breathe, and he was on top of her, pushing her onto the tarmac. Her cheek was pressed against the filthy, gravelly road, and her vision was blurry, but she could still see the yellow light, her porch light, glowing steadily. "I'm coming home," she whispered, as he yanked her to her feet, hooked his arm around her waist, and began dragging her back to his car.

Her only defense was to adopt passive resistance, making herself a dead weight. He was panting, struggling, and sweating despite the cold temperature, when he was suddenly illuminated by a spotlight. "Drop your weapon and release the woman," ordered a familiar voice. It was Barney's; she'd know it anywhere.

"It's okay," protested the sheriff. "I'm Sheriff Murphy, and I'm arresting a perpetrator . . ."

"Drop the gun and release the woman," repeated Barney. "You're under arrest."

"There's been a misunderstanding . . ." The sheriff let go of her, and Lucy dropped to the ground. He instinctively reached for his holster, finding it empty, and a single shot rang out, a warning. Realizing he had no other option, Murphy raised his hands over his head.

He was immediately apprehended by Officer Todd Kirwan, who had him neatly cuffed in a few seconds. "You have the right to remain silent . . ." he began, walking him back to the car.

Barney Culpepper was attending to Lucy, cautioning her not to move and reassuring her that the EMTs were moments away.

"How?" she asked, her voice a whisper.

"Your phone."

"Dropped . . ."

"You must've hit nine-one-one because it picked up everything. We were on the way right from the get-go."

She could hear the siren; the ambulance was coming. Far down the road, the yellow light was still burning, and a figure was running down the hill. It was Bill, she realized, as her eyes closed and she slipped into unconsciousness.

Sometime later, after she'd been x-rayed and IV'd and given painkillers, she was comfortably tucked under a heated blanket in the emergency room at the Tinker's Cove Cottage Hospital. Bill was beside her, holding one of her bandaged hands and apologizing profusely.

"I saw the blue lights and figured it was a traffic stop, one of those speeders that go roaring by all the time. I never dreamed it had anything to do with you. But then I heard more sirens and thought it must be an accident, so I decided to see what was going on down there at the bottom of the hill. I thought it might be one of the neighbors and maybe I could help. But then I saw your car hung up in the woods, and I thought you'd managed to crash the SUV . . ."

"I'm a good driver," protested Lucy.

"Yeah, but things happen. Could've been a deer or a moose and you swerved to avoid it."

"If only. It was terrifying." She shuddered at the memory of the sheriff's leering face, pressed against the car window. "You can see evil. I saw it in his eyes."

"I should've got off my butt sooner. I can't believe this was all happening to you on our own road."

"I could see the porch light. It gave me hope."

"I should've realized it was you. I saw the blue lights right after you left the house."

"It's okay, Bill."

"You forgive me?"

Lucy was saved from answering by the arrival of Todd and Barney, both holding their caps in their hands. They shook hands with Bill, then turned to Lucy.

"How are you feeling?" asked Barney.

"I'm pretty drugged up," she confessed. "Feeling no pain."

"And no broken bones," added Bill.

"Just soft-tissue damage, which is just as painful." She sighed. "But I'm grateful to be alive, which I wouldn't be if you hadn't come when you did."

"We owe you guys a big debt," said Bill, his voice breaking.

"We're the ones who owe Lucy," said Todd, twirling his hat. "We'd been investigating the sheriff. The DA was getting a lot of complaints about him, but we could never get anybody who was willing to testify. They wouldn't even file an official complaint; they were too afraid of him. We finally got the break we needed yesterday. The ME found a bullet lodged in Gabe McGourt's spine, and it matched the sheriff's handgun. I was actually on the phone with DA Aucoin working out how to arrest Murphy when your nine-one-one call came in. It was all we needed. The problem was getting to you fast enough."

"In the nick of time," said Lucy, smiling. "It was great hearing Barney's voice coming out of nowhere."

"I wanted to kill him," admitted Barney. "When I saw him mauling you like that, I wanted to beat him to a pulp."

"There's nothing I hate more than a crooked cop," said Todd. "We're entrusted with so much power—life and death sometimes—and we need to respect it. Our job is to protect people, pure and simple. To serve."

"Yeah." Barney nodded. "That's the motto on our shields, and it means to serve the people, the citizens, not ourselves."

"So you have an open-and-shut case against Murphy?" asked Bill. "Because I can see him getting some fancy lawyer, and next thing you know he's back on the job."

"Believe me, the DA is going to work very hard to make sure that doesn't happen," said Todd. "And now that he's been arrested, I think people will get braver about coming forward. He was operating a pay-to-play system, and everybody knew it. If you applied for a job, you were advised to make a donation to the Sheriff's Benevolent Fund. It was supposed to provide help for widows and the orphans of department employees, but it mostly went to Murphy. There were also compulsory donations taken from the paychecks of department personnel, and he collected 'supervisory fees' whenever the prisoners went out on a work detail. He even got a kickback from his admin, Nora. The money just poured into his pockets, and now he's going to have to account for it all." He turned to Barney. "But the worst crime, of course, was killing Gabe McGourt. We've got the physical evidence. What we don't have is the motive."

Lucy's eyes were closing, but hearing this, she rallied. "Gabe felt bad about killing Melanie Wall and wanted to confess."

Todd saw the implications right away. "And that would have revealed the sheriff's involvement in a cover-up."

Lucy managed a nod before her head began to droop.

"We should go," said Barney. "Lucy looks like she's having trouble keeping her eyes open."

"Yeah, she's going to spend the night, just as a precaution," said Bill.

"Well, take good care of her," said Barney, clapping Bill on the shoulder.

"I will," promised Bill, but Lucy didn't hear him. She was already fast asleep.

# Chapter Twenty

Lucy was still pretty fuzzy-headed the next morning when she was released from the Tinker's Cove Cottage Hospital and Sara came to take her home.

"You're all over the news," Sara told her, as she helped her mother with her jacket. Lucy's injured arm was in a sling, so she could only use one sleeve; the other hung empty. She couldn't zip the jacket because of the sling, but Sara was able to fasten a few buttons at the top and bottom. "This will have to do. Good thing it's not too cold out today."

"Are there reporters outside?" asked Lucy, aware that she didn't look her best. Her face was swollen from the cuts and scratches, she had a black eye, and her hair was a mess.

"There was a WCVB truck here when I came," said Sara, going over to the window, "but it's gone now. Your fifteen minutes of fame must be up."

Lucy glanced at the clock on the wall, which read a few minutes past ten. "They're over in Gilead, for the arraignment. It's big news when a sheriff is arraigned on murder charges."

Sara sighed. "Yeah, but will he actually go to trial? And if he does, will the jury actually find him guilty? Seems to me these guys always manage to get off. Cops hardly ever get convicted."

Lucy looked out the window at the milky sky and the bare trees, their branches like skeletons. "I'll testify," she said.

"Do you think they'll believe you? You're part of the fake news."

Lucy looked at her daughter, struck by the fact that she was so cynical at such a young age. "Things are going to change, I really believe it. People are going to demand an end to corruption and abuse of power, in this county anyway."

"We'll see," said Sara, picking up her mother's big bag. "Gee, this is heavy. What've you got in here?"

"My life's in that bag," said Lucy, suddenly panicking. "My phone—is my phone in there?"

Sara looked, rummaging through the contents. "No."

"I'll bet they took it for evidence," said Lucy. "I'll need a new one. We can stop on the way home . . ."

"Later." Sara was firm. "There'll be plenty of time for that. Right now, you need to get home and rest."

"Not without a phone."

Sara sighed, yanking the string on the call button to summon a nurse. "Okay, okay. I'll get one of those cheap burners for you."

"Promise?"

"I promise. Now let's get you home."

"Okay," said Lucy, willing for once to let her daughter take charge. With conditions, to be sure—but actually she was grateful for Sara's bossiness.

The nurse arrived and insisted, over Lucy's protests,

that she had to be transported by wheelchair to the exit, where Sara would be waiting in the car. "That's how we do it," she said, making it clear that there was no point in arguing. Lucy shrugged and sat in the chair, while Sara went ahead to fetch the car.

The elevator was slow, so when the automatic lobby doors slid open, Sara was just pulling up in her aged Corolla. The nurse pushed Lucy's wheelchair right up to the car and insisted on taking her arm and helping her seat herself in the passenger seat. She shut the door and tapped the car, indicating it was okay to go and waving as they drove off.

"What a lot of fuss," fumed Lucy. "I'm perfectly able to walk. It's my arm that's hurt."

"It's because of insurance," said Sara, with a naughty grin. "Don't think they really care about you."

Somewhat chastened, Lucy found herself tearing up. "I'm glad to be alive, I was really scared. The cops and the EMTs and the nurses—they were all terrific."

"I know, Mom," said Sara, her voice breaking as she gave her mother's hand a squeeze. "I don't want to even think about what could have happened."

The sun went behind a little cloud, and the day darkened, and Lucy's spirits plummeted. "Why didn't your dad pick me up?" she asked.

"Oh, because Gram came home, first thing this morning, all upset. I guess she and Kate had some sort of falling out."

Lucy found herself perking up. "Really?"

"Yeah. It happened just when the hospital called and said you were ready to go home, so Dad sent me. He and Gram were going at it when I left."

"So is she mad at Dad or at Kate?"

"I don't know." Sara braked for the traffic light on Main Street. "I think both of them."

Lucy mulled over the possibilities as they continued on their way. Edna wasn't usually one to make a fuss; if anything, she was too passive having spent most of her life with a loving but somewhat overbearing and authoritative husband. Everything in their household revolved around Bill Sr. and his comfort: Nobody ever sat in his recliner or attempted to touch the TV remote, meals were provided on his timetable, and menus never included broccoli or what he termed "weird stuff" like kale or quinoa. In other words, thought Lucy, Edna had really been more of a servant than an equal partner, albeit a willing one. So it was rather difficult to imagine what had finally set her off. Had Kate gone too far, perhaps inquiring about her income or savings? That was the sort of thing Edna would have found intrusive. Or had she resented Bill's concern for her, believing he was trying to stifle her and control her just as she was finally trying her wings?

Those were her thoughts as they drove along Route 1, but when they turned onto Red Top Road she had a sudden panic attack. "That's where it happened," she said, spotting bits of crime-scene tape tied around a few trees. "I drive by this spot every day," she added. "I'm going to have to relive the whole nightmare."

Sara slowed the car. "It was a nightmare, but one you survived, Mom. You're a strong woman. You'll be fine."

Lucy turned away from the scene of the accident and looked up the hill, where their house stood tall, with its peaked roof and towering chimney. It was a safe haven, with strong walls that protected them from hurricanes and blizzards. It was a place where she and Bill had created a loving family, supporting each other and their children from physical danger and emotional slings and arrows, too. "I can't wait to get home," she said.

"We're almost there," said Sara, as they climbed the last few feet to the top of the hill and turned into the drive.

"Uh-oh," said Lucy, spotting Kate's rental car parked at an odd angle in the driveway and perking up. "This should be interesting."

When they stepped inside the kitchen, Sara and Lucy could hear raised voices coming from the family room. Their eyes met while Sara helped Lucy out of her jacket; then they went straight through to the next room, where Bill was waving a paper in front of Kate's face. Edna was sitting on the sectional sofa, her arms wrapped across her chest, looking small and stricken, with Zoe beside her. She made room for Lucy, who took her place and wrapped her good arm around her mother-in-law's shoulder.

"Good. I'm glad you're here to see this," declared Bill, handing Lucy the paper.

"How are you, dear?" asked Edna, patting Lucy's good hand. "What a terrible thing that sheriff tried to do to you."

"I'm okay; they gave me a lot of painkillers," admitted Lucy, trying to focus on the paper Bill had given her. It was his own DNA profile from Genious, and she noticed it did not include a reference to any sibling or half sibling, living or dead.

"What is it?" asked Sara.

"It's my DNA profile," said Bill.

"There's no reference to Kate," said Zoe. "It means she faked her profile."

Lucy turned to Kate, who was sitting in the rocking chair, almost like a witness in a courtroom. Or, more accurately, in this case, the accused. "Is that true?"

Kate gave an apologetic shrug. "It wasn't very hard. I got the real one and used it as a template; the computer made it easy. I just added a few changes."

"You're a professional con artist," accused Bill, practically spitting the words out. "You wanted to defraud my mother, all of us. What was the next thing? Were you hoping the will would never turn up so you could sue for a third of my Dad's estate? Was that your game? And now that the will's been found and you're not in it, you've switched gears. You're sucking up to Mom, taking advantage of a heartbroken, vulnerable widow. What next? Have you got some sort of con? An incredibly profitable investment she can't pass up? Or maybe a loan to get you out of some sort of trouble? Or maybe you'll just steal some checks and forge her signature? Or get her PIN number and borrow her ATM card? What lengths will you go to?"

Kate looked surprised, then shook her head sadly. "I understand why you don't trust me, but I had absolutely nothing to do with the missing will. I didn't even know about it." She twisted the strap of her handbag, which was in her lap. "And I would never, ever cheat Edna!" She lifted her face, her eyes brimming with tears. "I just wanted to be part of a family. Your family. I saw you all at the funeral, and I could see myself as belonging. I felt a pull; I don't know how to describe it. It was like you all were the family I never had, but should have had." She looked down at the floor. "I got my real profile, and I didn't have a single living relative. My grandparents were Holocaust survivors who lost their entire families in the camps, I never knew my father, and my mother was killed in a plane crash when I was in college . . ."

Lucy found herself feeling sympathetic to Kate, but Bill remained skeptical. "Am I supposed to believe this?"

Kate sniffed, wiped away her tears, and took a deep breath. "It's true, it's all true. I was married for a while, but it didn't work out." She paused and shrugged. "I couldn't get pregnant . . ."

"And your husband left you because of that?" demanded Zoe, outraged at this example of male infidelity.

"It was a bit more complicated than that," confessed Kate, with a weak smile. "I focused on my real estate career, and I've been quite successful, if I say so myself. A good part of my business was helping bereaved families sell their loved one's property, and that's when I started reading the obituaries, looking for potential clients." She was quick to defend herself. "It was nothing high-pressured. I'd just send the survivors a card to let them know I was available, if they needed a realtor." She chewed her lip. "But pretty soon, it grew into something more, and I found myself attending funerals, kind of pretending to be a member of the bereaved family."

"And then you found us," said Bill, unmoved, "And figured you'd found an easy target."

"No." Kate shook her head. "It's really kind of funny that you think I'm after your mother's money. The truth is I have much more money than I'll ever need. Like I said, I've done very well for myself, but it turns out that cash is very cold comfort." She took a long breath. "When I was at your father's funeral, I truly felt as if you all really were my family. I know it sounds crazy, but I really felt as if I belonged with you."

Lucy, who was sitting beside Edna, felt her mother-in-law pulling away from her embrace, sitting up straighter and turning her attention to Kate.

"So you faked a DNA report?" asked Sara.

"Yeah. I had one that I used as an example, and it was easy with my computer and printer, a little cutting and pasting, and I used the info from the obituary." She gave a little nod. "I thought it looked pretty convincing."

"But I still can't get past the fact that you took advantage of my mother when she was at her lowest, weakest . . ."

"I saw it differently. I was offering myself as a friend when she needed someone."

"That's right, Bill," said Edna, using a tone of voice he hadn't heard since he started to shave. "Kate hasn't hurt you or our family. If anything, she's offering to share herself with us."

"What?" demanded Bill. "Don't you see what she's done to you?"

"She's telling the truth. What she's done is befriend me, at a time when I needed a friend. She's opened up my life to new experiences and given me a lot to think about. I've been trying to decide what to do with the rest of my life. Should I move to Maine to be close to you, or should I stay in Florida, where I have friends and a lively community?"

Bill was quick to provide an answer. "You should move up here; in fact, I'm working on a condo project that would be perfect . . ."

"I don't want to live in a condo." Edna shook her head. "I like my house in Florida, but I know it's too big for me to manage alone. That's why I think it would be nice to have a roommate, someone to share it with."

"What are you saying?" demanded Bill, narrowing his eyes.

"I'd like it very much if Kate would consider moving in with me. Would you, Kate?"

Kate smiled. "Only if you let me share costs . . ."

"Of course," said Edna. "And you can deal with the plumbers and landscapers . . ."

"Absolutely," said Kate, crossing the room and giving Edna a big hug.

"I'm not convinced this is a good idea," insisted Bill.

"Oh, Bill, enough," said Lucy, taking his hand. "It's only natural that you want to protect your mother, but Edna is an independent, smart woman who knows what she wants. This could be a very good thing, for both of them, and for us, too."

"What Reverend Marge calls a win-win situation," said Zoe.

"Right," said Edna, in a decisive voice. "Now, what's for lunch?"

Back at work on Monday, Lucy discovered she could type on the keyboard despite her sling if she rested her arm on a pillow in her lap. She was busy writing up her own first-person account of her frightening encounter with Sheriff Murphy when Assistant DA Kevin Kenneally showed up.

"Can I help you?" asked Phyllis, in a rather challenging tone of voice. Her authoritative manner was somewhat undermined by the fact that her hair was still bright green and she was wearing shamrock earrings, several green Mardi Gras necklaces, and a green sweater picturing a leprechaun raising a brimming mug of beer.

"I'm here to see Lucy," he said, displaying his winning smile.

Phyllis gave him a look that indicated he'd better not budge from the reception area until he got an okay from her, even though Lucy was clearly visible at her desk. "Lucy, do you want to see Assistant DA Kenneally?"

Lucy couldn't help smiling at her friend's protective attitude. "Sure," she said.

"All right," said Phyllis, in a begrudging tone. "Lucy will see you now."

"Thank you," said Kenneally, before advancing into the office area and greeting Lucy. "I came to, well, offer Mr. Aucoin's best wishes for your recovery and to let you know that there are some changes moving forward regarding the sheriff's department."

"Thanks," said Lucy. "Take a seat," she offered, indicating her visitor chair with her good arm. "Tell me all about it."

"George Blaine, who's the most senior deputy, will be the acting sheriff, but he will be closely supervised by DA Aucoin. I think we can expect a real housecleaning in that department as time goes on."

"Will there be criminal charges?" asked Lucy.

"If they're warranted." Kenneally paused. "Sheriff is an elected position, so I imagine there will be a number of candidates and a lively campaign to win votes."

"Long overdue," said Lucy.

"I agree." Kenneally seemed sincere, but Lucy wasn't entirely convinced of his change of heart. In the past, he had displayed no sign of disapproval or disagreement with Sheriff Murphy. On the contrary, he had appeared to be actively seeking the corrupt sheriff's approval.

"I think the sheriff's department, and the DA, too, will have to work quite hard to regain the people's trust."

"We're aware of that," said Kenneally, perking up a bit. "As a matter of fact, that's the other news I want to share with you. The Hibernian Knights have reached out to the Irish Festival planners and are coordinating efforts to make this St. Patrick's Day celebration an event that truly involves the entire community."

"That's wonderful," said Lucy, rather surprised. "So what changes can we expect?"

"Well, first off, we've asked Rosie Capshaw to march with her puppets in the parade . . ."

"That's great," said Lucy, opening up a new file. "Tell me all about it."

Tuesday morning dawned clear, crisp, and mild with a touch of spring in the air—perfect weather for a parade. Lucy and her family, including Edna and Kate, had put out chairs the night before and had a prime viewing spot. Like many others, they'd brought an ample supply of treats to sustain them: a thermos of coffee, donuts, and Irish soda bread, and shared them with friends and neighbors.

As always, the parade's starting point was indicated by two ladder trucks, one from Gilead and the other from Tinker's Cove. The trucks had their ladders extended to their highest point, and a giant American flag fluttered beneath them. Everyone's eyes kept wandering to the flag, checking for the beginning of the parade.

At last, the approaching honor guard could be seen, uniformed members of the VFW carrying the American and state of Maine flags. Everybody in the crowd stood up and crossed their hearts as the honor guard marched past.

Next, of course, was the vintage green Cadillac convertible containing the grand marshal, but this year James Ryan had invited the other candidates to ride with him. Eileen Clancy and Brendan Coyle both had broad smiles as they waved to the people lining Main Street from the back seat; James Ryan was in front, next to the driver, sporting a bright green suit instead of his usual banker's gray.

The grand marshal's car was followed, as always, by the entire Murray family on bicycles, tricycles, and unicycles. They were a large family, at least twenty strong, and were greeted with cheers and applause as they tossed candy to the crowd.

A pair of handsome Clydesdale horses clomped by next, pulling a hay wagon filled with preschoolers from Little Prodigies Child Care Center, all wearing construction-paper leprechaun hats they'd made themselves. These cuties were greeted with plenty of oohs and aahs, and only little Timmy Anderson cried, undone by all the attention.

The Gilead board of selectmen came next, identified by a banner held by two high school girls with green-and-white-striped mufflers. The three women and two men all had green carnation boutonnieres, and all five members carried green balloons, which they distributed to watching kids.

The high school band marched by, followed by a squad of motorcycle policemen; the state governor and his wife sailed by in a convertible; a bagpipe band set all the dogs to howling: and a green tractor from MacDonald's farm pulled a flatbed trailer with costumed step-dancers from Eileen Clancy's school.

Then, getting applause and cheers from the crowd, Rosie's giant puppet of St. Patrick appeared, carried by none other than a beaming Rob Callahan. St. Patrick's head bore a glittering halo, his hands were raised in blessing, and his green robe fluttered in the breeze. He was surrounded by a sea of writhing, fleeing snakes carried by members of the Tinker's Cove High School dance team. A number of wailing banshees followed St. Patrick and the snakes, emitting recorded groans that delighted everyone.

Rosie herself carried Mother Jones, a forbidding figure

with a huge head and one arm ending in a loosely jointed, wagging finger; she was dressed in a green plaid dress and carried in her other arm a placard that read JOIN THE UNION. Not everyone seemed to approve of Mother Jones, but those who did were enthusiastic in their cheers and applause.

But as the parade rolled by, with marchers representing the Gay Vietnam Vets and even contingents displaying Black Lives Matter signs and support for the Me Too movement, Lucy sensed a genuine sea change in attitude. People seemed more open and cheerful, friendlier, and less judgmental than in the past. And for the first time ever, when the end of the parade was signaled by fire engines rolling by with lights flashing and sirens wailing, the police officers assigned to the parade were heard commenting that it had been remarkably peaceful. In contrast to past parades, there had been no brawls, no scuffles, and no fisticuffs at all.

As the parade ended, many people made their way to Tinker's Cove, where the multi-cultural Irish Festival was taking place on the town common. Numerous tents and canopies had been set up around the perimeter, and the town bandstand provided an open-air stage. When Lucy and her family arrived, the town band was playing a medley of Irish tunes, featuring Billy Hawkins on the pennywhistle.

Bill's first stop was at the beer tent, where he met Sid Finch, and they both ordered black and tans, watching intently as the bartender first poured a clear golden ale into the glass and then topped it with Guinness stout, careful that the two did not mix. Satisfied with his result, he beamed proudly as he passed the two glasses to Bill and

Sid. "Slaínte," he said, when they added a generous tip to the tab.

"It's a neat trick," said Bill, licking some of the heady Guinness foam from his lip.

"And it tastes good too," added Sid.

Lucy watched the pair with tolerant amusement; she didn't really approve of drinking so early in the day, but it was St. Patrick's Day, after all. "Let's see what they've got to eat," she suggested, and they all trooped over to the refreshments area, where they found offerings ranging from entire corned-beef dinners to Cornish pasties and classic hamburgers and hot dogs. Also green pizza, which nobody wanted to try.

After refueling with a hot dog, Lucy spotted Rob Callahan and Rosie, and went over to speak with them. "Fabulous display in the parade," she began, congratulating them before turning to Rob. "So how does it feel to be a free man?"

"Pretty great," said Rob.

"And does Ted want you to write a first-person account of your experience in the county jail for *The Courier?*"

"How did you guess?" he asked.

"I know Ted."

Rob gave Rosie a smile. "It's going to be my last story. I'm moving back to Cleveland . . ."

Lucy was surprised, and also pleased that Rob was clearing out, although she didn't want to admit it after all he'd been through. "What made you decide to leave?"

"I guess Rob's really a city person," volunteered Rosie, taking Rob's arm. "Rob's going back to his old job at the Plain Dealer. He'll have a lot more opportunities there."

"Well, good luck to you." She smiled. "And, Rob, try to stay out of trouble."

"Believe me, I will," he promised.

An announcement on the PA system said the talent show was about to begin, and Lucy hurried across the common to join Bill, his mother, and Kate, who were sitting in the front row. She joined them on the folding lawn chairs they'd brought from the parade and waited expectantly for the show to begin. They clapped heartily for the Irish tenor, the stand-up comedian, and the Little Theatre Players' dramatic scene from *Dancing at Lughnasa*, but held their most enthusiastic applause for Sara and Zoe's step-dancing routine.

At first, the two girls seemed like traditional step-dancers, togged out in thickly embroidered, stiff costumes and clunky black shoes to the accompaniment of an Irish fiddle, but the performance soon went awry as it turned into a comic tug of war between the two girls, eventually culminating in a rowdy hip-hop as the fiddler gave up his instrument and began to rap. The audience went wild, and the girls got a standing ovation, which ended only when they left the stage and headed for the dressing-room tent.

They emerged a few minutes later in their usual jeans and sweaters and joined the family, enjoying congratulations and smiles from the people seated nearby. Kate was especially enthusiastic and surprised them each with a bouquet of white roses tied with a green ribbon.

"You made it look easy, but I know you worked very hard on that routine," she said.

"Gee, thanks," said Zoe, burying her nose in the fragrant flowers.

"What a nice gesture," said Sara, giving her parents a glance. "I think you're going to be a great addition to our family."

"I'm sure gonna try," said Kate, gathering the two sisters into an embrace.

Bill started to hmpf, just like his father used to do, but Lucy gave him a gentle kick in the shin, and he ended up laughing instead. "We may not be Irish, but I guess we're all one big happy family on St. Patrick's Day."

"For today, anyway," said Lucy, under her breath.